THE ART OF LETTING GO

THE ART OF LETTING GO

Chloe Banks

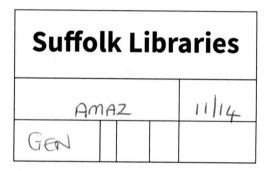
This edition published in 2014 by:

Thistle Publishing
36 Great Smith Street
London
SW1P 3BU

www.thistlepublishing.co.uk

ISBN-13: 978-1-910198-20-9

For Paul, whose constant love and faith makes it all possible.

I was walking along a path with two friends – the sun was setting – suddenly the sky turned blood red – I paused, feeling exhausted, and leaned on the fence – there was blood and tongues of fire above the blue-black fjord and the city – my friends walked on, and I stood there trembling with anxiety – and I sensed an infinite scream passing through nature.

Edvard Munch (1863 – 1944)

ROSEMARY

The sea was the colour of madness on the day I first met Ben. Not Slate or Ash, Gunmetal or Battleship, just grey. It was one of those autumn days that had lost its way and ended up in summer; storm clouds puffing up beyond the horizon, the wind gathering itself out in the bay. And into that grey world came Ben – an unwelcome splash of colour.

Even now, after all this time, I find myself wondering how Ben would start our story. As if it mattered. Chances are he wouldn't think of it as our story at all, and he wouldn't start with grey, I'm sure of that. He'd make that day a melodrama full of crashing waves, howling wind and colours with fancy names. It wasn't like that. Not how I remember it. I remember an ordinarily dull June day – the kind where holiday-makers stayed in the shelter of the caravan park arcade and I could sit on the rocks to watch the storm approaching with only barnacles and guano for company. The grey sky, the grey sea, and me. I'd thought it was just me, anyway.

"Don't move." His voice came from the point where the rocks met the wet sand. "Keep looking out to sea, I'm nearly done."

Nobody ever told me what to do. Nobody had presumed to order me around since October 1967. Maybe that's why I did what he said. The chalk steps up to my house on the headland would be impassable within minutes of a downpour starting, yet as the first fat drops of rain splattered on the rocks around me I found myself frozen in place. A minute passed and then another, and my window of opportunity slammed shut with the arrival of the wind, belching on to land in a splutter of sea spray.

"OK, all done." The figure crouching in the periphery of my vision rose to his feet two minutes too late for me to avoid a soaking. His voice had lost its urgency. "You can move now."

He might have been a couple of decades younger than me, but he wasn't as young as he'd sounded. Approaching 50 perhaps, with the first peppering of grey at his temples. A paint-flecked shirt ended halfway down goose-pimpled forearms, ripped jeans were caked in sand. He had a pencil tucked behind his ear and a sketchbook under his arm. I knew at once I wouldn't like him. No, that's not true – and I'm not scared of the truth anymore – I knew at once I didn't *want* to like him.

"Ben Summers." He held out a wet hand. "I'm renting Anchor Cottage for the season."

He jerked his head at the tiny building sitting a few feet from the furthest reaches of the Spring Tides. It was Mrs. Baxter's cottage. That alone should have warned me.

I didn't take Ben's hand. "It'd be courteous to tell me why you've kept me out in this rain."

"Of course. Sorry." He flipped the sketchbook open and held it out. "I should've asked before drawing you, but you looked so perfect I didn't want to ruin the moment."

Raindrops were already blurring the edges of the pencil and soaking through to the page beneath, distorting the fragmented lines. I tried squinting, but it made no difference. "Doesn't look anything like me."

He laughed, and it was one of those annoying laughs that only the truly good-natured can pull off. A laugh that is certain one day you'll be remembering this moment together round a log fire, wine glasses in hand. A laugh that doesn't allow for the possibility of not being the best of friends.

"I guess that sums up what I do." He shut the book again and stuck it under his shirt. "I paint and draw stuff that doesn't look like what it's meant to be."

"How ridiculous."

"You think so? Why don't you come up to my cottage and see for yourself?"

"No thank-you."

"Please. I feel terrible for keeping you out in this weather." He shivered, shirt already clinging to his collar bones under the weight of rain. "Come and have a cup of tea at least."

"I don't think so."

"Just a quick one?" That laugh again. "I don't bite."

I should've walked off by that point – made my way home the long way, past the caravan park. I don't know why I was still there. Perhaps it was his eyes. I remember noticing then, right at the start, how peculiar they were. They weren't blue-grey, or green-grey; they were true grey, the colour of madness. They were holding me in place as firmly as his voice had done moments earlier, pinning me to the sand. I was only halfway through refusing his invitation for the third time when the weather decided to take his side of the argument. That summer was one of the wettest on record, and this was not the first or last in a long line of rainstorms, but it was a particularly bad one. When Nature took off the handbrake, there was nothing for it. Without another word, we ran for the cottage.

That was where it started, I think. In Ben's cottage, as I stood dripping on the mat, was where the insanity of both our lives took its hold. Not that I could see it at the time. As Ben picked a damp towel off the floor and presented it to me for my hair, I was only concerned with ignoring the offer – in staying there with him as little time as possible. I wasn't on my guard. But I suppose madness is rather like that, isn't it? Only visible in hindsight. If we could see it coming, blowing whistles and waving streamers, it would have no hold over us. We'd cross the road, avoid eye contact, remember that bus we had to catch. We'd run for cover as soon as the rain started.

If that summer – Ben and the man who became Michael and all the rest of it – taught me anything, perhaps it was how madness makes puppets of us all in the end. It steals over us as a creeping grey shadow, disguising itself as the best course of action, the easy decision. We find ourselves in situations – as I did that day in Ben's cottage – we never consciously chose, doing things we never meant to do. All because of one decision, one moment in time. And then suddenly we'll see it – we'll feel the jerk of the strings – and in a moment of lucidity, we know it's too late. We're already soaked to the skin.

The cottage was tiny. Apart from the cupboard containing what Mrs. Baxter must've thought passed for a bathroom, there were only two rooms – a living space for eating and sleeping, and a studio for painting. I couldn't believe Mrs. Baxter had found someone foolish enough to fall for the romantic artistic ideal of living in such a poky place.

"Can I get you a cup of tea, Mrs... Mrs..."

I gave him my hardest stare. "*Dr*. Blunt. And I don't drink tea."

"Coffee then, Doctor?" He pulled two half-clean mugs from a basket of crockery under the bed. "Everyone drinks coffee. You can have a look at my paintings while the kettle boils." He nodded towards the interior door. "Go on through. Don't be shy."

I had no desire to go on through. The only reason I did so was to avoid making further conversation with Ben as he tried to persuade the ancient kettle to get up steam on a hot plate the size of a jam jar lid. Anything was better than small talk.

The studio was three times bigger than the living space and was painted all white. Large windows would've framed a view of the sea if water hadn't been pouring down them off the gutter-less roof. Along the back wall a trestle table was covered in a chaos of palettes and brushes, tubes of paint and dirty rags. Around the rest of the room unframed canvases were leaning against the walls. Some were blank, others were covered in more abstract rubbish.

"Mrs. Baxter's letting me have the place at a very reasonable rate." Ben came into the room behind me. "On account of there being no heating and this being about the only place that needs heating in the middle of summer."

I hoped my silence would be enough of a hint that I didn't want to talk, but apparently Ben didn't take hints easily. He stood a little too close and tried again. "Do you know Mrs. Baxter?"

"Everyone in Brackton knows everyone, more's the pity. Mrs. Baxter considers herself central to life in Brackton."

Strictly speaking, Mrs. Baxter didn't live in the village. Her mock-Tudor monstrosity occupied the opposite headland to my own grey stone house. Whereas I lived a couple of minutes from the outskirts of Brackton itself, Mrs. Baxter lived on the fringes of the caravan park. It was her biggest insecurity and, I suspected, the reason she'd bought Anchor Cottage in the first place. The cottage was the only building on the beach – it was her way of staking a claim on the whole place. She wasn't content with spying on the sand; she had to own some of it too, even if it was only a poky cottage with a twee name.

Ben joined me at the trestle table. "What about you, Dr. Blunt?" he said. "Are you central to village life? Have you and your husband been joint-presidents of the gardening committee for 40 years, or did you retire here when you stopped being a doctor?"

"You don't stop being a doctor. You either are a doctor or you're not – retirement has nothing to do with it. Physics is still physics." I wiped my fingers on the least filthy of the rags. "And for your information, I've never seen the need for a husband."

"Right. Of course." Ben looked uncomfortable for the first time since we'd met. He floundered for a minute, then said brightly, "I suppose becoming a doctor of physics was quite an achievement in your day."

"My day?" I gave him another look. "When was that exactly?"

He was saved by the whistle of the kettle from the other room and I hoped his embarrassment might delay his return, but in only another two minutes he was back, as cheerful as before. "What do you think of my paintings then?"

"You're right." I took a mug from him and sniffed the contents. The coffee was instant. I might've guessed. "They don't look like what they're meant to be."

"You don't know what they're meant to look like."

"Dog sick?" I waved at the nearest canvas. "A bumble bee that's been run over by a bike?"

I wasn't trying to be funny. I was trying to offend him. He laughed. "What about this one?" He selected a small canvas from near the window. "I did it in Tenerife a few years ago. It's one of my favourites. It's meant to look like the sea on a hot day."

I set my mug on the table and pushed it away from me. "Then why doesn't it? Why don't you paint things how they really look?"

"What's the point? We have photographs if we want to make a poor copy of something beautiful. This way I'm creating something new – inspired by reality but not mimicking it. See?"

I had no intention of seeing. "You won't sell anything like that round here."

Brackton was not a place for a budding abstract artist. One or two of the more adventurous residents probably had a driftwood sculpture hidden at home somewhere, but family photographs in seashell frames and cheap prints of watercolour flowers were more Brackton's style.

"I only came here to paint. I do all my selling in London."

"People buy them do they? Pictures of dog sick?"

"If I gave it the title, '*Fido's Dinner: The Return*', I'm not sure it'd sell. As it happens that picture is actually a representation of the atmosphere on rush-hour tube trains. And yes, people buy them. Hugh Grant's got one of mine in his bedroom."

I suppose I was meant to be impressed by that. I think Ben wanted me to be many things in those brief weeks we had together, and I nearly always disappointed him. When I didn't say anything, he picked up the packet of Hobnobs lying open on the table and walked over to the big easel in front of the window. It was angled to catch the light on the canvas, five feet wide by four high. Tendrils of orange and yellow curled from the top left corner; the rest of the canvas was blank.

"This is my newest project. It's going to be God." He held out the packet. "Hobnob?"

I didn't take one. "That's ridiculous. How can you paint God? You don't know what he looks like."

"How can anyone know what he looks like if nobody paints him?"

Perhaps Ben thought a physicist would be bowled over by his infallible logic. I remained firmly on my feet. I walked past the canvas and stood instead at the window, looking out at the grey world.

"I'm not being flippant," Ben said. "I'm just sick of only getting snatches of God." He came to the window too. "I'm sick of spotting him in the smell of coffee or in that fragment of tune when a car drives past with its windows down, and then never seeing him for real. I want to get a proper look at him."

"Gods don't exist in smells and music."

"Then maybe they exist in oil on canvas."

The rain had eased to a steady drumbeat. The wind no longer wuthered at the cliffs enclosing our narrow cove. For a minute we stood side-by-side, watching the greyness lift to leave a trail of destruction behind it on the sand. My house loomed out of the low-cloud on the clifftop.

"It might not work," Ben's voice was softer. "I have to try though. A picture's meant to paint a thousand words, but that's not good enough for me. I want to paint things you can't take a photograph of; things you can't ever describe – not really – not even in a thousand words."

"Like God?"

I turned away from him and tugged at the zip on my coat. Before I could reach the door, Ben's hand was on my arm, drawing my eyes back towards his. "Yes," he said. "Like God."

And so it started: Ben and God and me. I don't suppose Ben would start our story with madness, and if he did, it would be all neon polka dots and luminous stripes, not grey. For Ben, madness was what happened later, not at the start; it is in endings, not beginnings. And maybe I'm not sure which of us is right after all.

BEN

If I have any hope of justifying myself I have to start where it all started. Trouble is, I don't know where that is. It could've been when I first met Rosemary Blunt, or when I decided to move to Brackton, or at some unheralded point in my childhood, or when I was first born. Maybe it was at the dawn of time itself when we were single cells floating in murky swamps. But I think perhaps it all began with *The Scream*.

My parents had a print of *The Scream* hanging in the hallway. When I was young and they were working late, I'd sit on the staircase, staring at it through the banisters long after I should've been in bed. That tortured face – too familiar now through countless horror movies and Halloween masks – horrified me. And, like all things that horrify small boys – nose bleeds, broken bones, road kill – it fascinated me too. Blood red sky, anxiety, an infinite shriek of nature. Matisse or Mondrian could've done it, Klee or Dali might've been to blame, but I think if anybody has to take responsibility for my ambitions of being a painter, it's Edvard Munch. If it hadn't been for him, I might've been content with being a architect or an accountant, or any of the other respectable professions that keep the world spinning.

When I agreed to rent the cottage in Brackton Cove for the summer, it wasn't the beginning of everything, although it was meant to be a start of sorts. And on that third morning, as the storm rolled in, I was still in that blissful state of naivety; I still believed in new beginnings. I didn't realise it wasn't any sort of start – it was the twist at the end of the tale, that final scene that makes the play drag on too long.

Brackton hadn't been a careful choice. Anchor Cottage popped up during one of my hurried searches for short term rentals which were cheap and within touching distance of London. I'll confess I had some childish fantasies about being the mysterious new arrival in a small community; I'd harboured hopes of being asked to open fêtes or give talks to the WI, but that was as sinister as my motives got. Even when I first laid eyes on Rosemary, I wasn't thinking of London and India, not even about striking up a conversation. I only wanted to draw her. The grey sky, the grey sea, and Rosemary.

She looked perfect. The waves were crashing on the rocks just feet from where she sat – Slate Grey and Celadon. There was something about the loose strands of hair whipping round her face, and the way she sat bolt upright, staring into the storm as it approached over the sea that was striking – regal maybe, despite the anorak and walking boots. I'm not a cubist but even I couldn't resist drawing her in angles and distorted depths, the women and the waves blending into one. As the wind howled about us, I had to capture that sense of the unknown – a stranger watching a stranger.

My first impression of Rosemary, as an obliging woman who had stayed up on the rocks at my request out of sheer amiability, was shattered the first time she opened her mouth. From her dismissal of that sketch and her first short and short-tempered visit to the cottage, all the way through the rest of that stormy summer, she managed to avoid being obliging and amiable at all times. Until the end, I suppose. And I still don't quite know what happened then. Perhaps she was mad.

Of the three women I found myself entangled with that summer, it's Rosemary who I remember in bright colours and sharp edges, even though she wasn't the first I met. Jenny was my first acquaintance, though she, as with everyone else in Brackton, has already faded now to a series of pen and ink drawings. Naive sketches of people.

Jenny turned up at my door the day after I'd arrived, with a red face, lowered eyes and looking lost inside an oversized cardigan I was pretty sure she couldn't have known was back in fashion. She thrust a tin into my hands a little harder than I think she'd intended. Everything about her was abrupt, apologetic, uncertain.

"I'm Jenny Gribble. I brought you scones."

I'd come to Brackton on the bus from Lockhaven station with only one bag and had spent a merry morning lugging the remainder of my life's possessions down the cliff path from where they'd been delivered to Mrs. Baxter's house. I was ready for a tea break and a friendly face.

"You're too kind, Mrs. Gribble." I opened the tin and inhaled the warmth. "They smell divine."

"I'm not Mrs." She blushed deeper. "Please call me Jenny. Everyone else does."

"Then you must call me Ben." I stepped back to clear the doorway. "Won't you come in? The place is a bit of a mess – I'm a typical artist I'm afraid."

Jenny stepped inside and stopped, her eyes sweeping the chaos to find something they could politely rest upon. She settled on the print sticking to the wall above my bed. "Edvard Munch?" she said. "*The Scream?*"

"You're an art-lover?"

"Gracious, no." She was either surprised or horrified, I couldn't tell. "I'm not clever enough for that. Dad and I get no more highbrow than *Songs of Praise*. I've always liked the colours in this painting though. Very cheerful."

"You're the first person I've heard describe old Edvard as cheerful." I ushered her to a box so she could sit down. "Lucky bastard had insanity and tuberculosis running through his family like bad news through the Mother's Union." I caught a glimpse of Jenny's face. "I beg your pardon. I only meant that most artists would kill to have a muse like that. My parents were disgustingly healthy and not one of my relatives has ever ended up in an asylum."

"No, I should hope not."

I realised I wasn't making the best impression on Jenny. The first neighbour who'd shown an interest in me and I was wishing consumption and madness on my family. To tell the truth, I've never been very good at impressions. I prefer to concentrate on first *expressions* instead. It's how you make people feel, rather than what they think of you, that matters. Feelings, rather than truth – that's what expressionists were all about. And we have photography of all things, to thank for that.

Until photography was invented realism in paintings was the most important thing. If you wanted a family portrait there was no sudden flash and bit of dark room magic, just long hours sitting for a painter. When cameras *did* come along, it changed the face of painting completely. Monet and his lot stopped trying to imitate life exactly and gave an impression of a scene instead. Critics hated the visible brush strokes and intense colours. They didn't want to know what Renoir thought when he saw a boat drifting down a river; they wanted to know what he'd actually seen. So when the expressionists came hot on the heels of those impressionists – discarding realistic viewpoints and accurate colours for feelings and emotions – I don't think the world was ready for them. It wasn't ready for people like me.

I tried to explain all this to Jenny, as we sat munching warm scones, toes tucked up against our boxes. In a smaller way I tried to explain it to Rosemary the next day when I first met her too. I'm not sure either of them ever got it, but at least Jenny made a pretence at interest. Before I'd realised it, I'd had her trapped there for half an hour, listening to me blather on about impressionism and expressionism, truth and beauty, lies and reality. I'm not sure I let her get more than a few words in the whole time. Poor Jenny – it was always that way with her. She was too polite to escape from conversation – even if it was Mrs. Jolly at the post office complaining about the road-works again – until the last possible moment.

"I promised Dad I'd take him to his doctor's appointment," she said at last, edging her way back to the door, every movement an apology. "It's been a pleasure to meet you though. Let me know if you need anything – I live two doors down from the church."

"You're an angel. I'll look you up as soon as I run into trouble with the locals."

"I'm sure you won't do that, Mr. Summers."

"I don't know. We artists are a misunderstood bunch." I held the door open for her. "You're welcome to pop down any time you like. I'll always be happy to see you."

She flushed and muttered her goodbyes, almost falling over herself as she tried to escape on to the sand. I watched her picking her way down the beach past the lazy wrinkles of seaweed abandoned by the tide. She didn't look back.

In the cottage, I took the last of my cooling tea over to Edvard. The red sky, the swirling, looping water in the fjord, the strange white face – none of it could've been true. And yet, the colour of sky and texture of water was only one kind of truth. Anxiety, fear, anguish – all he was trying to convey – that was another kind of truth altogether. Perhaps what I'd been trying, and failing, to tell Jenny was that a painting isn't ever a lie just because it contains exaggeration or substitution. It doesn't lie because it expresses something beyond the tedious truth of life, just as no person can be reduced to a list of historical facts. How people feel about you – emotional truth – that's what matters. That's what I wish Jenny and Rosemary had understood. That's the truest truth of all.

ROSEMARY

When we are alone, I can say whatever I want to you. While the nurses cram into their staffroom to discuss the broken people in their care, we have the place to ourselves. For 20 minutes, I don't have to act.

The room in which you lie decaying is too hot. The sunlight bullies its way past the bluebottle busy battering itself to death against the window-pane, and falls across the bed. In its strength your pale hands seem almost transparent; the blue of your veins might be the blue of the blanket beneath them. Your nails have been cut, squared off at the corners. The few remaining wisps of white hair clinging to your scalp have been trimmed. They always make you look respectable. I always wish they hadn't bothered.

I don't hold your hand. Time for all that later. Instead, I read aloud – *New Scientist, National Geographic* – anything that won't interest you; anything you'll hate. Because there's nothing you can do about it.

The squeak of trolley wheels, cutting across the monotonous buzz of the fly, gives me just enough warning. By the time the nurse backs into the doorway, I am in position, one of your paper-thin hands in both of mine.

"Morning, Dr. Blunt." She produces a smile and a tube of alcohol gel. "Time for your husband's exercise."

I join the bluebottle at the window, leaving you to it. Outside, the last traces of yesterday's rainstorms are evaporating away in the heat of the morning. Only hints of violence remain: a trail of mud, a scattering of broken twigs, a car spinning its wheels in the flooded car-park.

She's a quick worker. And I wonder if you're embarrassed to have her so close – to need each limb lifted for you, each joint flexed in turn. Or do you enjoy her closeness? It wouldn't surprise me. She's like you – pieced together out of contrasts: bright pink lips and scarlet fingernails; sharp face and soft waves of blonde hair; chirpy tone and officious name tag swinging from her hip pocket: Cheryl WARNER. She's different from the other nurses. Unlike them, with their salesman patter and pointless questions, she understands I don't find idle conversation comforting. Perhaps she even knows I don't need to be comforted. When she speaks it's only because she has something to say.

"Dr. Richards asked me to tell you something."

Of course he did. It's been a year. When we first came here, you and I, we were told, weren't we? A year is the limit of their patience. And we've tested that patience right to the bitter end; a year and a week and three days.

"He's on holiday at the moment," she says. "But when he's back he wants to arrange a time to have a chat with you about Michael."

The bluebottle begins to do slow, punch-drunk laps of the room. Cheryl bats it away from her and it skims over you, struggling to regain height.

"I know it's hard, Dr. Blunt." She fills the silence herself. "But we all want what's best – both for you and for your husband."

I let her finish her checklist without talking, and I don't come back to your side until I'm sure she's gone, the squeal of the trolley cut off by the fire doors at the end of the corridor. When I do return, you are as unreadable as ever.

"Did you hear that?"

No answer. Not even a flicker.

"Apparently we all want what's best for you." I know you can hear me in there. "That's nice, isn't it?"

. . .

Letter from Rosemary to Julia.

From: Dr. R. Blunt
The Lookout
Brackton-on-Sea
Tuesday 19th June

Dear Julia,

Don't be absurd. It's only six days since my last letter, that hardly constitutes abandonment. I don't know why you insist I write so much. You can't possibly find me interesting after all this time, especially when I never have any news.

You seem to think being in Brackton is like living in St. Mary Mead. You wouldn't be alone – half the village seem to think I'm a Miss Marple figure. I daren't take up knitting or I'd be called in to solve every crime going, not that that would take long. This is the only place in the world Hercule Poirot could come on holiday and have a well-earned rest. As soon as the postman is found dead with a scrap of cloth in his hand, or Mrs. Baxter turns up strangled in Smuggler's Cave, I shall be so grateful for the excitement I'll get down to sleuthing straight away. But it won't happen, Julia, because nothing ever happens here.

The closest we'll get to crime this year will be at the Village Show. Last year Martin Hussingtree nearly punched Mr. Gribble after his carrots in Class 32 were tampered with. We only avoided bloodshed by Jenny Gribble whisking her father away with one of her loving smiles of goodwill to all men. It's impossible not to like Jenny a little bit, though I try very hard. After I've talked to her I always feel as if I need to pull my socks up and take a dose of Milk of Magnesia.

I know what you'll say. The non-existent crime and people like Jenny are the reasons I came here. I should attend coffee mornings and join the flower arrangers. After a whirlwind life of pointing at things on a blackboard, I need a rest. And you're probably right. No doubt you'll meet Jenny one day and think she's simply marvellous. You'll become best friends, leaving me to sit alone in my house without even a cat for company. Do you think I should get a cat? I don't think Miss Marple had one. Perhaps it might help.

The current gossip feeding the village, is that Mrs. Baxter has finally let the cottage on the beach to some artist fellow. I accidentally saw some of his paintings and they're not what I'd call art. I expect I'm a terrible philistine because he says Hugh Grant has one in his bedroom. Or was it his bathroom? Bathroom might make more sense.

Anyway, you needn't be excited at the arrival of an artist in Brackton because he doesn't look anything like one. I suppose he does act like one though. I saw him coming out of the post office today and he tried to greet me as an old friend. Even suggested that I came down to his cottage to try my hand at painting. Can you imagine it, Julia? Me?

With love, Rosemary

Letter from Julia to Rosemary.

From: Mrs. J. Braithwaite

15 The Warren

Eastmoore

Wednesday 20th June

Dearest Rosemary,

I can't see you as a Miss Marple. Sherlock Holmes, maybe. Anyway, if I picture Brackton as the sort of place where aristocratic detectives intimidate lowly peasants into revealing the village secrets, it's your fault – you never describe anything properly. After six years I still have no idea whether your village green has a maypole and duck pond, or is one of those modern ones with bins for dog mess.

What about this artist? How can you say nothing ever happens? It's so romantic to have an artist on the beach and you haven't told me a thing about him. What does he look like? What does he paint? Of course you must paint with him. I shall never forgive you if you don't.

You could invite me to visit, you know. Then you wouldn't have to describe everything. I'd be very good. I won't bring any grandchildren and I'll try to dislike Jenny Gribble. I'll even come to the Village Show and roll my eyes at the rural charm if you want.

I won't bore you with my tales of domesticity, other than to tell you Rory has finally persuaded Alison to marry him in the New Year – after she's had time to lose the baby weight – and Jacob got his 50m swimming badge this week. Secretly, I'm hoping Alison has a girl this time. At my age there are only so many times I can play in goal before I need a nap.

Lots of love, Julia

PS: Get a cat if you want, but don't tell the grandchildren. After your last visit, they're convinced you're a witch.

Letter from Rosemary to Julia.

Friday 22nd June

Dear Julia,

What can you possibly find interesting about Brackton? It's hardly the jewel in the seaside crown. The beach itself has no amenities to speak of – no pedaloes or ice-creams or shops selling saucy postcards. The one public toilet is in a shed which only gets unlocked if somebody from the Parish

Council remembers, and as everyone on our side of the bay has as little to do with tourists from the other as possible, that's rare. The Green has both a duck pond full of seagulls and a bin for unspeakable messes, but no maypole except on May Day. What else would you like to know? The roofing material on the post office? (Slate). The colour of the vicarage window ledges? (Blue).

I don't know what you're complaining about. I've sent you so many pictures of my house and garden. As you told me my house looked like it suited me perfectly – did you mean because it is an austere and ugly pile of grey stones, or because it stands apart from everything else? – I daren't send you more for fear of what other conclusions you'll draw. Besides, it's such a faff getting photos printed and I have no intention of joining you in the Polaroid club. You're the only person I know who still thinks Polaroid cameras are cutting-edge technology.

As for Ben – what's there to say? He's middle-class and journeying through middle-age with reasonable wear and tear. He wears clothes for people 20 years younger and could do with getting out in the sun a bit. Had I realised there was to be an exam I would have studied him closer. He paints the sea and the smell on trains and God. Now you see why I can't like him and shan't paint with him.

Come to visit if you must, but not until autumn. You would find the Show so utterly delightful I wouldn't be able to bear it. You'd ruin my reputation as a miserable hag by having a go on the coconut shy and buying local honey. And then I'd probably find myself running a stall at the Christmas Fair. No, you may come in the first week of October and not a moment sooner.

Congratulate Rory for me and give my best wishes to Alison. About time too.

Love, Rosemary

PS: Shan't get cat – think I'm allergic. Will consider toad instead.

Letter from Julia to Rosemary.

Sunday 24th June

Dear Rosemary,

I've booked my train tickets to Lockhaven for Monday 1st October and if you change your mind I'll know you're hiding some sinister secret from me. An insane husband in a padded room? The Polaroid will be coming too (I don't think they're cutting-edge technology, thank-you very much,

I just happen to find them convenient), and I intend to take photos of everything.

What colour eyes does Ben have? What does God look like? You simply must go to see him again. For me? You might even like him if you give him a chance. What harm could it do?

Love, Julia

Letter from Rosemary to Julia.

Wednesday 27th June

Dear Julia,

You're getting your genres mixed up. I'm sure Jane Eyre isn't cosy crime. At any rate, if I had an insane husband I wouldn't need to lock him in a padded room. I'd send him to the Bowls Club with the rest of them.

Ben is a bohemian with grey eyes, and, as far as I can see, God is mostly Burnt Amber. I've been to see him again – Ben, not God – purely out of loyalty to you. He was no less irritating than before and makes coffee as if he's never drunk it. He's disgustingly good-natured and absolutely refuses to be offended, however hard I try. You'll love him.

Now for the rest of my Tales from the Country... The Show is on Saturday and you'll no doubt be delighted to know that I may have volunteered to be a judge for the children's science competition. I'm not entirely sure. I had the misfortune of sitting next to Jenny all the way to Lockhaven on Monday – despite the bus being only half full. When Jenny talks I find it easiest to keep up a steady nod, interjecting an occasional, "Oh, I quite agree." It leaves me free to think on more interesting things, but does mean I have little idea of what I've agreed to by the time I've shaken her off.

I'm cross again, can you tell? I'm cross because the sun is blazing down like nobody's business and the horrible little tourists are making the beach look untidy. One nice bit of weather in amongst all this rain and you'd think it was the last chance anybody had to go on holiday. I'll probably spend all tomorrow morning picking the litter off the high-tide mark and it's not even the school holidays yet. Why can't these people be bohemians too and go travelling in Thailand instead of sunbathing in Sussex?

Grumpily yours, Rosemary

Letter from Julia to Rosemary.

Friday 29th June

Dear Rosemary,

I AM jealous. I wish I had a grey-eyed artist painting an amber God as my neighbour. Instead, on one side I've got an elderly couple who scowl at anybody who talks above a whisper, and on the other side I've got an elderly couple who smile at everybody and try to entice you in for tea and dry scones. But perhaps now we're in our seventies I shouldn't call other people elderly.

I would've thought you'd be interested in a painting of God with your upbringing. Or did three decades in the science department drill that out of you? Do you remember that awful picture of the Sacred Heart that hung in the assembly hall at school? When we were naughty we were forced to kneel and 'look upon the bleeding heart of our saviour and repent'. I spent a lot of time looking at that picture. Not you though – you probably never once knelt before it. I never understood why your parents sent you to St. Boniface. Didn't they think Roman Catholicism was of the devil?

Perhaps if you prayed to the Mighty Burnt Amber, he might make everyone go to Thailand for you and you can stop being grumpy. I bet Ben's been to Thailand, hasn't he? I expect he's been everywhere. He sounds terribly romantic. Is he impoverished? I do hope so.

Affectionately, Julia

BEN

When I opened the door to Rosemary the second time, she scowled.

"I'm not here because I want to be." She swept past me into the cottage. "My friend wants to know what colour your eyes are." She pushed a packet of ground coffee and a cafetière into my hands. "Drink instant and you may as well drink dishwater."

While I put the kettle on and rinsed the least filthy of the mugs, Rosemary disappeared into the studio. I could hear her pacing up and down. Every now and then the footsteps would stop, as if something had caught her eye and disapproval. When I got into the studio however, she wasn't looking at my paintings. She was examining the table. The tubes she'd arranged into neat blocks of six had returned to their natural state in amongst the rags and brushes. A new packet of Hobnobs towered dangerously over my abandoned palette.

"They're grey," I said as I handed her a mug. "My eyes I mean."

"I know."

"Somewhere between Dark Slate and Smoke, if your friend likes details."

Rosemary smiled as if she wasn't quite used to it. "Julia eats details for breakfast, lunch and dinner. I'm trying to wean her off them." She adjusted a paintbrush to line up parallel with the edge of the table, then glanced over her shoulder at my easel. "How's God coming along?"

"I'm currently trying to work out whether he's more Burnt Amber or more Tangelo." We walked over to the canvas. Bands of colour rippled out from the top left-hand corner. "What do you think? Yellow or orange?"

She considered the question for longer than I expected. For a brief moment I even thought she might be appreciating the brushwork. Then she shrugged and said, "The yellow is certainly less offensive. I wouldn't like to say which was the more divine."

And that was all she had to say on the matter. In another second she was back at the window, staring out at the one sight that didn't offend her.

"You don't think a lot of modern art, do you Dr. Blunt?"

"I try not to think of it at all."

"Shame. We could've done a deal. I could've taught you to paint, and you could've taught me about science."

"I can't see that being very agreeable for either of us."

"I don't know. Scientists make great painters. It's the attention to detail that does it – that and already knowing how to be misunderstood."

It wasn't an award-winning joke, I'll admit, but Rosemary could at least have attempted a smile. She didn't even look at me when I joined her, just continued to stare at two seagulls extracting polystyrene from the seaweed with equal amounts of effort and disappointment. People were beginning to spill out of the caravan park and down the cliff path by Mrs. Baxter's with towels and cool-bags, dressed for the Caribbean, arms folded against the stiff breeze.

Rosemary took a sip of her coffee and grimaced. "It's scorched. You poured the water on too soon." She gave me a university-professor look. "You need to wait a minute and a half after the kettle's boiled before pouring."

"I hadn't realised that coffee-making was such an art."

"It's not." She looked around unsuccessfully for somewhere to put the offending drink. "It's a science."

"That would explain why I'm not very good at it."

"Rubbish. Anybody can be good at science, even with the shoddy education most schools give nowadays."

I seized my chance to pique her interest. "I was home-schooled actually. My parents were OK with most stuff, but they weren't so hot at science so they only covered the basics."

Rosemary clicked her tongue. "I can't stand all that hippy nonsense. Why parents think they'll be better at teaching their children than a qualified teacher, I'll never know."

I began to explain my story, telling her all about a childhood spend travelling round Europe, never staying long enough in one place to attend school. I'd hoped it was a romantic tale but I'd picked my audience badly. Jenny might have been fascinated by the thought of being home-schooled by artists, but I wasn't scoring any points with Rosemary.

"I was taught a lot that other kids didn't hear about – politics, philosophy, art. My mum was a sculptor and my dad a painter, and they'd let me sit up with them all night as they talked to other artists – it was an education in itself. I learned my times tables and stuff like that, but I learned far more than that too." I took a swig of my coffee. It tasted fine to me. "It's only science I fell behind with."

"You could still learn," Rosemary said. "Science isn't hard – it's just thinking about things in a certain way."

"So is abstract art."

Stand-off. We stood in silence for a minute until Rosemary took another mouthful of coffee, wincing as obviously as she could.

"It's still a no," she said.

"What is?"

"Teaching me to paint. I'm still not going to agree to it."

"I don't have to *teach* you. Come and paint whatever you want and I won't interfere unless you want me to."

I'm not sure why I was so keen for Rosemary to visit me again. I wasn't so lonely – no more so than I had been in London – and I hadn't been starved of human contact. Jenny had been down to the cottage a couple of times and my daily trips to the village had put me on nodding terms with most of the locals. Perhaps then, it was the challenge of Rosemary that attracted me. If we'd been teenagers I'd have said that her determination to dislike me was a crush, or that my fascination of her dislike was an indication of a spark between us. But we weren't teenagers and there was nothing to cause a spark. There was just something about her complete abhorrence of my paintings, that made her interesting, that was all. She intrigued me.

"What makes you think I have any interest in starting to paint?" She looked at me over the rim of her mug. "And even if I did, why would you want me to? I'd only be disturbing your divine mission."

"I want you to because the only coherent conversation I've had for the last two days was when Mrs. Baxter asked me if I intended to start using the door-mat, or pay for a professional cleaning company to come in after my lease is up."

After a struggle, Rosemary allowed herself to smile. "I can believe that."

"So you'll come again?" I asked. "For the sake of my sanity?"

She made a show of considering the issue. "As I wouldn't wish Mrs. Baxter on anybody, I'll see if Julia has any more questions for you." She drained the last of her sub-standard coffee. "If she has, then I'll come next week some time." She pushed the mug into my hands. "You needn't think it means I like your paintings though. I still think they're terrible."

CHERYL

I don't feel bad about it. Everything I did that summer I'd do again. Most things anyway. Forget what the papers said afterwards, it was Lauren who went panting after Ben in the first place. When we met him at the Brackton Village Show I didn't even think he was that good-looking, never mind the fact he was old enough to be my dad. Lauren, on the other hand, thought he was George Clooney or something and, boyfriend or no boyfriend, she had to drag me over to speak to him.

It was my idea to go to the Show. Only once we'd got there did I wonder why I'd bothered. We kind of thought it would be fun – something a bit different. There was nothing to do in Lockhaven on a Saturday except the usual options of crowded coffee shops or crowded swimming pool, and neither of us was feeling rich enough to go into Brighton for the day. Catching the bus to Brackton for a free event seemed like a good idea at the time. Trouble was, once we'd watched the welly-wanging and the ferret racing and had a go on the tombola, there wasn't much to do.

I'd forgotten that Dr. Blunt lived in Brackton. I suppose I must've known at the time because the address was written on the front of the hospital notes, but it was two different worlds. The people I met as I worked the wards at the hospital were nothing to do with what I did on my days off. You did bump into relatives of patients in Tesco sometimes but that was the only time I'd think of them outside work. Not that I didn't like my work. I'd only been a nurse for a year and I wasn't exactly bored of it by then, it was more that it had hit me that I'd started a career. Not just a job – a Career. If I didn't think about it, I could probably work for 40 years straight before retiring and wondering what had happened to life. That's what Ben brought to me I think – the realisation that there was more to life than I knew; the fear that I'd never know it.

Lauren didn't understand that. She thought she did, but she didn't. By the time I graduated and was applying for every nursing job I could find in London or near my uni in Manchester, Lauren had been a beauty therapist for two years. When I finally got sick of NHS rejections and agreed to come home to take a job in Lockhaven Private Hospital Lauren was I-told-you-so all over. She'd thought I was stupid to rack up all that debt at university. As I moved back in with my parents, Lauren was moving into her first flat and that was what she counted as ambition – not having the best out of life, just getting to each base before everyone else. I wanted something different. Ben was different.

We were in the beer tent sampling Harvey's Kiss and wondering if we should move on to cider when Lauren spotted him. He was alone at the far end of the make-shift bar, half-empty plastic pint glass in hand.

"Something to look at, three o'clock," Lauren said in a stage-whisper most people in the tent could hear.

I glanced over at him. "Seriously? He's old."

"Daniel Craig isn't exactly young – didn't stop you drooling over him in the cinema."

"Yeah, but Daniel Craig is James Bond." I took a sip of the taster glass. "That guy is probably some weirdo with no friends."

"I think he's pretty fit." Lauren wasn't even pretending not to stare any more. "I wouldn't say no."

"What about Lee? Or do you forget about boyfriends when you see potential sugar-daddies?"

"No harm in looking is there?" She leaned over the bar and smiled at the barman. "Two halves of Appledram, please." She scooped her change out of a puddle and winked at me. "No harm in talking either. Come on."

And before I could argue she was wiggling her way toward her prey.

"You look lonely." She stopped too close to him. "Thought we'd come and keep you company."

"That was nice of you." He swapped his pint to his left hand and held out his right. "I'm Ben. I don't know many people in Brackton yet."

"We're from Lockhaven." She thrust her hand and breasts in his direction. "I'm Lauren, and this," Lauren practically pushed me into Ben's arms, "is Cheryl."

Ben shook hands with both of us. "I think you're the first people I've seen between the ages of 10 and 50 all day."

This made Lauren giggle and go off into one of her super-fast monologues where she took on the persona of a soap opera barmaid, dropping aitches as if she'd gone to Redhill Park on the east side of town and not Lockhaven High School. I never got why she did it, but it nearly always seemed to work. I'd heard the act so many times I wasn't really listening and didn't even realise Ben had told her he was an artist from London until she squealed. "Oh my God – like a real artist? A painter?"

"Yup." Ben took a swig of his beer and looked nonchalant. Or tried to. "Though I don't paint your traditional stuff. I do abstracts."

I knew for a fact Lauren didn't like art. She'd only chosen it for GCSE because she was no good at either music or PE, and didn't want to have to take German as well as French. She spent the whole two years complaining about how rubbish Van Gogh was and how there was no point painting anything now we had cameras on our phones.

"If you find yourself in Brackton again, you're welcome to come down to my cottage and take a look at my work," Ben said. "I'm staying at Anchor Cottage – it's on the beach, you can't miss it."

He addressed this last comment to me, so I had to make eye contact. And I could kind of see what Lauren was talking about. I still wouldn't have said he was gorgeous, but there was something about him. Nice eyes. His smile took over his whole face and it switched from dipped to full beams in a second.

Before I could think of a reply Lauren had answered for me, "We'd love to. Next time we both have a day off we'll be sure to come down."

"What do you do?" Ben said.

"I'm a beauty therapist."

He smiled a dipped smile and spoke with an easy charm that might've been smarmy if he wasn't dressed in old jeans and carefully avoiding staring at her cleavage. "I can see you must be good at your job."

Lauren giggled again. "Cheryl's a nurse."

"And I suppose I should say I hope you never have to find out if I'm good at my job," I said.

Ben laughed and Lauren looked annoyed. Not annoyed enough however, to abandon her match-making. "Cher looks after people who are in comas and stuff. I couldn't do what she does. It's an amazing job."

Ben half-raised his glass in my direction. "I'm sure it is." He drained the contents. "If you'll forgive me, I have to go and give out some prizes, but I'll hope to see you again soon."

He was barely out of earshot before Lauren was on my case. "Well?"

"Well what?"

"Oh come on – you have to like him, even if he is a bit old."

"Yeah, he seems nice enough."

"Cher, you'll never get a boyfriend if you only think someone like Ben is 'nice enough'."

"Who says I want a boyfriend?"

I did want one – and she knew it – but I wasn't desperate. Not desperate enough to go after a man more than twice my age. There had been two boys at uni who'd filled the time from halfway through first year to final exams, but nobody since graduation. Lauren said I was too picky, whereas Mum always told me I was too flighty. Mum said that about everything though. When I happened to mention I might not want to be a nurse forever, she acted like I was running away to the circus not discussing some distant career change. She accused me of always looking for the next thing, never being content. She was right in a way, but I didn't see why that was a character flaw. Ambition isn't a fault.

"You've got to admit that knowing an artist would be pretty cool," Lauren insisted. "You *do* want to see him again, right?"

"I wouldn't mind."

She gave me an I-bet-you-wouldn't look. "You're always saying that Lockhaven is boring and you can't wait to get out." She sighed at me over the top of her glass. "You spend more time on job websites than you do on Facebook, and you're the only person I know who puts aside a bit of money every payday not for a flat or a car but just for 'escape'. Then somebody actually interesting turns up and you act like you can't even be bothered to talk to him."

Lauren was right, I guess. Ben was the sort of person you didn't meet in Lockhaven. There were plenty of better places for people to live if they wanted to live in Sussex. Who'd choose a small run-down town, nearly 10 miles from the sea, when they could live in Brighton or in one of the cute villages on the coast? Ben didn't actually live in Lockhaven, but Brackton was only a bus away and he was more of an attraction that most of the men at our local.

I suppose I decided then. As Lauren and I sipped our cider I decided that if she went to see Ben at his cottage, I'd go with her. That was all. We'd go and we'd look at his paintings and then we'd return to Lockhaven and forget all about him. It would shut Lauren up and she'd move on to the next thing. That was what I thought anyway. I honestly didn't expect anything more than that.

ROSEMARY

Saturday arrived with a blaze of sunshine even I was grateful for. There could be nothing more dreary than watching people toss the sheaf in drizzle. I read Julia's latest letter on my way to the fields on the far edge of the village. She was right about one thing – my upbringing should've made me more interested in Ben's painting of God. But upbringings are funny things – they can fill you with lifelong passions or with lifelong wariness. Mine had done the latter.

My mother was an Anglican: fiercely loyal, devastatingly dogmatic. It was a shame she couldn't abide Catholicism because the local priest was as big on hellfire as she was. Dad had a softer approach. He played along with my mother, but while her god stood before her, making her copy lines from a blackboard, I got the impression that Dad's god was ensconced in a corner of a pub, offering gentle advice over a pint of ale. Growing up in that atmosphere made the god of my childhood something obscure – a cosmic cross between head teacher and secret diary. He made sure I behaved when nobody else was watching, and had the power to grant me wishes. He was a jukebox god; if I paid my money I expected to be able to pick the tune. That's how I treated him back then – back when he still existed. Before I lost him. Before I stopped caring if I'd find him again.

I'd finished Julia's letter and composed most of the reply in my head, by the time I reached the showground. The marquee was already closed for judging and I was accosted by Jenny as soon as I pushed my way through the flaps. She was looking agitated. "Dr. Blunt, there you are. I thought you'd forgotten us." She gripped my arm. "So kind of you to judge all the children's classes. This way."

She released me and began to trip her way to the back of the tent, past rows of trestle tables covered in vegetables.

"All the children's classes?" I hurried after her. "I thought it was just the science."

Jenny pulled the clipboard from under her arm. "That's odd. You're down to do it all." She looked at me with a smile full of confidence. "You won't mind doing it, will you? There's only 20 classes for children – it shouldn't take long."

Before I had the chance to protest, Jenny had thrust the judging guidelines into my hand and joined the other judges huddled round the rhubarb. I looked at the first bullet point:

- *When assessing the entries, consider effort as well as overall achievement*

That was ridiculous for a start. Anybody who needs to be awarded marks for effort isn't cut out for the job. I scrunched the paper into a ball and dropped it into a bucket under the table. There were too many entries to bother with all that. After decades of waiting for data to be processed and marking first-year essays I had learned a degree of patience, but there were only so many decorated eggs and homemade biscuits I could look at. By the time I was halfway through the second category – *Best Handwriting: Infants* – I was bored. I clipped the red winner's card to the only legible one I could find, scribbled 'Well done!' on all the other entry cards and moved on.

I think it's fair to say I wasn't cut out to be a children's judge. Mediocrity seemed to me to be an odd thing to celebrate, and there wasn't much that wasn't mediocre as far as I could see. It soon became tiresome to think of platitudes for all the comment cards and so I lapsed into Latin. If it wasn't for fear of a mob of irate parents, I might have been honest in my appraisals, but it wasn't worth the hassle. Latin and the sayings of Confucius filled up the cards nicely, were not obviously rude and had the advantage that I probably wouldn't be asked to be a judge again next year.

The last category was the science projects. After all I'd had to wade through to reach them, there were only two entries. A bunch of forlorn daffodils, stained blue with food colouring, wilted next to a single bulb and switch connected to a battery. I tried the switch. The bulb flickered and died. For a few seconds I wavered between the two uninspiring offerings. I'd just chosen the daffodils – chiefly because I hadn't realised it was even possible to grow daffodils in June – and was scribbling on the cards, when somebody spoke from inches behind me. "*Parturient montes, nascetur ridiculus mus.*" Ben was reading the card over my shoulder. " 'Mountains will be in labour and an absurd mouse will be brought forth'? That's Horace isn't it? Why are you writing that on a card for some seven year-old?"

"What are you doing in here? It's judges only."

"I know." Ben perched on the edge of the table. "I *am* a judge. Jenny asked me to do photography and watercolours."

"Then why don't you?"

"I have. But I didn't write Latin on the cards. Should I have done?"

"Depends on whether you were taking it seriously or not."

"I tried to, though God knows it was hard not to laugh at some of the entries. One or two good ones though – care to take a look?"

I shuffled together the remaining cards. He was trying to get me to meet his eye, I could feel it. And from there it was only a short step to trying to get me to like him.

"Not really."

"It's not *my* art, Dr. Blunt. You might actually like some of it. You're not going to pass up the opportunity to take a sneaky peek at the entries while we've got privileged access to the marquee, are you?"

It was only then I realised we were the sole people in the tent. Beans had been snapped and cakes sliced, and the other judges had gone, leaving a scattering of coloured cards behind them.

"Rumour has it that competition was pretty fierce in the beetroot class this year." Ben hadn't given up yet. "And I've heard there was a scandal in Class 71, *Arrangement of Flowers in a Teacup*." He leaned in closer and lowered his voice. "Apparently – and you didn't hear this from me – somebody used a mug."

I turned away from him and began to walk down the rows of tables, pretending to be interested in feathered asters. After six years it still baffled me why anybody entered the Show – perhaps proving that I never was cut out for village life. Why should anyone care whether their marrows were bigger or rhubarb straighter than the marrows and rhubarb of their neighbours?

"Listen to this." Ben had drifted off to another table and was holding up a comment card. " 'What a shame you didn't think to consult a recipe before attempting this tart.' " He held up another. " 'What a shame you've produced a jam sponge instead of the requisite Victoria Sponge Cake.' I hadn't realised we were allowed to be spiteful." He ran his finger along the edge of a plate, licking off a smudge of cream. "If I'd known, I could've had a lot more fun."

My uninterested path past the exhibits brought me to the opposite side of the trestle table Ben was leaning over. One entry caught both our eyes at the same second.

"Oh dear." Ben leant over the plate. "That doesn't look too bright." He poked at a sad-looking pizza with the wrong end of a knife. "Congealed cheese and soggy ham flavour. Still, looks like it's the only entry so an easy win for Competitor 51 at least."

"It would be if they'd won." I pulled a blue card from under the plate. "They've been given second prize."

Ben's mouth twitched. Before he could say something witty and insightful, the flap of the tent was turned back.

"Look out," he whispered. "It's the What a Shame gang back again."

It was only Jenny. "Mr. Summers, Dr. Blunt – I didn't realise any of the judges were still in here. Do you need more time?"

"Dear me, you've caught us in the act." Ben switched on his biggest smile. "Dr. Blunt and I were being terribly naughty and looking round the other classes while we had the chance. Would you care to join us?"

He advanced on Jenny and tucked her arm into his. She beamed up at him, blushing in that ridiculous way she did whenever anybody was the least bit nice to her.

"I can't thank you enough for letting me be a judge," Ben continued. "Such an honour when I'm only a guest in your village."

"It's us who should be honoured." If possible Jenny went even more red as she allowed herself to be steered towards the watercolours. "Coming, Dr. Blunt?"

"I think I'll leave you to it." I headed for the exit. "I've seen quite enough for one day."

Outside the marquee, the crowd had grown. A few dozen competitors, all pretending not to be bothered, took a step towards me as I came out.

"Not quite ready yet," I announced to nobody in particular. "Shouldn't be long now."

The fields were filling up fast. Coach-loads of tourists spilled out of the parking area to mob the nearest stalls. Over by the white elephant, children gathered for the sack race, and behind the beer tent a brass band played the tunes their grandfathers had played half a century earlier. To an outside observer – who didn't know about the family feuds and village politics – it was picture-perfect. It was iced lollies and cream teas, lemonade and innocence; Britain in an age of manners and common sense, when crime didn't exist and everyone knew their place. It was twee and villagey and just the sort of thing Julia would've said I needed in order to feel settled. Right then, I didn't feel as if I needed it. And I didn't feel settled.

I paused at the edge of the arena to watch the Huntmaster demonstrate hunting calls on his horn. As the pack of dogs milled around him he beckoned to the watching children to come under the ropes to meet them.

"Good day, Ms. Blunt."

I turned to find Mrs. Baxter at my shoulder. She said my name as she always did, emphasising the Ms., clipping the t to a spike at the end.

"I didn't expect to see *you* at a community event."

It was a fair point. I shifted my gaze back to the arena. With so many new playmates the hounds weren't interested in imaginary foxes and instead of obeying the calls, they were pouncing on each child, burying them under an avalanche of fur.

"I was judging the children's classes in the marquee," I said.

"*You* were?" Mrs. Baxter's eyebrows disappeared into the brim of her hat. "I suppose Miss Gribble asked you, did she? I really don't understand why they let her pick the judges."

Nothing would have delighted Mrs. Baxter more than seeing me offended. Fake, gushing apologies were her speciality. She lived in a constant state of paranoia that the rest of Brackton looked down on her for living on the wrong side of the cove. If she'd realised the truth – that nobody in Brackton thought of her at all if they could help it – she might never have got over the shock.

Mrs. Baxter was the sort of person who wanted the last word in every village matter, but as it was always the same word and never a positive one, nobody listened. Putting people down and then pretending to be surprised when they took offence at the 'misunderstanding' was just one of her many hobbies, which also included raining on parades and bullying her husband into writing letters of complaint to the council. She probably had some redeeming feature, but in the decade we'd occupied the solitary houses on opposite headlands, I'd seen no indication of it. I had no intention of letting her rile me.

The Huntmaster was racing round the arena, brandishing his whip, trying to rescue the sobbing children and return them to their parents. The yelping, piddling hounds were growing more frantic by the minute, until at some secret signal they lost interest in the game and rushed from the arena *en masse* to hunt out lost ice-creams.

"Did you enter any of the classes this year, Mrs. Baxter?" I asked. "The tent was full to bursting."

"Three." She ticked them off on her fingers. "Six pods of beans – broad. Floral arrangement for a gentleman's buttonhole. Pizza with own choice of topping."

I felt suddenly cheerful. "You have been busy. I hope you win a prize. Especially for your pizza."

Mrs. Baxter frowned. "Did you see my tenant in the marquee?"

"He was judging the art classes when I was there."

"I'm not surprised Miss Gribble asked *him*. Having a professional judge adds an air of respectability to the proceedings, don't you agree?"

"If you can call him professional."

"You'd know more about that than me, Ms. Blunt. You're the one who's been in and out of his cottage since he arrived."

I'd been to his cottage twice. And both of them unwillingly.

"Of course Miss Gribble's been there too. It must be so nice for him to have somebody his *own* age to talk to." Mrs. Baxter gave a smile that missed her eyes, and shifted her gaze to the opposite side of the arena. "I think my husband is trying to get my attention."

I looked over. Mr. Baxter seemed to be engrossed in conversation with a group of men, and not at all eager to alert his wife.

"A wife's always on duty as you know... well... as I'm sure you can imagine, anyway." She gave a little laugh. "Goodbye, *Ms.* Blunt."

Conversation cut off by his wife's arrival, I watched as Mr. Baxter allowed himself to be dragged off to the marquee, then I walked in the opposite direction, towards the top of the field. I tried to picture Mrs. Baxter's face when she found her pizza.

"What's so funny?" Ben appeared at my side without warning.

"Nothing. Where's Jenny?"

"Peace-making among the legumes in the marquee. Some guy called Martin making a fuss." Ben shrugged. "I left her to it."

"Not very gentlemanly."

"I suppose not."

I didn't like to have Ben's company imposed on me, especially when I had no definite plan of where I was going. I hoped the mud, churned by hundreds of feet already and sticking to his designer trainers, would've deterred him from tailing me as we slipped our way up the hill. No such luck. We'd nearly reached the top before Ben said, "You haven't been to see me for days."

"Should I have?"

"I thought you might've wanted to."

"I can't think of a single thing I've said or done that might've given you that impression."

There was silence for another few seconds before Ben said, "No. Neither can I."

A fence separated the field we were in from the one beyond the crest of the hill. Not knowing what else to do, I leaned against a post, looking out over the fields, inland towards Lockhaven. I wanted Ben to go away.

"Why don't you like my paintings, Dr. Blunt?"

"I don't see the point in painting the smell on trains and God and all those... other things."

"Is that why you won't come to paint with me? Because I'm trying to find God?"

"You finding God or not is nothing to do with me. I won't come to paint because I'd be terrible."

"You don't know that."

I was expecting another of his speeches, but it didn't come. He didn't speak at all for a good few minutes, until in a tone that was unexpectedly harsh he said, "It's alright for you. You understand how it all works." He waved an arm in a circle that took in the sky and the trees, the people resting further along the fence and the fields stretching to the horizon. "You've got physics to explain it all. It might not matter to you whether God's behind all those equations that tell you how the universe works, but if you wanted it to be God, then it could be. I don't have that."

Ben glanced at me and laughed an embarrassed laugh. "Thinking out loud," he said. "Bad habit of mine." He pulled out his phone. "You know, we can hardly see a single building and yet in a few seconds this could tell me the nearest place to get a takeaway."

"And?" I couldn't see the connection.

"And so if I was a software engineer I could work on an app that tells people where they can find God. But I'm not. I'm an artist. So I have to work on finding God in my own way."

"Perhaps people are more interested in where they can get a pizza than where to find mythical higher powers."

A cheer from the Country Pursuits enclosure made us both turn to look back down the field. A steady trickle of people wandered up and down the slope, eating ice-creams and clutching jars of chutney.

"Got quite the rural charm, hasn't it?"

"If you say so. You're the artist."

Another cheer announced a new record in the welly-wanging and I turned to watch the crowds milling about. On the edge of it, two young women stood, heads bent together, laughing. And, without knowing why, as soon as I saw them – as soon as I saw that flash of blonde hair – I knew I had to leave. Immediately. The unsettled feeling that seemed to lurk at the edge of my consciousness, but that I could never name, prickled into life. I didn't stop to question it. It never answered me if I did. It was never wrong either.

I headed for the nearest stile, Ben still in tow. "I have to go."

"What's the rush?"

"Things to do."

"Then why not go back the way we came?" he said. "It's far quicker."

I dropped down into the next field. "I fancy a walk."

"Cool." Ben hauled himself up on to the stile after me. "I'll come with you."

"I'd rather walk alone."

Ben hesitated then shrugged and jumped back down into the field we'd come from. "If that's what you want." His smile flicked back on again. "I'll go to investigate the beer tent instead, on one condition." He winked. "I'll leave you in peace now if you promise you'll come to paint with me. By this time next week, I want to have seen you at my cottage. No excuses."

JENNY

It was the week after the Show that Ben and I became friends, rather than merely neighbours. In the previous fortnight I'd taken to popping down to the beach every few days with a loaf of bread or a few slices of cake, but it wasn't until that Tuesday that we got talking properly. I never understood why he bothered with me, when nobody else in the village ever did. But he did bother. Because of that, some people said that I ought to have known about him. And perhaps on those lazy days at his cottage, when he taught me about art, he was trying to tell me more than I realised, but I didn't see it then. I'm not sure I'd see it now.

The Show was a success and we were lucky with the weather – barely one dry day in the whole of June and God gave it to us. It was always my favourite day on the Brackton calendar; the one day where I mattered. For a few hours there was something that couldn't be done without me. I'd been allowed to pick the judges for years, but I'd never dared ask Dr. Blunt before. She might not have been as thorny as some liked to make out, but she could be rather like her name – blunt, brusque even. I only plucked up the courage to approach her and Ben the week of the Show itself and I was so glad I did. In the end they proved to be the most enthusiastic judges, remaining in the tent long after the other judges had finished. It seemed only polite to take a seed cake down to Ben's cottage a few days later as a sort of thank-you present, and we ended up eating it together on the sand outside his front door.

"This is gorgeous." Ben spoke with his mouth still half-full. "You're the best cook I've ever met."

"I don't know about that. I just thought you could do with some feeding up."

"I'm hardly wasting away." Ben laughed and patted his stomach. "But I'm more than willing to let you feed me delicious cake whenever you want."

"Are you enjoying Brackton?"

"It's splendid. Nothing like London."

"I thought perhaps you'd find it lonely." I brushed the crumbs from my fingers. "Life in a city must be so much more lively."

"You can be lonely in a big city more easily than you can in a small village, I can assure you. Though it would be rather nice to get to know people here a bit more intimately. Nodding to people in the shop isn't quite a friendship is it?" He glanced at me and then back towards the water's edge where a game of rounders was in full swing. "You've been very kind to me. Wasting your time coming down to indulge me so often."

"It hasn't been a waste. I've enjoyed it."

It was true. Ben's appreciation was novel to me. It wasn't that the vicar and the cricket team didn't thank me for the sandwiches and scones, but they were all used to it. What's one more ginger cake after 25 years of ginger cakes? Ben wasn't bored with my baking yet.

"I'd love to be able to talk to someone about art," Ben said. "Nobody down here seems too bothered by it – except for one or two photographers and they hardly count."

"You could talk to me." I felt stupid as soon as I said it. "I don't know anything about it of course, but I... I'd love to learn. All those things you taught me about the impressionists and expressionists last time were fascinating."

Actually, it had mostly gone over my head, but I'd appreciated the effort.

"Would you really like to learn?" Ben shifted on to his side so he was facing me, stretched out on the sand. "I rather thought I'd bored you. If you wouldn't mind indulging me then you must let me take you to dinner some time in return – make it worth your while." He craned his neck to follow the rounders ball as it splashed into the sea. "Good shot."

I didn't dare say anything to that at first. Had he just asked me out to dinner? He'd said it so casually, as if there was nothing to it. As if asking me to dinner there, on the front step of that cottage was no big deal. As if history could repeat itself without consequences – without causing time to stand still or my heart to freeze in my chest. It was one of those throwaway comments people make and don't mean – I'll call you, we should do this again sometime, let's do dinner – and Ben couldn't possibly have known about the cottage after all. He wouldn't have known what his words meant. Nobody would have. There was nobody who could've told him about Tom.

It was because of Tom I'd nearly walked into the cottage without knocking the first day I came down to see Ben. Only at the last moment did I knock and wait for him to come to me. It'd been a long time since I'd set foot in there, and Mrs. Baxter's renovations had made it almost unrecognisable inside. From the outside however, it was almost the same. It was too much the same. When I'd left again, picking my way through the seaweed to the cliff steps, I knew I should've looked back, should've waved. I hadn't dared. I wasn't ready to see another man standing in the doorway to the cottage, smiling at me. And then there I was with that man, on that step, only a few weeks later, not knowing what to say. Unsure of whether I should say anything at all.

It'd been 20 years since I'd last been asked out to dinner by a man – not counting Dad. And when I had been asked it had been so different from the casual way Ben had tossed the suggestion into the breeze between us, it was almost comical. There had been nothing casual about Tom. He'd stumbled over the words, talking round the subject until neither of us could look each other in the eye. Then I'd accepted his offer so fast it had only made things worse.

That first date, when we'd sat on the front step of his cottage, eating fish and chips with our fingers as the sea turned orange in the setting sun, would've looked like something of nothing from the outside. To me – to us – it was perfect: full stomachs, greasy fingers, the trace of salt and vinegar on my lips, and the understanding when he walked me home that we were something more than we had been. Even if nobody knew it.

I wasn't comparing Ben to Tom as we ate seed cake together. Tom was shy and reclusive, barely leaving Brackton if he didn't have to; Ben was wild and impulsive and had been everywhere and done everything. The date with Tom had been a long dreamed of event; Ben's invitation had come out of the blue. But when I'd caught my breath and my heart had begun to thump again, when I was no longer giddy with ancient history, I realised I did want to go to dinner with Ben. I wanted him to talk to me about art. About anything.

"I'd like that."

It was only after I said it I realised how long I'd left a silence before replying. At the far end of the beach the ball had been rescued and the game was back in full swing. Ben had drained his tea and was frowning at the phone he'd pulled from his pocket. He dragged his eyes from the screen and put the phone face-down on the sand next to him, looking at me with confusion.

"Dinner I mean." I tried to sound as casual as he had. "Dinner some time would be nice."

"Great." His face cleared. "I've been meaning to try The Royal Oak ever since I got here. We'll have to arrange a date. You can indulge my pretentions at being an art lecturer in return for a couple of glasses of house white. I won't go earlier than the 1890s though, I promise. Nothing earlier than the fauves in my lecture series."

"Who were the fauves?"

"They were the fathers of abstract art. *Les fauves* – the wild beasts. You'll have heard of some of them I'm sure." He looked at me. "Braque?"

I shook my head.

"van Dongen?"

I wondered if I should lie, but shook again.

"Matisse then?"

"Oh, I've heard of Matisse."

"There you go – he was a fauve. And like the others he didn't paint total abstracts – birds still looked like birds and boats like boats – but he painted with pure, unmixed colours. Skin could be yellow, leaves purple, water green." Ben sat up and pulled his knees to his chest. "They weren't a refined school of art, just a group of friends. When somebody asked van Dongen about that, he admitted they didn't have the principals and theories the impressionists did, they only thought the colours the impressionists used were a bit dull and decided to do something about it."

"Reality was too dull for them?"

"Exactly. So they changed it."

And so began my second lesson. Drawing squiggles in the sand with a twig, Ben taught me how the fauves manipulated their audience with the mundane. Instead of painting weird stuff, they painted the everyday as if it were extraordinary. They used brilliant colours to twist, entertain, dazzle. A view of a river, a glimpse of a woman in a hat – the ordinary made larger than life, the truth hidden in plain sight, buried beneath the lie of fantastic colour. I'd never been interested in art before, but there was something infectious in Ben's patter, something in the ideas I found intriguing. An ordinary life, made to stand out, celebrated; hung on the wall for everyone to see. I liked that.

"Sorry – there I go again." Ben dropped his twig and gave me an apologetic smile. "Forcing you to listen and I haven't even bought you dinner yet."

"I did ask."

He laughed. "And you'll know better than to do that next time." He picked up his phone again and scanned the screen. Frowning, he returned it to his pocket.

For a few seconds we both sat, staring out past the handful of bobbing boats, to the horizon.

Without unfixing his gaze, Ben said, "They were doing the world a service, you know – the fauves. They were giving people a new way of looking at things that would otherwise be overlooked. They knew that deep down people don't really want to know the truth about something or someone, even if they think they do." He did look at me then, as if willing me to understand something I didn't yet know I needed to understand. "They want to be astonished."

BEN

Two days after the Show I had to make the first of my flying visits to London. It took place in inappropriately glorious sunshine; the necessity of the trip had not put me in the mood for good weather. It didn't last. By the time I was back, eating cake on the beach with Jenny, the clouds were coming over, and when Rosemary showed up the following day, a uniform blanket of grey stretched out in every direction, fitting perfectly with the expression on her face. She was wearing old clothes – as if planning on painting a ceiling rather than a picture – and her lips were already pursed.

"Go on then." I didn't try to make small talk as we made our way into the studio. "Paint something."

I'd already set up a canvas for her on an easel next to mine. My tactic was to not be too friendly. If I didn't try to instruct her, or jolly her along, I hoped she might find me less irritating.

Rosemary was clearly resigned to the morning ahead, because she didn't argue, only stood at the table, rummaging through the tubes. "What shall I paint?"

"Whatever you want."

"I don't *want* to paint anything."

I stood back to get a better view of my own work, avoiding her eyes. I'd promised myself we'd get through at least 10 minutes without arguing. "How about painting a feeling – how you feel when you wake up before the alarm, or that jolt you get when you nearly fall down the stairs?"

The silence radiated from Rosemary, boring into the back of my head. I gave in immediately. Sometimes losing a battle can help win the war.

"Or paint the view from the window if you want."

This must have been an acceptable idea, because Rosemary settled to work, and I found that her industry had an odd effect on my own painting.

Instead of fretting over colour and direction, I found myself relaxing. The picture began to breathe and grow. And I found it strange that Rosemary's hostile presence was a muse to me, when all the bashful admiration that Jenny cast my way hadn't helped one bit. It wasn't that I didn't enjoy Jenny's company – her timid chatter took me out of my bubble long enough to keep me sane – but in all the weeks I lived in Brackton, she never inspired me, never connected me to my canvas in the way Rosemary could without trying.

Rosemary and Jenny were quite alike in a funny sort of way. Chalk and cheese on the outside, but with both of them what you saw was what you got. Jenny's honesty came from an inability to be deceitful. It was natural, un-calculating. Whereas with Rosemary I got the impression she was honest because not being so was too much effort. To be dishonest – to portray yourself as something you're not – you have to care what people think of you. Rosemary didn't give a damn about what anybody thought. I was jealous of her for that.

During that first painting session, we worked side-by-side for over an hour before I looked at her canvas. The bottom third of it was covered in a range of sludge colours – Taupe, Buff, Wheat – with flecks of Onyx here and there.

"You need more white." I pointed at the real beach beyond the glass. "You see? Everywhere the light catches wet sand it looks white because of the glare."

"Hmmm." Rosemary dumped her palette on the folding table between our easels. "You can see why I concentrate on sub-atomic particles and not painting beaches."

"It's not bad for a first attempt."

"You're squinting."

"No I'm not." I moved in to examine it closer. "It reminds me of India. Amazing country, India."

There I was again, still trying to bait Rosemary into asking me questions – showing any sort of interest in me. And there she was resolutely refusing.

"It reminds me of sick."

"India does?"

"Not India." Rosemary didn't laugh. "My painting. It looks like vomit."

"Didn't you say that about one of mine too? It should fit in nicely here."

"True." She narrowed her eyes at the offending picture. "Perhaps I should see if Hugh Grant wants to buy it for his downstairs toilet."

This sounded perilously close to a joke. I took it as an invitation to make conversation. "You should go there sometime."

"Hugh Grant's toilet? No thank-you."

"I *meant* India." I carried our empty mugs through to the sink and put the kettle on to boil again. "You'd like it. It's a place where you catch those glimpses of God everywhere you look."

"Unlike you," Rosemary said, "I don't feel the need for a God."

"Like you don't feel the need for a husband?"

"Exactly. If I wanted someone meddling in my private affairs I'd hire a cleaner."

Rosemary took her brushes to the table and began to clean them inexpertly but methodically. It had the same deliberateness about it as everything else she did. She didn't waste a single movement, not half a word, as if she'd long ago programmed herself to do everything she might possibly be called on to do in her whole life. She never stumbled over her words or picked up something she didn't need to because it was next to her hand. She was totally in control, permanently on guard. I'd never met anyone like her.

"You never wanted to go to India then, Dr. Blunt?"

"Not to see God."

"Everyone wants to see something of the world." I leaned against the doorframe, watching her sort the brushes and paints. "Even physicists must travel."

"If by travel you mean what we used to call 'taking a holiday', then yes, I suppose some physicists do. Some of us were too busy lecturing."

"What about the university holidays?"

"Too busy not lecturing." She gave me a sharp look. "What is this? Spanish Inquisition?"

Unprompted, Rosemary gathered a new handful of tubes – the blues and greens of the sea – and returned to her easel with the clean brushes. I tried not to look victorious.

"I didn't mean to pry." I went back to my own canvas. "I'm just interested in people's lives. I'm always trying to get Jenny to tell me about people in the village."

"A fruitless exercise no doubt." Rosemary snorted. "She only ever says anything good about people and she's hopelessly dim. Nothing nice ever happens to her because she's too afraid to ask for anything out of life."

Rosemary's tone surprised me. It wasn't vicious, but it was dismissive, and that seemed rather cruel – like making a point of telling the fat girl she'll never get a date for the disco, when she's painfully aware of it already. Jenny's timidity didn't seem a fair match for Rosemary.

"She doesn't bitch about people, if that's what you mean," I said. "She's a good woman, and she asked me out to dinner yesterday – don't you think that's a nice thing?"

"*Jenny* did?"

Rosemary's surprise was not surprising. I would've said Jenny was more likely to miss church or even take up sky-diving than ask a man out to dinner, but she'd asked me outright while we were eating cake on the beach the previous day. I'd said yes partly out of duty – she'd been good to me since I'd arrived as a stranger – but I did think it would be rather fun. I liked Jenny in a funny sort of way, I honestly did. She was one of those people who nobody took seriously, but nobody could dislike either. Life in Brackton couldn't have been all that fun for her, yet she never appeared bitter or discontent. In fact, she was the only truly content person I've ever met. It was her contentment that came across as silliness, but whether it was or not, I never quite worked out. Anyway, she asked me and I said yes. And I was looking forward to it too.

"Wonders will never cease." Rosemary looked sideways at me. "I'm not sure I'd count it as a turning point in Jenny's life, but it'll be up to you whether it's nice or not."

"Maybe a glass of wine will loosen her tongue. I'll ask her everything about everybody – starting with you."

"Being nosey isn't a virtue, Mr. Summers."

"I'd much rather you called me Ben. Especially if you're going to tell me off."

When Rosemary didn't answer, I risked asking, "Do you mind if I call you Rosemary? Dr. Blunt seems rather formal for friends."

"For friends it would be."

"Is that a no?"

She gave me a withering look. "You can call me what you like."

Maybe that's where I should've started the story of summer. Those seven words: *you can call me what you like.* Not exactly an invitation to intimacy, but the first crack in the armour, the crumbling of mortar in the castle wall. Rosemary had allowed for the possibility of friendship. It would be a bizarre friendship, and I would have to work hard for it, but there it was, the moment when impossibility faded from shot. Rosemary still had her secrets and God knows I had mine, but our paths had just become entangled in ways neither of us could have guessed.

ROSEMARY

Vegetable: a plant or part of a plant commonly used as food.

Vegetable: a person incapable of conscious response or activity.

Vegetable: the man in the bed. Michael. You.

Your face is shrivelled, skin stretched taut across the bones; cheeks hollow where the life has been dragged out of you. Hands motionless on the blanket, fingers curled into not-quite fists.

Cheryl is smiling at me as she scribbles on your checklist. "You live in Brackton, don't you? I went there on Saturday – to your Show. Did you go?"

"No. I was busy."

"Shame." Your blood pressure cuff beeps. "It was nice. Really old-fashioned." She pulls at the Velcro. "Nice place too. I can see why you two moved there."

Dr. Richards's head snakes around the open door. His eyes scan you, then Cheryl, and then fix on me. "Dr. Blunt, I was hoping I'd catch you. Do you have time for a chat today?"

No more avoiding it now. The one-year chat. Are you ready? Am I?

It was six months when he first warned me it would come to this. That was when you were given your first diagnosis: Persistent Vegetative State. Dr. Richards had been wanting to slap that label on you ever since I'd transferred you from Lockhaven General. He already had one eye on The Chat even then. Your sand was slipping through the glass. And now it's trickled away to nothing.

You are not asleep. Dr. Richards does admit this at least: PVS is not sleeping. You do sleep, but you wake too, just like everyone else. Only, you don't know it; you're unconscious of it. Or that's what he says. Those times when you grunt, when your fingers spasm on the blanket and your eyes roll – all those times that make me jump from my skin and search your face again – they don't mean anything. You've no idea you're doing it. You're no more aware of your memories and movements than a crab on the sea floor dreams of the Himalayas. Sometimes you even yawn or smile, and Dr. Richards hastens to tell me again that it's a reflex – not your choice. And *that* I can believe. You've not chosen to smile for a long time.

Cheryl slips from the room. Perhaps you hear her go. Perhaps you don't.

"I'm sorry to have this conversation with you, Dr. Blunt." Dr. Richards sinks down into the chair on the other side of you. "You'll probably find it difficult and upsetting and I would strongly encourage you to take some time to think about what I've said."

He knows I know what's coming; I don't have to speak yet. I couldn't have come here for 12 months, Mondays and Thursdays without fail, and be surprised now.

"Your husband's condition hasn't changed for a year. We've run brain scans and done various tests and found no evidence that he's conscious of the world outside, or even his own body."

A pause. He waits for me to take it in – places the plus sign between the two and the two and lets me make four on my own. I was always good at maths.

"It's the opinion of Michael's entire medical team that continuing to support him is not in his best interests – or yours. There's practically no chance now of Michael making any sort of recovery." He takes a deep breath, pushes his glasses back up his nose. "Dr. Blunt, we'd like your permission to start the legal process of withdrawing nutritional support from Michael and allowing him to die."

He talks on, but I don't listen. I know it all already. Instead, I watch you and wait. Watching and waiting for a flicker. Do you understand what he's saying? It's all paperwork now. If I agree to kill you then we'll go to court to ask permission. And they will grant it, you know. They'll say yes. More paperwork and then sedation – a precaution only, you're not meant to be able to feel anything, are you? – then starvation. All for the best, of course.

I wonder what it feels like to starve.

"It will be very peaceful. He won't feel anything and we'll continue to maintain hygiene standards for Michael through to the end."

Another pause. My turn now.

"Thank-you for explaining things, Doctor." I drag my eyes away from you to him. "Do you need a decision straight away?"

"Not at all." An earnest shake of the head. "In fact, we recommend you talk to your friends and family about this and, if you think it would be helpful, we can arrange for you to see a trained counsellor who has experience of similar situations. Nothing will be done to your husband until you're happy with the decision. We understand how hard this is for you."

It's always 'we'. Never personal. The system is sympathetic, the system feels my pain. And what does the system expect from me? Grief? Weary resignation? I look at Dr. Richards but he leaves no clues behind him as he goes, only a ticking clock. Only time slipping by until the moment we must come to in the end: the moment we kill you; the moment I lose my husband for the third time in my life.

...

If there was one person who might have disapproved of Ben even more than I did, it would've been my mother. Pop music, rock-and-roll and artists – she despised these things even more than she despised Catholics. Not that she was really that against Catholics when it came down to it. Rather like Dante's Inferno, my mother had different degrees of devilry and a Catholic school with weekly church services was one step further from damnation than a heathen grammar school. Failing my 11-Plus to go to the Secondary Modern would've placed me in the jaws of Satan himself, shoulder-to-shoulder with Judas. So St. Boniface it had to be. And she had to admit they did give a good education. Good enough for one or two of us to even think about university.

It was assumed that the girls at St. Boniface might take on suitable employment – nursing or teaching perhaps – until we found husbands and settled down. That wasn't for me. Everyone, even my mother, had to accept I was going to university, and two terms through my A-levels I had my heart set on Cambridge. I think I might even have started to fill out the forms when Julia asked me to the party.

I never went to parties. The boys from the private school down the road seemed to have them most weekends, but I steered clear. I didn't even pay much attention to the Monday-morning gossip of which records were played and who danced with who. But when Julia's 17th fell on a Saturday she insisted I should go to that week's Big Event with her. She even did the lying to my mother for me – told her that I was staying the night at her house but would be back in time for church – so I didn't have an excuse.

The irony of it was that Michael wasn't even at the party officially. It was hosted by his younger brother while their parents were away and Michael had promised their mother not to let anything bad happen. I suppose baby-sitting your brother's friends wasn't a fun way for a 26 year-old to spend his Saturday night, so he was keeping himself to himself. I don't think anybody even knew he was there.

Compared to today's standards the party was tame. This wasn't the swinging-60s yet. I'm sure somebody had laced the fruit punch with something or other, but we weren't passing vodka bottles or smoking the kind of thing I would smell on my students three decades later. The record player was at full volume and people were dancing in the hallway, but that was as wild as it got. Most parties then were conducted with parental supervision, complete with ice-breaker games and stilted conversations in the kitchen. Some boys were determined to make the most of being adult-free and by half past nine I'd seen enough of their flirting and feeble attempts to emulate the jive moves they'd seen at the pictures. I went in search of somewhere I could disappear for a few minutes.

In the end I had to settle on the walk-in linen cupboard. I waited until the landing was empty, then slipped into the darkness. The smell of warm, clean laundry was soothing after the bustle of the party below.

"Who are you trying to avoid?"

The voice in the blackness had me reaching for a light switch. The bare bulb revealed a blonde-haired man, sitting on the floor, just inches from where I was standing. His eyes were screwed tight against the sudden brightness, but when he did eventually open them, the irises were so pale blue they seemed almost colourless. I didn't know what to say.

"Watching the boys trying to impress the girls not your thing either?" He smiled. "I've been in here over an hour, trying to avoid it. Nobody's found me yet – other than you – and I'd like to keep it that way. Would you mind awfully turning the light off again?"

If my mother was still alive, she'd say I wasn't brought up to shut myself in dark cupboards with strange men. But if I wasn't then I can't explain why I did.

"What's your name?" the man asked when it was dark again, as if the situation was normal.

"Rosemary Shelley. I don't really like parties."

"I'm Michael Blunt – David's brother – and neither do I." I could hear him shifting into a different position. "What do you like, if you don't like parties?"

"Reading." It wouldn't have occurred to me then how much of a swot I must have sounded. "And maths."

"What do you read?"

"Everything." I thought for a moment. "I like Dickens best."

"*A Tale of Two Cities* is my favourite."

"Mine too." I sank down into a sitting position as well. "Though I think *Dombey and Son* is underrated."

And that was it. We stayed in that cupboard for nearly an hour, until I was sure Julia would be frantic. Having avoided the opposite sex like the plague until then, I was suddenly captivated, in the way only teenagers can be. Michael talked to me as if I was a proper person, not a school girl, and he talked about important things like politics and literature. I couldn't see him and we didn't so much as shuffle an inch closer in all the time we were there, but by the time we came out of that dark cupboard I'd seen a light. My eyes had been opened to a world beyond essays and exams, even if essays and exams were still my priority.

When the time came to go, Michael squeezed past me to the door. He opened it a crack and looked along the landing. "All clear." He grabbed my hand and pulled me into the light. "Wouldn't want anybody to think we were up to something in there. Would we?" He didn't let go.

He insisted on driving Julia and me home in his clapped-out Austin, and waited until we were standing on the road outside her house before leaning across the passenger seat and winding down the window.

"May I ring you next weekend, Rosemary? We could go to the pictures or something?"

I could almost hear Julia's eyes extending on cartoon stalks.

"If you'd like to." I tried to look casual as I wrote down my number, and knew I was failing. "That would be fine with me."

As he pulled away again, I could feel Julia watching me.

"Thanks for inviting me to the party." I slipped my arm through hers. "I think I actually enjoyed myself."

. . .

Letter from Julia to Rosemary.

Wednesday 4th July

Dear Rosemary,

You haven't written for a week now and you must know that I'm dying to hear about the Show. It's mean of you. Spare me no details or I really shall come next year and then what will you do?

Is there no news for me? Not even the whiff of a scandal I can get excited about? No missing pearl necklaces or mystery of the third slipper? Anything that's more exciting than the washing machine repair man coming round again, or accidentally being delivered next door's post would be quite something in Eastmoore. I know I like it here for the suburban dullness, but I do want to feel that something more exciting is going on in the rest of the world. You could save me a fortune in overdue library fees if only you'd tell me what goes on in Brackton. You know how slow I am at reading and your letters are much more manageable than a whole Ruth Rendell.

Do you remember how cross you used to get with me for being so slow? I always asked you to do my homework for me – especially maths – and you never would. You'd try to find some new way to explain the problem and then get even more frustrated when I still didn't understand. I don't know how I survived that last year without you. If I'd been doing maths A-level it would've been a disaster. Domestic Science, English and History were just about in my powers, though I got nowhere near a distinction. Not like you. You would've got a distinction in everything – you with your Grade Ones in every O-Level you took. That's why it was so unfair. It should've been you that finished A-levels, not me.

How is our artist getting on? Has he found God yet? I hope you've been letting him bewitch you with his tales of travelling. Tell all.

Love, Julia

CHLOE BANKS

Letter from Rosemary to Julia.

Friday 6th July

Dear Julia,

Ben has been doing no bewitching whatsoever. Not of me anyway. I've seen Jenny popping into his cottage at least twice this week, whereas I've only been to paint with him once – and only then for your benefit. The things I do for you. I've no idea if he's found God yet, though when I saw him coming out of the post office in the rain yesterday he didn't look particularly enlightened.

The Show was exactly as expected – a mixture of faux-1930s charm and the regular feuds. Mr. Gribble won one more vegetable class than anybody else which led to the usual petty rumours of corruption on Jenny's behalf, even though Jenny is the least corruptible person imaginable. There was bunting made from an old alphabet quilt by Emma Jolly – a woman who does not live up to the promise of her name – which had accidentally been hung to spell out a very rude word, and the head of the parish council got drunk just before he had to make the vote of thanks to the organisers. There's no need for you to come next year, the same things will happen again.

I fulfilled my role as children's judge to the best of my ability, considering the tripe I had to work with. I gave first prize in Junior Creative Writing to a story about a princess who kissed a frog and ended up turning into a frog herself as a result. I thought it was quite insightful. Other than that there was nothing that could possibly make me want to look at another crayon drawing or peg doll ever again.

Don't be silly – you had as much right to A-levels as I did. More in fact. Anyone who gets themselves pregnant to a man 10 years older than them while still at school isn't really Cambridge material. Not back then. Nowadays teenage mothers can probably get fast-tracked to Trinity under some scheme or other.

Talking of pregnancy, how is Alison coming along? The baby must be almost due if I've got my maths right – and my biology for that matter.

With love, Rosemary

PS: No pearl necklaces or slippers, but somebody has been letting their dog foul the Green. Quite a scandal. R

CHERYL

We were almost at Brackton when Lee called Lauren. She hadn't told him she was going out for the day. Hadn't told him about Ben either I expect. Lee should've been at work anyway – Saturday was the busiest day for Lockhaven Property Rentals – but it turned out he'd taken the afternoon off to surprise Lauren, then found she wasn't at her flat.

"I'll have to go back," Lauren said, flipping her phone shut with a snap. "He's got the cinema tickets already and he's going to take me to Bella Italia for dinner. Can't say no to that."

It was annoying. £4.80 on a return ticket to Brackton only to have to turn round again the second we got there. Only we couldn't. The rattling bus that took us to the Green in the centre of the village wasn't due to make the return journey for nearly an hour. And of course, instead of going for a drink in the pub like nay normal person, Lauren insisted we should go and find Ben.

When he opened the door it took him a few seconds to place us. "It's... Cheryl, right? And Lauren. From the Village Show."

"That's right," Lauren said. "You said we should come down and take a look at your paintings." She spread her arms wide. "Here we are."

He welcomed us inside, nudging piles of clothes and bags out of the way with his feet and we wove our way to the studio door. He went in ahead of us and hesitated as if unsure where to start.

"This is my current picture." He tapped the side of the canvas resting on the easel in front of the window. "And these are previous ones of mine." He waved at the pictures round the perimeter of the room. A few were hanging on the walls, most were stacked together on the floor.

Lauren caught my eye as Ben turned his back to deal with his abandoned paint brush. She wrinkled her nose. Not her kind of thing. I don't know what would've been Lauren's kind of thing, but she made it pretty clear in that one look that squiggles and geometric shapes were not it.

Ben turned to face us again and Lauren snapped back into character. "God, they're amazing," she said. "You're so clever." She pointed at the nearest one. "What's that one about?"

"Have a guess?" Ben grinned at her and I could've sworn gave me a little wink as Lauren began to flap.

"Oh... ummm... is it a desert? Or maybe a maze or something?"

Ben looked at me. "What do you think?"

I studied the canvas. I wasn't much better than Lauren at art, but I did kind of like Ben's style. This one was striking. The background faded from deep brown in the centre out to nearly-white at the edges. Orange and brown swirls spiralled inwards, the outer ones large and loose, the inner ones small and tight and melting into the background. Everything about the picture seemed to be sucked into the centre.

"I don't know," I said. "It kind of makes me feel as if it's hard to breathe. As if I'm choking."

Ben studied me as if I was one of his paintings, then nodded slowly. "You're very perceptive. It's called *Atmosphere on the 17:22 from Elephant and Castle* and it's about the suffocation of rush-hour London." He crouched in front of it and ran a finger along the edge of the wooden frame. "You're the first person down here who's got it. Somebody else told me it looked like dog sick."

Before I could stop myself, I laughed.

"You think they were right?" Ben was smiling again.

"Maybe a bit. It's more like what you said it was though."

"Thank-you, sweet lady." Ben stood up and took my hand, kissing it with a melodramatic bow. "My ego is restored."

I could sense Lauren battling with herself next to me. Bless her, she loved nothing more than to set me up with every half-suitable man she happened to stumble across, yet she couldn't bear it when I was getting the attention. Even though Lee was in a well-paid job and treated her more like a princess than she deserved, she couldn't quite be content with that.

"I like this one," she said, drawing Ben's away from me. "It's the sea, right?"

It wasn't an inspired guess. Anyone could've worked that out. Blues and greens with foamy flecks of white rolled across one of the smallest canvases. Ben was gracious about it though.

"That's right." He joined her in front of the picture. "I can see I've found some true art critics at last. I'm going to have to raise my game."

For another 10 minutes we looked at his paintings while he told us what they were. My favourite was *Time and Punishment* – a tall, narrow painting with thin black lines painted horizontally across it. At the top they were close together like a barcode over a mess of vibrant colours; at the bottom they were far apart with only one or two blurred shapes in red and blue. Supposedly it was to do with time slowing down in an office as five o'clock grew closer, but to me it just looked like an organised mess – one that caught your eye among all the other organised messes.

"I'm sorry, I haven't offered you tea yet, have I?" Ben wandered back towards the door. "Or coffee, if you'd prefer?"

Lauren glanced at her phone. "We've got to be going. Bus to catch."

"I'll have a tea," I heard myself saying. "Milk, one sugar." I turned to Lauren. "No point both of us shooting off so soon. Your boyfriend isn't going to want me hanging around with you all afternoon. You go. I'll catch the next bus instead."

For a second she looked irritated. I'm not sure she'd been planning on mentioning Lee in front of Ben. In another second though she was giving me her most knowing smile. "Sure. Good idea."

I watched Lauren from the picture window as Ben made the tea, wondering why I hadn't gone with her. She was the one who'd wanted to come, I'd only joined her for the ride. Now I was alone with an artist and nothing to talk about. A couple of weeks later that wouldn't have bothered me – I soon learned Ben was capable of talking for two people – but watching Lauren puff her way up the cliff steps, I wasn't sure what I'd let myself in for.

"You mind if I crack on with my work?" Ben said as he came back in with the tea. "You're welcome to stay and watch, or look at the view, or whatever."

He dragged a stool out from under a pile of newspapers and I took it to the back of the room. Ben started mixing colours on his palette, whistling to himself. "It's going to be God." He nodded at his easel. "Hope so, anyway."

"God?" I took a Hobnob from the packet he'd placed on the table next to me. "You believe in all that do you? Most people don't."

"You don't think so?" Ben examined his picture, head on one side. "I suppose God is rather out of fashion at the moment. But I've seen a lot of stuff in my time that I can't explain. Might not be God of course, but there are more things in heaven and earth, Horatio... and all that."

"I guess being an artist is a bit more exciting than being a nurse. You've probably seen tonnes of stuff that show God exists. In hospital I've seen tonnes of stuff that suggests he doesn't."

"I've certainly seen a lot of things in my time. My parents were taking me all over the world practically as soon as I was born." He selected a brush. "But your job is a different kind of reality. A harsher one. A braver one."

I didn't know what to say to that. So I didn't say anything. I sat and watched as Ben worked. It was as if I was hearing him thinking out loud with his brush. Each stroke he made was so precise, it was hard to see how they were going to build up into anything as wild as his other paintings, let alone a God. For half an hour he dabbed and slashed at the canvas, sometimes talking, sometimes silent. I didn't talk, but I didn't mind being the silent one. Ben had that way about him. In conversation with him you'd always feel involved by the little glances he gave you, the touches on your arm, the sudden explosive smile. Somehow it always felt as if you were talking as much as he was. It was as if he wanted to transport you into a world he'd seen for himself and couldn't wait to share. It was a jigsaw world – abstract art and strange ideas, cubists and futurists – but when Ben talked about it, it felt more real than the real world. Or more important anyway. It was a world where people didn't need careers and life plans; where you weren't trapped by your choice of degree or your obligations to HMRC; where adventure and ambition weren't things you thought about only on your holidays.

I didn't know how long Ben would paint that first time. I had it in my head that once artists started work they went straight through for 20 hours or something without stopping. But after 30 minutes, Ben dropped his palette back on the table and scowled at it, as if it was a child who'd interrupted his train of thought.

"It's not working today," he said. "Something's wrong. There's no point carrying on." He picked up his mug. "More tea?"

We drank our second cups perched on the edge of his bed, front door wide to let in the rare sunshine July had managed to find from somewhere. Ben was quiet now, and with no paintings to look at, I found myself watching him instead. I'll admit I saw more in him than I had done at the Show. In his natural environment – or what I assumed was his natural environment – he was different: better-looking, relaxed, attractive even.

"Do you have a studio in London?" I said when the silence had gone on for half a mug already.

Ben shook himself from thought. "Yeah. Nice place in Soho. Share it with a few other artists."

"It all sounds pretty glamorous. Not like clearing up vomit and sponge-bathing old men."

"We don't do a lot of that, no." He leaned back against the wall, shifting his weight to look directly at me. "Don't you like nursing?"

"It's alright. It's what I wanted to do. It just freaks me out that nursing might be what I do now. Forever. I feel as if I want a career change, but I'm afraid that if I had one I'd get bored of that too within a year. And then what?"

"What would you do if you could do anything at all?"

I thought about it. "Doesn't every girl want to act or model or something? That'd be pretty cool. But I wouldn't mind one of those fast city jobs – advertising or events management or something. Something with a bit of excitement."

"I reckon you could be a model if you wanted to be." Ben balanced his empty mug on the bed post. "I know loads of art studios that would give you work in London."

I wasn't stupid. Ben wasn't the first person to tell me I could be a model and I was no Heidi Klum. It was different though with Ben. The other guys had been immigrants working cash-in-hand for sleazy photography studios, handing out cards in the street to any teenage girl who walked past, or were men who promised the earth as they ogled my cleavage in the kind of cheap bars all pub crawls had ended up in at uni. Ben wasn't promising Hollywood or the cat walk, not even clothing catalogues. He was suggesting something much tamer than that. But modelling for artists was still much wilder than nursing the comatose.

"When you say you *know* the studios..." I said.

"I've worked with them – or in them." Ben sat up and stretched. "If ever you're in London when I've moved back you should look me up and I'll see what I can do."

Hours later, lying on my bed at home, I relayed this snapshot of conversation to Lauren. She'd called from Bella Italia between the mains and puddings to get the gossip.

"Oh my god, he SO fancies you."

"Don't be stupid."

"Ummm, hello? Middle-aged man gets the undivided attention of a blonde woman half his age and suggests he could get her some modelling work. And you don't think he fancies you?"

"He didn't say it like that." I felt defensive for some reason. I didn't want Lauren twisting nothing into something. "He was professional about it, not creepy."

"I'm sure he was. Doesn't mean he doesn't like you." She squealed and I pictured the other couples in the restaurant eyeing her over their dough balls. "You ARE going back to see him again, right?"

"Maybe. He said I could."

Actually, I'd asked him. On the front step as I was leaving, I suggested I might like to come again and he'd seemed open to the idea if not outright enthusiastic. And I did want to go again. Not only because he'd said I could be a model. I liked him and I liked his paintings.

"Oh my god, *this* is what you've been waiting for, Cher. I *knew* the whole degree-career thing wasn't you. Didn't I tell you? This is the excitement a girl like you needs on top of all that stuff." She squealed again. "Oops, got to go, Babe, Lee's coming back from the loo. Call you tomorrow, yeah?"

And she was gone before I could say anything.

ROSEMARY

At 16, when I first realised my period was late I wasn't worried. It sounds naive now, but I'd only started them a year earlier and they were still irregular. It wasn't until I was more than a week overdue that I began to wonder. Some women say they can tell when they're pregnant even before they have any symptoms of it. I'm not one of those women. Or at least, I wasn't one of those girls.

Walking out with Michael had necessarily been a secret at first. My mother was determined that no daughter of hers would have anything to do with boys – much less men – until an unspecified appropriate age. Therefore I spent the whole Saturday following the party longing for and dreading Michael's call. As luck would have it, it was Dad who answered.

"It's for you Rosemary."

I don't know why he didn't say it was a young man on the other end of the line. An act of loyalty to me, perhaps, or the wisdom that came with being married to my mother for 20 years. But as I passed him in the doorway, he looked at me with an expression I've never been able to forget. The expression of a father who knows the moment has come when he'll never be the only man in his daughter's life again – pride, fear, sorrow. When I returned to the room five minutes later I couldn't look at him. I went instead, to my mother.

"Can I go to the pictures tonight with Julia?"

"That depends on what you're planning to see."

I clutched for a film that would get past my mother's obscenity filter. There weren't many that would. Nearly all the girls had been to see *Jailhouse Rock* during the Christmas holidays, but it'd been out of the question for me.

"*South Pacific*. That new Rogers and Hammerstein one."

My mother had a soft spot for Rogers and Hammerstein.

"You can go if you're back by half past nine and promise not to spend your money on that awful popcorn."

Dad didn't say anything.

Even if I'd known how to do my hair nicely or put on make-up I couldn't have done so without my mother smelling a rat. In the end, all I dared do was put on the one dress I had that ended half an inch above my knee and put in the hair slide covered in tiny flowers that Julia had lent me for the party. I don't suppose I looked anything much, but I felt special.

I waited until my mother was in her sewing room before leaving my bedroom. I crept downstairs and grabbed my coat from the back of the kitchen door. Dad was sitting at the table. His gaze took in the hair slide, my dress, my best shoes.

"You look lovely." He sounded sad. "Have a nice evening with Julia."

I'd reached the door before he said anything else. "Rosemary?" He waited until I'd turned back to face him. "Be careful, Love."

It seems funny that after all this time I should remember which film I told my mother I was going to see, but not which one we saw. I don't suppose it mattered to me then. All I could think about was the man next to me, holding my hand from the second the lights went down until the credits had ended and we were the only ones left in the theatre.

Michael played the part of the gentleman to perfection. He paid for my ticket and the popcorn I'd promised I wouldn't buy, and he had me home at half past nine on the dot, delivered to the end of the drive with a kiss on the cheek that had me dancing on air.

Dad was still at the table. "How was the picture?"

"It was good." I couldn't stop myself smiling. "Really good."

He hauled himself to his feet and bent to kiss my cheek. "Good. I'm glad."

Michael and I couldn't meet often over those first few weeks, but when we did I had a willing accomplice in Julia. We were silly schoolgirls for whom a first boyfriend was a terribly exciting adventure and she was more than happy to provide me with alibis. In the following 54 years – between Michael turning up in my life and Ben doing the same – Julia wouldn't change a bit. She remained the same person from the day I met her as we took adjacent desks in the First Form at St. Boniface, to today. But I was a different person then. 16 year-old Rosemary didn't like secrets. And Michael was a big secret to keep.

To be fair to him, Michael was the one who wanted to make everything legitimate. I felt guilty about Dad, but I wasn't in a hurry to tell my mother anything.

"When are you going to ask me home for tea?" Michael asked, a month after the party. "Not ashamed of me, are you?"

"Of course I'm not. I'm just not sure what my parents will think – what with you being so much older than me."

"You'll never know if you don't ask."

And in the end, it wasn't so bad. My mother only kicked up the minimum amount of fuss and Dad was as polite as always. For his part, Michael pulled out all the stops. In one afternoon his polite questions and unabashed flattery of our house had melted the ice of my mother's first greeting into a tight smile as he left.

Secretly, I think my mother was rather pleased. She didn't say so, but I'm sure she was hoping I'd choose marriage over university. There was no shame in an educated woman, but she considered them inferior to a good housewife. A daughter courted properly – by a man who visited the house on a Sunday afternoon and drank tea from the best china – had an air of respectability about her. Had Michael been a Teddy-Boy, I would've been locked in my bedroom until I was 21, but he could pull off a sober suit and already had a job as a junior manager in the biggest department store in town. Before long, it was my mother who was asking him to come to the house.

I don't suppose any of us thought to wonder what Dad made of it all.

Michael didn't ask me to have sex with him for over three months. By today's standards he was a model of restraint, but at the time it'd never occurred to me that one could do that sort of thing outside marriage. We'd all heard the nuns' warnings about girls who'd fallen into the gutter, but we hardly listened. After all, it was avoidable, wasn't it? Nobody *has* to have sex if they don't want to. And I never considered that I might want to. Sex was one of those irksome duties that came with the security of marriage as far as I could see.

It was about the time of our lower-sixth exams. My meetings with Michael had to be snatched between the hours of revision I'd set myself. He didn't force me into anything. He didn't have to. I would've done anything for him and I trusted him completely. I only had hazy ideas about contraception, but Michael was blasé about the whole thing.

"I won't let you get pregnant, Rosie. I promise. Only people who aren't careful get themselves pregnant and we'll be very careful. Nobody need even know we're doing it."

Nobody needing to know inevitably meant doing it in the back of his car. In my mind the whole act was meant to be bathed in dusky pinks and a warm golden glow. We should've been whispering sweet nothings while classical music played in the background. But it wasn't like that; everything was over so fast. No fireworks, no earthquakes. It wasn't anything, and then it was something, and then it wasn't anything again. All over. I hadn't realised I would need to grit my teeth the first time, or that I would hardly feel a thing by the third. As I lay on the back seat, skirt hitched up round my waist, waiting for Michael to catch his breath, I didn't feel womanly. I wondered what the fuss was about.

Michael enjoyed it. Enough to want to do it whenever we were alone and, idiot that I was, I was flattered into thinking that was because I was something special. He treated me like a queen before, during and afterwards. That was enough for me. The cramped space, the steamed-up windows, the eerie gloom of the lane outside didn't seem to bother Michael; perhaps that's what sex did look like to him. To me though, it didn't look like what it was meant to be.

It must have been the seventh or eighth time that it happened. The condom must've split, or perhaps it was one of those things – we might have been unlucky. Bad luck on top of stupidity. But when the nausea started and hadn't disappeared after a week, I knew I had to tell Michael. And once I'd told him, there was only one thing we could do – we had to tell Dad. And my mother.

It was Dad who insisted I should be allowed to say goodbye to my school friends. One of the few times I ever saw him overrule my mother. From the afternoon Michael and I sat in our front room, listening to my mother calling down hellfire upon us, I didn't go to school. I wasn't even allowed to see Julia, until Dad put his foot down and insisted I should be permitted one visit at least.

We sat in the car outside the school gates for quarter of an hour, neither of us saying anything until I finally plucked up the courage to open the door.

"You don't have to do this, Rosemary."

I thought Dad was talking about visiting school. My mother had already told the nuns I was leaving – probably played proud-mother-planning-a-wedding to perfection, though she wasn't kidding anybody – so it wasn't as if I had to go inside. If I'd wanted, Dad would've driven me home again and thought no less of me for it.

"I do have to."

Months later it dawned on me that he hadn't meant that at all. He had meant Michael. I didn't have to marry Michael, whatever my mother said. Dad would make sure I was alright. If only I'd known.

He waited in the car as I climbed the steps and rang the bell. The head-teacher didn't even look at me as she led me along the dingy corridors to the classroom. When she ushered me inside, I regretted coming at once. I'd been missing for less than a week and the girls in front of me already seemed like strangers; people who hadn't ruined their lives in the back of an Austin. The eyes that fixed on me were wide with confirmed rumours. Only Julia smiled.

"Miss Shelley has come to tell you something," Sister Agnes announced.

I was Miss Shelley now, not Rosemary; no longer any pupil of hers.

"I... ummm... I wanted to tell you..." I locked my gaze on to Julia. "I wanted to tell you that I'm leaving school. I'm getting married."

I didn't add that the wedding would be in three weeks time with a dress designed to hang loosely round my waist and hips. They already knew. Only my mother would keep up the pretence. She would pretend to be crying tears of joy as I walked down the aisle and would be delighted and astonished when I announced my pregnancy on the day she deemed acceptable. When the baby came she would make a show of being anxious about how prema-ture it was and, in time, she might even forgive me.

"I'm sure we're all very happy for Miss Shelley." Sister Agnes spoke in a monotone. "Everyone here at St. Boniface will want to wish her all the very best for her marriage."

She couldn't even bring herself to talk to me directly. And as the door clicked shut behind me, I just caught her next words – probably the last time she ever mentioned me.

"Let that be a lesson to you, girls. Dance with the devil and he'll have his wicked way with you."

But Michael wasn't the devil then. That didn't come until later.

BEN

I watched Rosemary fussing at a white splodge of paint that almost looked like a seagull. "You know I reckon you should give up on painting the beach."

"I thought you said I was getting better?"

"You are." I took a slurp of tea. "But that painting doesn't tell me anything about you. A picture should always tell you something about the artist."

"She put her brush down and walked over to my canvas. "So what does this say about you? That you liked yellow but you're now swaying toward blue?"

"Perhaps it says I'm a bit mixed up." I laughed until it was obvious Rosemary had no intention of joining in. "What's wrong with *you*?"

"You take everything with such good grace." She turned her back on me. "You're impossible to annoy."

"Don't give up now. Not when you've been trying so hard."

I let Rosemary sulk while I examined my progress. I was pleased with it so far, despite the absence of God. The colours grew in tendrils from the top left corner of the canvas, inching its way towards an invisible point in the centre. The yellow creeper was cut short by hard-edged blocks of blue and green, and the blocks themselves morphed as they made their way to the right; the fierce angles of one side gave way to a sinuous curve on the other. The first flecks of Rust were spitting from the centre of each block.

"I don't know why I come here," Rosemary said, not content to let the tension pass. "I don't know why *you* ask me here."

"You come here because you can't stand not being able to do something perfectly. Until you've given painting your best shot you can't stop, even if you hate it."

"Rubbish."

It wasn't rubbish.

"And I ask you here because I enjoy your company."

"You can't enjoy it," she said. "I disapprove of your paintings, I don't understand art and I criticise everything you say."

"But you don't tell me to wipe my feet."

"If I did, would you stop asking me to come?"

"Straight away. Scout's honour." I headed for the door. "Another coffee?"

When I returned Rosemary was glaring at my canvas. She didn't give me time to gloat over her interest.

"Which bit of this mess is meant to be God?"

"He'll show up." I said it with confidence. I think I was still confident then. It didn't occur to me at that point, that God might not appear in time to save me. "*Crede quod habes et habes*," I said, and paused a moment before translating. "Believe that you have it and you have it."

"I know what it means. Some of us went to a proper school." Rosemary took the mug without thanking me. "But belief doesn't make something exist. It's a sad state of affairs when people believe something because they believe it."

"What some people call gullibility, others might say was being open to possibility." I knew I should drop the subject – riling Rosemary wasn't meant to have turned into a hobby. "When I was 25 I spent a year travelling in the USA. I meant to do it all but in the end I didn't leave the deep south even for a day. For the bible-belt you wouldn't believe what weird stuff went on there. There was this one motel in Arizona..."

"I hadn't realised motels were the epicentre of spiritual activity."

"They are if you have a Ouija board."

I waited for the interest, for the questions. I waited for Rosemary to act as Jenny would've done. She didn't. Of course.

"Some girls in a motel had a board they picked up at a flea market somewhere," I carried on as if I had a captive audience anyway. "They wanted somebody to join them. It was just a glass and some letters, I didn't think we'd actually get through to anyone."

"I suppose you're going to tell me you did?" She wrinkled her nose.

"Some local 17th-century Sioux chieftain, I think he said he was."

"A Sioux chieftain?" The look she turned on me was one of the Rosemary Blunt specials. "In *Arizona*, you spoke to a long-dead *Sioux* chieftain?"

"Stranger things have happened."

"I doubt it."

"Anyway," I put my mug down and pulled a crate of blank canvases from under the trestle table, "we're here to paint, not talk Native Americans. It's time you tried an abstract painting." This time I didn't wait for her to speak. "Can't knock it until you've tried it, Rosemary. Think of something to paint you can't take a photo of." I selected one of the smallest, cheapest canvases I could fine. "Something that's hard to describe."

"String Theory."

I should've known she wasn't going to make it easy for me. When did she ever? Despite her truculence, however, I was still enjoying her company. Jenny was always a welcome distraction, but nothing more than that, and as for Cheryl and her friend – whose name I must've known once – they were positively toxic.

I had no objection to Cheryl coming to see me. Of everybody, she was the one who seemed to get my paintings, if only in a small and insignificant way. But there was something about her that was all wrong. I thought so from the start, despite everything. She was good-looking and smart, even if she did wear clothes that were a size too small, but she was almost too charming. She didn't turn on the charm in the obvious way her friend did – not all breasts and eyelashes – but in subtler, more dangerous ways. I think she had a game plan all along. I might not have been able to put that into words then, but there was something about her – some corruption – that made it impossible for me to paint while she was there. She ruined God. Unlike Rosemary. I could paint with Rosemary.

"I wasn't really thinking about String Theory," I said. "More an emotion, or something you've experienced that's unique to you."

Rosemary thought about it for about two and a half seconds. "Nope. Can't think of anything."

Not sure why I was bothering, I dragged Rosemary over to the table. "Describe jealousy to me."

"What?"

"Humour me. Describe what jealousy is like."

Rosemary folded her arms and gave a deep sigh. Only when she realised I wasn't going to give in did she say, "Ugly."

"Good. What else?"

"Green?"

"Right. How about messy?"

"If you like. What's this about?"

The tubes of paint were half in the arbitrary order Rosemary liked to impose on them and half in my usual chaos. It took me a minute to find what I wanted. I selected three tubes of green: Olive, Forest and Hunter. I squeezed a thin sausage of each on to a sheet of cartridge paper.

"What are you doing?"

Plucking a thin brush from the nearest jar, I began to swirl the three colours together; round and round until they'd blended into one mess of green, with blotches and streaks of the individual colours showing through. When I'd done enough, I took a thinner brush and drew a jagged black line around the edge of the swirl.

"You say jealousy is messy and ugly and green." I held up the soaked paper. "I say it's like this. Now – describe God."

This time Rosemary really didn't reply. The silence built between us, growing in volume until I couldn't ignore it.

"Describe God for me, Rosemary."

"Invisible."

Touché.

"Apart from invisible," I said.

"I don't know."

Talking to Rosemary was usually like one of those bright winter days – bracing, chilly round the edges, but somehow invigorating. At that moment, however, a wall of dank autumn fog came down between us and I had the uneasy feeling I might have wandered into a minefield unawares.

"OK, how about describing how God makes you feel instead?" I tried.

"I don't know." She said it louder this time. "This is ridiculous."

I should've left it there, of course. There was something going on in that fog I couldn't see, and I, of all people, should've known not to pry. But I thought I was invincible.

"It's not ridiculous. Painting jealousy or God isn't more strange than describing them in words, is it? What about happiness?"

No answer.

"Describe happiness for me – like you did with jealousy. What's it like to be happy?"

Rosemary wasn't looking at me. She stood motionless. And I still didn't see it for what it was – the sucking back of the tide before a tsunami.

"I'm just trying to explain how it works." I went for a tactical withdrawal. "I wanted to explain how people like me think."

"People like you?" Rosemary's head snapped up. "People who think that because they can hold a paintbrush they're something special – they have a right to know God?"

"I can't quite tell who you're angry at." I tried to sound amused – as if we could laugh off the sudden tension. "Me or God." It was a mistake.

"Take a wild stab in the dark."

I chose optimism over sense. "God?"

"I don't get angry at things that don't exist."

It didn't seem like a good moment to explore that avenue of thought, so instead I said, "Me then. Why?"

"Because you're a FRAUD!"

The word exploded out of her and hit me full in the chest. Crazy as it sounds, I believe I actually staggered backwards under the force of it. It wasn't the venom that took me by surprise, it was the fear I felt at hearing that word echo round the white walls

"You think you can pinpoint God – put him on the wall for everyone to see?" Rosemary jabbed her finger at me. "Well you can't. You can only paint shapes and sell them to people with more money than sense. You can't make God exist, whatever you think."

"Rosemary, I never said I could. I..."

"Forget it." She grabbed her coat and barged into the next room. "I'll leave you to your make-believe and you," she flung open the front door, "leave me to the real world."

The door slammed behind her. And as if on cue, my phone began to buzz with a number I recognised all too well. Still baffled by what had just happened, I let it ring out then turned it off. It was the last thing I wanted to deal with. He'd call back. He always did. That was the problem.

ROSEMARY

Letter from Julia to Rosemary.

Sunday 8th July

Dear Rosemary,

Alison is due in two weeks and tells me that the wedding dress diet starts in three. I'm not sure she'll be saying that after a week of no sleep, but we'll see. I do wish they'd found out whether they're having a boy or a girl. I've got blue and pink wool all ready, but it's not fair to expect me to knit booties at a moment's notice. Maybe I should have gone for yellow.

I can't believe you actually painted with Ben! Why didn't you give me more details? What did you paint? Did he teach you everything he knows? I'm sure it wasn't the ordeal you make it sound.

You mustn't let Jenny monopolise Ben. You complain that life is boring in Brackton, but you don't seize the opportunity when something exciting happens. Have you been to see him again? If not then you must do so at once before he falls in love with Jenny and gets married. If he marries he'll almost certainly become dull.

The Show sounds marvellous. I wish we had something like that here. The closest we've got is the primary school fete. Guessing how many sweets are in the jar doesn't sound as fun as drunken announcements, vegetable feuds and obscene bunting.

It's not true, Rosemary. You didn't deserve to leave school as you did. And even if you had deserved it, you certainly didn't deserve everything else. Nobody could have deserved that. I'm still ashamed that I didn't do anything – that I guessed what was going on and didn't even mention it. When you got yourself into university I was so proud. It's not very British to say so, but I've never been more proud of anyone. And I wasn't just proud, I was relieved too. It meant that I could stop feeling guilty for all those years of silence.

How long ago that all seems! Thinking back to our teens makes me feel old. Are we old, Rosemary? I suppose we must be.

Yours in decrepitude, Julia

PS: Any suspects in the Case of the Dog Fouling yet?

Letter from Rosemary to Julia.

Tuesday 10th July

Dear Julia,

Must you be so insufferable? You know I'm terrible at describing things. What do you want to know? I tried to paint the beach with lots of variations on beige and very little success, and the sea with blues and greens and hardly any more. That was all there was to it. I went back to finish it off and was subjected to more of Ben's absurd stories straight out of the Boy's Own Paper or the Idiot's Guide to Gap Years. The ability to get on a plane and get off it again somewhere new doesn't seem to me to be any great skill to boast of. He doesn't seem to realise that if I wanted to learn about the world, I'd have done it by now. I'm interested in how the universe works not the spiritual life of a group of people on a mountain in some country I've never heard of. That's why I'm a physicist and not an anthropologist. Or an artist.

Anyway, I won't be doing any more painting, so Ben will have to find somebody else to bore with his tales of Ouija boards and road-trips. And, for your information, Jenny is welcome to him. God knows it would do her some good to have a man. I doubt the poor woman has so much as been pecked on the cheek in her life. Let's see how she handles a bohemian.

As for being old, Julia – you're 72, and so shall I be at the end of next month. But that doesn't mean we have to be old, whatever our hips and knees might be telling us. If thinking back to our teens makes you feel elderly then take a leaf out of my book – don't do it.

It doesn't matter whether you knew about Michael or not, you had nothing to feel guilty about. I could've done things differently and I didn't. 10 years is a long time to be pathetic – I only have myself to blame. You not mentioning that you knew anything about it was the only thing keeping me sane. You were my respite.

Give Alison my love. I'll be thinking of her.

Affectionately, Rosemary

PS: I suspect Martin Hussingtree and his brute, but have been unable to obtain evidence so far.

Letter from Julia to Rosemary.

Wednesday 11th July

Dear Rosemary,

You can't stop going to see Ben now. If you liked it enough to go twice, why not a third time? It's not as if you're on the Gardener's Club committee or too busy rehearsing for the village pantomime. There's a reason you don't want to return, isn't there? You're not just being miserable. You didn't want to go before, but you still went. Something's changed. He didn't try to ravish you, did he? Answer me properly or I shall come straight down, seek out Jenny Gribble and make friends with her.

I wouldn't mind listening to Ben's stories. They sound exciting. I've never been further than Italy. Did he really play with a Ouija board? If he's still in Brackton in October I shall ask him all sorts of questions while you sulk on the beach outside. I want to know everything about him. I can just picture him working his way round the world, scraping a living by selling sketches, immersing himself in local culture, bungee-jumping off Sydney Harbour Bridge... Wonderful!

Washing machine broke again today. It's all go here.

With love, Julia

Letter from Rosemary to Julia.

Friday 13th July

Dear Julia,

If you were anybody else I'd tell you to mind your own business. If I don't want to paint with Ben, why should I? But if you really want to know why I won't go back to the cottage, I'll tell you. I could make up something to appeal to your over-developed sense of the dramatic, if you want, but the truth is rather more crass. I don't want to go back because Ben asked me to describe happiness. And you know what, Julia? I couldn't do it.

I could describe jealousy, fear and anger. If pushed I might even be able to describe the satisfaction of an equation working out how it's meant to. But happiness? No.

Even since I stormed out of his cottage (and I did storm, Julia – I was quite disgraceful about it) I've been wondering how to describe it. Is happiness warm? Is it round and yellow? We both know that I'm terrible at describing anything, but what if that's not why I couldn't do it? What if I can't describe happiness because I've forgotten what it looks like?

If I go to the cottage, Ben might try to make me paint happiness and it won't work. I know it won't. It won't look at all how it's meant to be.

Rosemary

...

Nothing makes you fall out of love quicker than having to marry. Wanting to marry might be a different matter – I wouldn't know – but *having* to marry is the end of romance. Not that I'm sure you could call what Michael and I had romance. Infatuation, maybe. For three months he'd been the moon and stars to me. I would've sworn before my mother's god that I wanted to be with him every minute of my life. And suddenly I had to be. And it all looked a bit different then. Life with Michael loomed before me in glorious Technicolor, and it wasn't the same anymore.

Michael did at least seem anxious to do things properly. My mother said we were to marry at once, and he agreed with as much apologetic enthusiasm as he could muster. He even continued to tell me that he loved me. By the wedding day he was settled in a tiny end-terrace I'm almost certain Dad had sorted out for him, and for a little while I thought that everything would be alright after all.

During those few short weeks before the wedding I did my best to concentrate on being delighted at the prospect of marriage and on not being more pregnant than I could help. But at night, the dead dreams I was leaving behind haunted me. Those fantasies I'd had of cycling through the streets of Cambridge between library and lectures, scarf trailing behind me, were only that – fantasy. As I lay awake, choking the tears into my pillow, hoping that my mother was not listening with smug satisfaction the other side of the wall, the fantasies drifted further and further from view until they were nothing more than smoke on the wind. When I woke on the morning of the wedding – it was always *the* wedding to me, never my wedding or our wedding – I decided to pull myself together.

Marrying for love is a very modern ideal. And a very western one. There are plenty of successful, even happy marriages between people who hardly knew each other before they made their vows. Michael and I had a head-start on those ones at least. We might have been marrying for all the right reasons and none of the good ones, but it didn't mean the outcome was inevitable. We'd be fine as long as we took our marriage vows seriously. And for almost seven months, we did.

JENNY

Ben was on the Green when I finished my shift in the post office. He was talking on his phone, pacing from the oak to the bench and back again. It had started to spit with rain in the half-hearted way of summer clouds that haven't worked their way up to a storm yet and can't decide whether they mean to. The handful of dog-walkers sharing the grass with Ben, held out their hands, shook their heads at each other, rolled their eyes at the audacity of another British summer. The loose canines scuffled about their feet, sniffing at each other, sniffing at Ben when he came within range. Ben didn't seem to notice. He didn't even greet the people he brushed past on another length of the Green. Even from where I was standing on the kerb, I could see he was frowning. He was pressing the phone to his ear, head dipped as if trying to whisper and shout at the same time.

It took me less than a minute to cross the Green to the church gate. I was already through it when Ben called after me. No sign of the phone now, he was jogging to catch up.

"Dinner," he said, still catching his breath. "Saturday or Sunday?"

I don't know if I was being particularly silly that day or if it was the strange briskness with which the question was asked, but I didn't understand him.

"I need to have dinner with you," he said again. "Are you free this weekend? I can do Saturday or Sunday – whatever suits."

The expression on my face must have said more than I intended it to because Ben laughed and the curious intensity about him vanished.

"Sorry, haven't even asked how you are." He squeezed my forearm. "Didn't want to keep you out in the rain too long, you see. And I did want to fix a dinner date. Like we said we would."

"But of course. I'd love to."

I felt flustered, rushed almost. I'd convinced myself Ben must've forgotten about his casual invitation to dinner. And now he seemed keen again – eager, as if I'd already turned him down and he was desperate to change my mind. I think at the time I took it for embarrassment, though I couldn't see why Ben should be embarrassed.

"Sunday then?" he said. "Eight o'clock at The Oak?"

"That would be... lovely."

"Splendid." He released my arm. "I'll see you there."

And he was gone, hurrying towards the cliff steps almost at a run. It wasn't until I had closed the lych-gate behind me that I noticed Todd standing in the churchyard, only feet away from where Ben and I had talked. He wasn't looking at me, leaning instead over his wife's memorial, but I had no doubt he'd overheard.

The old boys' network in Brackton was extremely efficient. It was only a few hours later that Dad cornered me in the kitchen. Todd was his best friend and anything Todd knew, Dad knew. Not that there was anything to know as far as I was concerned. There was nothing significant in my trips to the beach – neighbourliness, that was all it was in my head. If only my heart hadn't been a different matter.

"What's this Todd's been telling me about you and some young artist chap?"

"I don't know, Dad. What *has* he been telling you?"

I was glad I had my back to him as I bent over the mixing bowl. He sat down on the stool behind me, tugging at his wellies.

"Says you've been seeing rather a lot of him."

"I wouldn't say that."

"Been at his cottage every day?"

"Not every day. Off and on. I've been dropping off food." I banged the bowl on the counter to settle the cake mixture. "You know what these artists are like – unable to feed themselves properly."

I tried not to be angry at Todd. He was a good man and had been as good as an uncle to me since Mum died. His wife had made sure I knew everything a teenage girl needed to know, relieving Dad of any need to discuss periods and bras and contraception. With Todd and Betsy's intervention Dad had made good work of being a single parent to a 13 year-old and we'd muddled through the next 28 years without too many mishaps. So I couldn't stay cross with Todd for long.

"I was meaning to tell you at lunch," I said. "It must've slipped my mind." As if Ben's invitation was every likely to do that. "I'm going to the pub for dinner on Sunday."

"And do I get to know the lucky young man's name?"

"Ben – but he's not young. No younger than me, perhaps a bit older."

"You're still young."

Dad was always trying to convince me of that. Ever since my 40th he'd made a point of reading out any mention he came across in his newspapers of women who'd married in their retirement, or had babies in their fifties. There was still time to see me married off – he needed to believe that, even if nobody else did.

"Can I meet him?"

"That's a bit formal, Dad. We're just two friends going for dinner."

He pulled on his slippers. "Well, that'll do for now. No sense rushing into things."

Dad didn't retreat immediately. He hovered in the doorway, watching me as I fussed around doing things that didn't need doing. "Jennifer, love – this cottage he's staying in – it's Mrs. Baxter's isn't it? The one on the beach?"

"What of it?"

I did look at him then, daring him to say the thing we were both avoiding. So what if it was that cottage? It'd been more than two decades. A whole other life.

"Nothing." He dropped his gaze first. "I was just wondering."

"There's no need to wonder." My voice came out sharper than I'd meant. "It's only a meal, Dad."

"Of course." He nodded and backed out of the room. "Course it is." He reached the door into the front room before stopping again. "I kept the money, Jenny. I want you to know that."

I wished he hadn't said that. More than that, I wished it wasn't true. He had no right to keep that money. It probably wasn't worth anything anymore – 20 years of inflation and what would a few hundred pounds get you? It was a waste. He was the only one who couldn't see it.

In 1990 I hadn't objected to Dad starting a wedding fund. I told him it was silly to do it only a week after I'd introduced him to Tom, but I had no doubt we'd need it soon enough. Tom had talked of marriage almost from day one. He only had to finish his accounting course and find a job, and his first paycheque was going on a diamond ring – that's what he told me. I said we didn't need to wait for that – who needs diamonds? – but he insisted on doing it properly. I thought that was sweet then. There weren't many men left who still insisted on doing things the right and proper way.

Dad always joked that we would've been better off courting in Edwardian England than trying to start a relationship in the 90's. We didn't call each other Mr. Spencer and Miss Gribble, but we were old-fashioned certainly. Where most of our school friends went to raves, we sat in the living room after church, sipping sherry with Dad. Tom wore the clothes he'd inherited from his own father rather than the denim jeans and jackets of our time, and I don't think I even knew what slouch socks were. We might have been preppy, but not in the ironic, fashionable way of our peers. We were suited to each other because we were so unsuited to our age. I thought Tom was the last of the dying breed of English Gentleman.

Nobody in Brackton knew about us, I don't think. For once in his life, Dad was a master of discretion. I suspect he was saving it up for when he got to make the big engagement announcement down the pub. Poor Dad. With anybody else there would've been rumours within days, but I suppose people were unable to think of either Tom or me and romance in the same sentence. Tom's visits to our house went unnoticed – or at least uncommented on – and we were very happy to leave it that way.

I've never held to the notion that God's behind everything that happens to us. I'm not clever at theology, despite my years in church, but I can't see God as some puppet master making children die of cancer or good fathers get mown down by drunk drivers to teach us all a lesson. I do think he'd want us to learn from everything though – the good and the not-good. I tried to learn from Tom, I really did. I was determined that I wasn't going to count chickens with Ben, not because of one meal at The Royal Oak. He was a man who was charming and polite and smiled at me like nobody had for years, but he was also a man who'd forget me the second he boarded the train back to London. There was nothing to it. And I said that to myself as I made Dad's tea. Nothing to it. Absolutely nothing.

ROSEMARY

How do you picture Dr. Richards? From inside your body-prison, what face have you given to his voice? Let me tell you. His face is the face of a doctor who has known hardship at second-hand for 20 years; professional, concerned, distant. He has a way of looking at your bed as if you're not really real, and then looking at me as if I'm larger than life. He has one eye on the time and the other on protocol, and spectacle rims cut them both in half as he stares at me, blinking less than he should. Fingertips press together, resting on his chin.

"I've brought you a leaflet with some useful contact numbers on." He hands me a pastel-pink paper. "Counsellors who can talk through your options and discuss any issues you might have. It's not compulsory of course, but we find it helps most people in your situation."

My situation. Had there ever been anyone in my situation before? If there had I'd like to meet them.

No. I would not like to meet them.

"Thank-you." I make a show of looking at the leaflet. "I'll certainly think about it."

He shifts, uneasy in the hard chair and his position of authority.

"As I said, Dr. Blunt, you're under no pressure to come to a swift decision. Michael's medical team would, however, like me to emphasise the severity of his condition and the very minimal chances of recovery."

For his sake, I meet his bisected gaze. "I understand. I'll try not to take too long. I just need a little more time."

"That's quite natural." He checks his watch and gets to his feet. "I only wanted to make sure you're getting all the help you need. I'll leave you with Michael now."

I wait three minutes; wait until his footsteps disappear and show no signs of coming back before I tear the pink paper into strips. What would I have to say to a counsellor? Who could possibly know more about losing you than I do? I don't need a sofa and a box of tissues placed within easy reach. There's only one person I need to talk to.

"Are you awake in there?" I bend closer, feeling the whisper of your breath on my face. "I know you can hear me."

Nothing.

"Play your games if you want, but we both know the truth. You didn't get away from me, Michael. You're not dead. Not yet."

I knew it had to be Locked-In Syndrome from the start. You couldn't be oblivious to the world, sunk in blissful darkness. You had to be fully awake, totally conscious of everything around you, but paralysed. Every time you had an itch to scratch, or you wanted to clear your throat, or move into a new position, you had to know it. And you had to be unable to do anything about it. You had to be trapped. Because if it wasn't Locked-In Syndrome then it wasn't fair.

They told me it was impossible. They'd done tests. If you were conscious then they'd know by now; trust them, they're doctors. But so am I. I'm the expert on you – not them. There have been plenty of other cases – Locked-In people who everybody had given up on. It doesn't matter if things are different now – if the checks and tests are more strenuous – I *know* that you are not in oblivion. You can't be, or you will have won. If I look at you long enough, you'll flicker. Maybe a finger, maybe just an eyelid, but that's how I'll catch you. You can't play forever.

"They've done tests on people like you, did you know that?" I keep watching your face. "They ask them questions and get them to blink at letters to spell out their answers. It's quite interesting actually. They did a little survey – asked all these Locked-In people, if they wanted to die." Still no response. "Do you know what they said?

"Apparently they want to live. That's interesting, isn't it? I would've thought somebody like you would find dying a relief, but apparently you still find that life has some meaning."

I begin to gather my things, slipping the magazines you don't like back into my bag. "If you don't want to die, Michael, you only have to say. Tell Dr. Richards you want to live and maybe we won't starve you to death after all."

Because if you don't say anything – if you keep playing the game – it'll be up to me. I can tell them you're awake, or I can keep quiet. I can come to talk to you, or I can leave you totally isolated in your prison. I can tell them to kill you. Or not.

"They want to get rid of you. You're taking up bed space. They think you can't hear us when we're talking about your future." I head for the door. "What do you think? What shall I tell them to do with you?"

I walk down the corridor, nodding at the nurses who stand back to let me pass, and I wonder if I've left you screaming in there. Are you screaming to tell people you're alive, that you don't want to die?

Go ahead, Michael. Scream. Nobody can hear you.

BEN

When Rosemary stormed out of my cottage, I had half-expected her to storm
back in again the next day, either to finish the argument or pretend it had
never happened. She didn't. A week passed and I didn't even see her at a distance. Even then – especially then – I could've given you a list of my failings
a foot long, but for the life of me I couldn't work out what I'd done to offend
her. This wasn't about abstract art, I knew it.

When Saturday came round again, I took matters into my own hands
and went looking. I'd passed her house every day since I'd arrived though I'd
never dared so much as open the front gate. It was a austere building standing only a few metres from the kissing gate at the top of the cliff steps. It had
no immediate neighbours, and there was something about it that suggested
it didn't want any.

The grey stone was weathered from two centuries of storms and it sat
perilously close to the cliff edge. The front garden was small and overgrown
in a way that hinted at method rather than neglect, with a path that cut a
weed-free, no-nonsense line from crooked gate to black front door. To either
side of it the long grass was dotted with wildflowers, blending into flowerbeds
bursting with plants. Bees and butterflies busied themselves in the cacophony
of colour, but I couldn't see a single weed anywhere. It was Rosemary all over.

When three jangles of the bell had elicited no response, I trod along the
edge of the nearest bed and peered in through the window. It was a fruitless
exercise; Rosemary was either not there or didn't want to be found. And all
of a sudden I felt annoyed at her. Who was she to dictate when I could paint
God and when I couldn't? It irritated me to feel as if I needed her when she
didn't need me. All the same, I found I couldn't face going back to the cottage to stare at my half-blank canvas for another morning. I had to get away

from the beach and the closed community of Brackton before cabin fever took hold here as much as it had done in London. So I set off East along the cliff path towards open fields.

In a conscious effort to rid my mind of Rosemary and God, I left myself open to any other stray thought that passed my way. That meant, though I hesitate to admit it now, thinking about Jenny. Not that I was plotting anything then – Jenny wasn't my Plan B – but she did drift to mind occasionally. The more I saw of her, the more I could see why nobody in the village took her seriously, and the more I wished they would. She was a good woman in the old-fashioned, biblical sense that doesn't mean anything to anyone anymore. She was a background person; a character in a TV drama who only exists to look shocked when the body is discovered. I had no intention of using Jenny the way Brackton used her. She was the lynchpin of the whole bloody place and even she couldn't see it; a mouse in a village of cats. OK, maybe the possibilities of our friendship had crossed my mind, but never seriously. I thought I still had time to pull something out of the bag – a grand plan, cunning scheme or willing god.

It didn't take me long to pass the outskirts of Brackton. From then on grassland stretched as far as I could see along the coast. I walked for a mile and half without seeing anyone, before pausing to watch a seagull riding a thermal above me. It wheeled in a lazy semi-circle then hung in the air, facing out towards the horizon as if able to see something beyond it. Then suddenly it dived in a controlled tumble towards the sea and I lost it as it dipped below the cliff edge. I didn't walk on at once. Instead I closed my eyes and imagined the gull as I would paint it, capturing it on canvas in my mind.

If I'd been a fauvist I would've painted that bird with those bright, bold strokes: greens and purples under the shadow of its wings, splashes of oranges and yellows where the light bounced off it. The sky would be improbably blue and the sun a deep red disc, tiny and eye-catching in the top corner.

If I'd been a cubist it would've been different. I'd would've painted the gull in tangles of triangles; here a beak, there the tip of wing. I'd have pulled it apart feather by feather and reconstructed it as a talon, an eye, a mess of shapes emerging from and blending into the endless swirl of blue behind it.

That had been one of my favourite games as a child – imagining all the ways I could paint something. Long car journeys sped by in the glimpses of cow fields and curious buildings. As I got older, painting became my way of trying to match the reality of the world in my head to the fantasy of the world I was part of. I don't think I ever managed.

When I resumed my walk, the first thing I saw was a bench with a figure sitting at the far end bolt upright, staring out to sea. Even from a hundred metres I could tell it was Rosemary. This was how I'd first seen her after all: straight back, motionless, eyes on the horizon.

She hadn't seen me, or, at least, she wasn't watching me as I approached. I tried – failed – to remember my annoyance with her. I'd wanted to see her so much, and now she was in front of me I wanted to slip away, to turn back unnoticed. I didn't though. I walked on until I was within touching distance of the bench.

"You mind if I sit?"

She looked over and then away again. I sat on the opposite end of the bench and followed her gaze to the first finger of cloud appearing on the horizon. "Nice weather we've been having – at last."

"I prefer rain."

She'd answered me. That was something. But it'd hardly been an invitation for a cosy chat. The only advantage of that was I had very little to lose.

"Why were you angry with me last weekend?" I said. "Why are you angry at God?"

"Who says I'm angry at God?"

"You do. Every time I mention my painting of him, you get annoyed."

"I still don't see the point in painting all those... those things that you paint. Maybe there are some things that shouldn't be painted."

"Maybe. But I don't see why God, or jealousy, or... what was the other one we were talking about?"

"Happiness."

"Right. I don't see why happiness fits into that category. You may as well say that music shouldn't represent real things. London sounds like car horns and people shouting into mobile phones, but nobody complains that Haydn conjured it in a symphony of woodwind and strings, or that Strauss made the Danube River a waltz. If you can make images with sound, why not feelings with paint?"

I was impressed with my argument, but Rosemary didn't answer. She didn't even give the impression she'd been listening. I didn't force the issue. I'd learned my lesson from last time.

"Why do you prefer rain?" I changed tack. "Rain would blot out the view. I'd like to paint this view sometime."

"But you can take a photograph of it, Ben. It's not a feeling or an atmosphere. Isn't it a bit beneath you?"

"I do paint real things too, you know. Just not the way everyone else does."

Rosemary rolled her eyes. I wasn't sure if I was meant to see it or not.

"I forgot. I'm not allowed to talk about all that rubbish, am I?"

"You can if you like." She folded her arms. "Just don't expect me to be impressed with your tales of the unexpected."

"Rosemary, I gave up on impressing you within 10 minutes of meeting you."

It wasn't true, of course. Certainly within 10 minutes of that first meeting I'd realised she was unlikely to ever allow herself to be impressed with me, and yet I hadn't stopped trying. I suspect I was beginning to find myself cheap – all those tales of travelling and art were a cheap way of making people interested in me. Rosemary didn't care who I was or what I'd done, so it didn't matter who I was or what I'd done. I was beginning to realise that could be better.

"Sensible man." Rosemary mustered the smallest of smiles. "Still, you've always got Jenny if you want someone to show-off to. I expect she's always eager to hear about your exploits."

"Whereas you are bored stiff with me?"

I waited for the cutting reply, but Rosemary said nothing. Her face, for one moment animated, turned to stone and I had that same sinking feeling – the one that told me I was close to warfare again. I couldn't work out how I'd managed to violate the peace treaty so quickly, so I decided to sit it out and wait for her to fire the first shot. But when she spoke it was in a small voice – not one I'd ever have associated with Rosemary then.

"We're very different people, Ben"

"I'll give you that." I said. "What's that got to do with anything?"

"You're an adventurous person. I've never travelled anywhere."

"Why not?"

Rosemary shrugged.

"Too busy lecturing?" I suggested.

"Something like that. Everyone always said I was married to my work."

"Is that why you never married anyone else?"

Again, she didn't reply, but the sudden hostility evaporated as quickly as it'd come.

"It's not too late." I shuffled an inch closer to her. "You could still go travelling."

"I'm 71, a retired physics professor and the sort of person who has kept an up-to-date passport in the drawer for 40 years without once stepping on a plane – constantly ready, but never brave."

"I don't see why that should stop you."

"Because I'm not the sort of person who travels, and I'm too old to become a different sort of person now. I'm a small life kind of person." For one second she caught my eye before looking away. "Some people live big, messy lives. Some people live small, neat lives. I'm a small-lifer."

The finger of cloud on the horizon was being joined by others. They formed streaks of grey, stretching towards the sun, racing to be the first to block it out.

"There's nothing small about being a professor of physics, surely? Especially in your... in your..."

I'd done it again.

"Day?" Rosemary raised an eyebrow.

"I never get that right, do I?"

"It's alright." Rosemary actually laughed. "In my day it *was* unusual for a woman to be interested in physics, let alone make a career of it. I was something of an anomaly."

"I've certainly never met anybody like you before."

It sounded rude. I started a stuttering attempt to clarify myself, and stopped. Rosemary knew what I meant.

"Come and paint with me again, Rosemary." The words came out before I even realised they were waiting to be said. "You don't have to paint a feeling. Paint String Theory – paint the bloody beach if you want to. Just come. I can't seem to paint God without you there. I miss being told I'm an idiot."

"I'm sure if you asked Jenny nicely..."

"I don't *want* Jenny to tell me I'm an idiot. Christ, Rosemary, she's the only one in Brackton who thinks I'm a good artist."

"I never said I thought you were a bad artist."

My face must have given me away because Rosemary laughed again.

"Hating your paintings isn't the same as thinking you're a bad artist." She stood up and stuffed her hands in her pockets. "Besides, you must be a good artist or you wouldn't have all those celebrity clients hounding you for your work in London. What does it matter what anybody here thinks?"

"I'm not sure I ever said hounding." The sky darkened as the first finger pulled the sun into its grasp. "Looks like we're going to get the rain you wanted."

We began to walk along the cliff path together, towards the village. I couldn't resist pushing my luck one step further.

"Do you really think I'm a good artist?"

I looked at Rosemary. She was smiling. "I never said that either."

JENNY

I was surprised to see them together. Dr. Blunt went walking every day but never with anybody else. I'd offered to go with her once and she'd brushed the suggestion aside without the formality of tact. And Ben of all people? I hadn't even realised they knew each other beyond a nod in the street.

I'd been on my way down to the beach with a batch of soup to keep Ben going until our dinner the following day. At the kissing gate I happened to glance behind me and I'd spotted them coming along the cliff path from the opposite direction – Ben bouncing along gesticulating and laughing, Dr. Blunt stiff-backed and stern. Before I could make up my mind whether to slip back to the village and try to catch Ben alone later, or brave out a sudden meeting, he saw me. Once he'd waved, I could hardly run away and so I waited by Dr. Blunt's gate, holding my pan and feeling awkward.

When they drew up next to me, Dr. Blunt didn't seem in a better mood for Ben's company. She suffered less than 30 seconds of small talk before opening her front gate and stepping through, firmly shutting us on the other side. "Can't stand here all day. Some of us have things to do."

She called back over her shoulder as she disappeared towards her front door. "You can use my garden for your liaisons but don't lean on the fence, it's rotten."

I wasn't at all sure what she meant – surely nobody could think that Ben and I... well, that Ben and I *anything*. Ben was quick to reassure me. "Ignore her." He laughed. "It was only Rosemary's way of telling us that by standing here we'll be spoiling her view."

"Do you think we should leave?"

"Not at all. Rosemary's bark is worse than her bite. She doesn't mind us being here a bit. She just had to say something. You know Rosemary."

I didn't really. Nobody did. Ben was the first person I'd heard refer to her by her first name. It'd taken the village two years to even find out what her first name was.

"I didn't realise you knew Dr. Blunt so well."

"I get the impression that she's not the sort of person anybody knows well." Ben shrugged. "But I could be wrong. You'd know more about her than me."

He wasn't wrong. Not as far as I could see. I didn't know a single person who'd set foot inside her house – unless you counted the tramp who'd collapsed on her front doorstep the previous summer. If he'd known what Dr. Blunt was like she might not have been his first choice for help when he fell ill, but I suppose he picked the nearest house. According to village gossip, he rang the bell at The Lookout and Dr. Blunt called him an ambulance, but I don't suppose that counts as getting to know her. He was the only person who had ever provoked her sympathy however, which is something. When people asked her about him the next day and she said he'd died on the way to hospital, she looked quite shaken and wasn't rude to anyone – even Mrs. Baxter. I remember thinking at the time how it showed she wasn't as cold as people liked to make out, but none of it meant any of us knew her any better than we had done before.

"I was bringing you this." I pushed the soup pan into Ben's hands, forgetting how hot it was. "Roasted tomato and red pepper."

"I think I would've starved by now if it wasn't for you." Ben balanced the pot on the fence that was meant to be rotten, while he pulled his sleeves down over his hands. "I'm looking forward to being able to thank-you properly tomorrow... so long as you haven't changed your mind?"

I had changed my mind so many times since Ben had forced a definite date for dinner on me, I didn't know where I was. I was desperately keen to have dinner with him, and terrified of having it in front of Dad's friends at the pub. What did you talk about over dinner? What would people think?

"If you still want to go, then I still want to come," I said as convincingly as I could manage.

"Fabulous. I'm going to continue your education with cubism tomorrow and cunningly find out all about Jenny Gribble while I do it." Big smile. "You'll have to be on your guard, Jenny – I intend to get to know you as well as possible."

On Sunday evening, I stood outside The Oak for a good five minutes before going in. It was only when it started to rain that I plucked up the courage. Ben was already there, lounging at a low table, reading a stack of tourist information leaflets. It was the first time I'd seen him in a shirt without paint marks and jeans without holes. It suited him. If he'd let me, I might have been too conscious of my own appearance to join him, but the second he saw me he was out of his chair and by my side. A kiss on the cheek and a Cheshire Cat beam, and I was seated opposite him before I knew what was happening.

"I'm not late am I?"

The pub was nearly full and I was sure most of the eyes in it were trained on us.

"It's a lady's prerogative to be late if she wants, but as it happens you are perfectly on time and I was early." He handed me a menu. "I was clearly too keen."

I scanned through the dishes, though I needn't have. The Oak was the only place Dad and I ever ate out and the menu never changed. The situation was different this time however. What was expected of me? Would Ben be offended if I offered to pay my half? Should I order the cheapest thing in case he wanted to pay for it all?

"Do me a favour will you, Jenny, and order something big." It was as if I'd spoken all my concerns aloud. "A gentleman can't possibly eat a proper meal if the lady he was treating only picked at something tiny, and I'm absolutely starving."

That was typical Ben. To put it that way, with no fuss and a laugh that had me at my ease in an instant, was him all over. I chose the steak and kidney and Ben ordered wine for both of us, and by the time the food came I'd almost forgotten the other people in the pub.

"I know so little about you," Ben said as he unfolded his paper napkin. "Who is this mystery woman before me?"

I felt hot under his gaze. "There's nothing to know – no mystery. I've lived here with Dad all my life and... that's about it."

There I was, opposite an artist full of tales of white-water rafting in New Zealand and painting the sunset over the Forbidden City in China, and what had I done? Orienteering on a school trip in the New Forest 30 years earlier was the closest I'd come to anything like that. That was the sort of thing Ben did before breakfast.

"Everyone's interesting when you get to know them," Ben said. "With some people there's just a bit of digging to do to find out what the interesting things are. What's your favourite colour?"

"Yellow, I suppose. I've always thought it rather cheerful."

"There you go, that's something about you. For an artist, somebody's favourite colour can be very revealing. Yellow means you've got a lot of energy but you're an introvert. You have a cheerful nature and you're logical. You're wise too, I'll bet. People underestimate you."

What was I meant to say to that? "I'm certainly too introverted."

"When's your birthday?"

"3rd of May."

"So you're a Taurus– warm-hearted, patient, reliable and love security?" He took another sip of wine. "I haven't known you long, Jenny, but I'd say we're on to something here."

He carried on with his questions throughout his fish and chips. It didn't seem to matter that I had nothing to say, he listened as if I was fascinating. He made me feel interesting in a way nobody ever had before – not even Tom. By the time the pudding menu came – and Ben insisted that we must have pudding – he understood more about me than the rest of Brackton put together.

We were halfway through our sticky toffee when I managed to steer Ben off me and on to art. Cubism he'd promised me and at least with that he'd have to do most of the talking. First though, he pulled a piece of paper from his pocket and unfolded it on the table, one corner soaking-up a splash of spilled water.

"*Girl with a Mandolin*," he said. "Picasso. Tell me what you see."

I looked at the picture. It was mostly browns and greys – nothing like Ben's art – and the shapes were all wrong and distorted. The natural curve of the mandolin stood stark against the unnatural angles of her hands. Other details jumped out of the confusion: a single breast, the suggestion of strings, her shoulder melting away until I couldn't see whether it was part of her or part of the wall behind. Her face was turned away but whether her eyes were cast down in modesty, concentration or not even cast down at all, I couldn't decide.

I said all this to Ben, feeling even more foolish than ever, and he nodded, leaned back in his chair, took another mouthful of pudding before saying anything. "The whole thing about cubism," he said, "was deconstruction. Cubists took the world apart and put it together again on their own terms. Where the fauves got rid of realistic colour, the cubists got rid of realistic shapes too. Picasso and Braque were trying to show you something from more angles than you would ever normally see, and yet never let you see the whole picture. They draw the viewer further away from reality until, by sleight of hand, the truth that had seemed obvious – a girl, a mandolin – disappears. It's all about perspective."

Perspective. I knew about that. I'd spent a lifetime trying to put events into perspective – see myself in my proper, insignificant place in the big story. And it was impossible. The world was made up of billions of tiny worlds, each with one person at the centre, each obsessed with seeing things from their own perspective. Everybody forces things into place – sometimes the right place, sometimes wrong.

"Are people interested in seeing things from different angles?" I said. "It doesn't seem to me as if many people are."

"You're right there." Ben sighed. "All anybody cares about is who you are, what you do, where you've come from. Somehow we've let that become more important than what you *could* be or what you dream off when you lie in bed at night. We love to have things clear and unambiguous, to know right from wrong, good from bad – to look at things one way and one only." He re-folded the picture. "Cubists weren't like that. All those distorted angles and uncanny depths, they aren't deception for deception's sake. They're meant to stop you looking at the bald facts about someone – *something* I mean – and make you wonder at it instead." He stuffed the paper back into his pocket and looked at me. "Is that such a terrible thing?"

And as with all Ben's questions, asked in that tight, strained voice, I found I both didn't know the answer and wasn't sure if wanted to know.

ROSEMARY

Letter from Julia to Rosemary.

Monday 16th July

Dearest Rosemary,

Did you really mean that? Can you not recognise happiness anymore? Is that what Michael did to you?

The best thing that man ever did was leave you. I do believe it might've been the only decent thing he did in his entire life. If the Australians were foolish enough to let him into their country then that's their problem. He probably isn't even still alive. Have you thought of that? He always liked a drink – he probably drank himself into a paupers grave in some Australian backwater 20 years ago. And good riddance to him.

Do you remember how you used to laugh at me? You said I was allergic to spite – that I couldn't be mean about someone to save my life. Gentle Julia you used to call me and I hated it. I wanted to be fierce and intelligent like you. All the girls had a crush on you. I bet you thought you weren't popular, but the other girls would watch as you passed by with your immaculate plait swinging from underneath your boater and I swear they'd get giggly. I was a somebody because we were best friends, but I wanted more than that – I wanted to <u>be</u> you. But I wasn't. I was Gentle Julia.

Well, I'll tell you something. If I could get my hands on Michael now, I wouldn't be so gentle. I'd tear his eyes out. All those things I should've said to him in our 20s, I'd say them all and more. For every bruise you tried to hide from me, I'd give him something to think about. I'd hold him down so you could hit him where it hurts, until he knew what it felt like. And if you'd do differently, you're a better person than me.

Don't go to Ben's cottage if you can't face it, but at least consider it. I'm sure he won't make you paint happiness if you don't want to.

Lots and lots of love, Julia

Letter from Rosemary to Julia.

Tuesday 17th July

Dear Julia,

I'm not a better person than you. Not even close. Sometimes I wonder whether I might not even be despicable, but it would be bordering on histrionics to say so.

I don't believe you for one moment when you say that all the girls had a crush on me at school. What nonsense! I was the boring one who always did her homework on time. Until I got pregnant. Then I suppose I was the one who wasn't meant to be talked about; the one that mothers warned their daughters about if they caught them getting silly over a photograph of Elvis. The fact that your mother still let you come to visit me after I left school says a lot for her character. And yours.

It was strange, wasn't it? Me, heavily pregnant and playing house in my own front room, while you sat opposite in your school uniform and told me who'd fallen out with who at lunch break. I was so scared you'd abandon me and I'd be left with only Michael for company. I've always been grateful that you stuck by me, even if I never quite put it into words.

I don't know if Michael leaving was for the best or not. What if he'd learned to love me? What if I'd learned to be loveable? What if Grace had pulled through? Perhaps it might all have worked out in the end. But there's no point thinking like that now.

I think you might be right about Ben. I saw him at the weekend – quite by accident – and he wasn't nearly so obnoxious as usual. Maybe I'll try my hand at painting one more time. Just for you, of course.

Love, Rosemary

. . .

Daughters are meant to become like their mothers, aren't they? I didn't. At least, I hope not. But, failing that, they should at least turn into their fathers. Not Grace. With Grace it was the other way round.

Labour was frightening. It didn't matter that I'd been top in mathematics every year or won a prize for handwriting. It couldn't help me. On the way to the hospital, in the same car our baby had been conceived in, Michael stopped to pick up my mother. When we arrived, he was more than happy to keep out of the way until the business was done.

"I'll be in the father's room, Rosie." He kissed the top of my head. "I love you."

I'm not sure if I believed him then. I know I still wanted to.

I was too scared of what was to come to care when the nurses pursed their lips in disapproval at my teenage face, but my mother hadn't organised a shotgun wedding for nothing. "This is my daughter, MRS. Rosemary Blunt. She's been in labour for three hours now."

Their eyes sneaked down to my left hand and the atmosphere got warmer. It stayed warm until the midwife did her first examination.

"Dear me, Mrs. Blunt, you've got a long way to go. You should've waited a little longer before coming. I don't know if we have room for you yet."

I would've been content with a home birth in the first place. It was more normal after all. But the new NHS coupled with the living conditions of that post-war era meant the government were beginning to herd more and more of us into the hospitals. Most people still preferred the midwife-at-home option, but hospital suited my mother nicely. If I was in hospital, her tales of doctors worrying over a premature baby – I was actually three days overdue – couldn't be contradicted so easily. And there I was being told I should've been at home after all.

I don't know how my mother managed it, but after a furious whispered conversation with the midwife, nobody said any more about leaving and a bed was found for me straight away. That was the last time I ever felt close to my mother. The distance my pregnancy had created and my hasty marriage had barely patched up, was gone. She was no longer the mother of a harlot, who'd spent seven months ignoring the smirks of the other women with their, "Honeymoon baby, is it? Rosemary looks awfully big already." She was now the grandmother-in-waiting; head of a dynasty. And I knew that in doing this one thing for her – producing a grandchild – we'd be alright again.

Labour stretched on into the night and through the following morning. It was long enough and difficult enough for a doctor to be summoned for the eventual delivery. He stood impatiently at the foot of the bed as I whimpered and pushed, looking for all the world as if I was prolonging the agony on purpose. Then, as the clock was striking midday on the 10th March 1958, my daughter arrived and the delivery room went silent.

"What is it?" I struggled to sit up. "Boy or girl?"

My mother sat frozen in her seat. One of the nurses hurried from the room. There should have been crying. I knew there should have been crying.

"It's a girl, Mrs. Blunt." The midwife spoke when nobody else seemed able.

"What's wrong with her? She's not... she's not dead, is she?"

"No. She's alive."

The midwife bent and gathered the tiny half-me-half-Michael into a bundle. She didn't hand her to me but turned instead to the doctor. He shook his head. And as the midwife pulled the blanket closer round my daughter, I saw her properly for the first time. Everyone's eyes fixed on me, as mine fixed on my baby, and I knew – before my mother said it – that this was my punishment.

Anencephaly is a rare thing. Nowadays I understand it can be diagnosed in pregnancy through ultrasound and serum checks, but there was nothing like that then. You got pregnant and dealt with whatever came out of you nine months later. There was no warning that your daughter might be born without a brain. Nobody told you that a major part of her skull would be missing so that her improbably large eyes, shut tight against a world she wouldn't long exist in, bulged up above the space where it should have been. It just happened.

The doctor eventually snapped back to life. "It won't last long."

It took me a moment to realise he was talking about my baby.

"She." I could hardly form the words. "She has a name. She's called Grace."

The doctor glanced at my mother's shocked face and then at me. He sighed. "Best not to get too attached, Mrs. Blunt." He nodded at the midwife who bustled out of the room, Grace still in her arms. "Your baby can't feel anything. It's blind, deaf, unconscious and unable to feel pain. It may have a few reflex reactions, but that's all." He patted my arm in the way he'd been taught at medical school. "The tiny portion of its brain that exists – the bit that's giving it a heartbeat and keeping the lungs going – won't hold out long. It'll be dead within a couple of hours."

"I want to see her."

"I don't think that would be wise."

"I want to hold her."

"It will be easier in the long run if you let us make it comfortable until nature takes its course, Mrs. Blunt. Try not to think about it."

I wanted to argue. How dare they treat my daughter – that fragile, deformed, beautiful ball of life that had shared my heartbeat for so many months – as if she was a monster, something dirty to be got rid of and hushed-up? But 19 hours of labour had taken the fight out of me. And so I never saw Grace again.

At some point my mother left and Michael came to sit by the bed. He was crying, I remember that. I don't remember what he said. All I know is that it wasn't, "I love you." I know, because those words never crossed his lips again. The whole reason we were married had been swept away from us in the silence of a newborn baby. The tiny back bedroom, painted in pastel colours, was worthless. For those few short months where a piece of him had sat restless in my womb, we'd been able to pretend that it was all going to be alright. Maybe it would have been. But as Grace lay dying in some hidden backroom, as the world juddered to a halt on its axis and the sun fizzled out, we became what we always really were – strangers.

There was no counselling then. At least, not for parents of good-as-still-born babies. There was nobody to take plaster casts of Grace's feet for our mantelpiece or suggest lists of songs for a funeral. When Michael got up to leave, he dried his eyes. And as far as I know, he never cried for Grace again. Neither did I. I suppose we both assumed that the other wasn't grieving. Perhaps that was our biggest mistake.

Decades later I came across an article on anencephaly in a medical science magazine in the departmental office at the university. Despite being a scientist by trade, it still came as a surprise to me to learn that a baby didn't develop without a brain because it had been conceived outside wedlock. It might have been that I didn't have enough folic acid, or it might have been nothing at all. One of those things again – like getting pregnant through a condom, or meeting a man in a linen cupboard at a party.

Perhaps it was then that I lost God. Love had gone, Grace too. God had to be next. Maybe while I was pushing as hard as I could to bring my daughter into the world, God was oozing out from under the door or leaking from the ill-fitting windows. While the doctor was explaining to me why I should forget I'd ever had a baby, perhaps God was tiptoeing away down the corridor, shutting the door behind him. I certainly never saw him again. Love, Grace, God – from then on it seemed only a matter of time before I lost Michael too.

Grace – unconscious, unresponsive, unfeeling – never had the chance to become like her mother. A good thing, probably. Neither did she become like her father. With Grace, it was the other way round. It took five decades, but eventually, Michael became his daughter.

BEN

On Wednesday I woke at the moment night was making its last stand against morning. From where I lay I could see the beach emerging from silhouette to colour in the dawn light. It would be some time before the sun overcame the shadow of the cliffs, but it was already a beautiful day. That patch of pale sky through the curtainless windows was the hopeful colour of summer – not a Sky-blue Crayola from a child's pencil tin, but a cross between Periwinkle and Cambridge, stretching away to infinity. And for a moment I was captivated. At a time when my head should've been full to bursting with everything I didn't want to think about, there was a stillness in that promising sky that made me forget there was anything other than the beach and the silence of the cottage and a half-finished canvas.

It was the seagulls that brought me back to the real world. With a clatter and hissing slide they arrived on the roof, calling to each other with hacking cries that conveyed the urgency I'd failed to grasp without them. They were trying to warn me, calling their cautionary tales through the window – tales of ticking clocks, of time slipping away. In some back-of-my-mind kind of way I did know I had to start making plans – seriously this time, not romantically, or half-heartedly – but it still didn't seem real. It sounds foolish, but I think it was more important to me to finish God than to find a way out.

I'd expected to see Rosemary that Monday – I'd counted on it to spur me on my way. After our chat at the weekend I'd thought I was forgiven for whatever I'd done, and after my dinner with Jenny I felt sure Rosemary would want to turn up to make sure Jenny hadn't seduced me into thinking I was interesting or funny. She didn't come. I spent Monday alone, dabbling with God and fussing with a sketch that was no good and was never going to be.

CHLOE BANKS

When the knock came on Tuesday morning, just before noon, I was so desperate for inspiration I ran to open it, only to find it wasn't Rosemary after all.

Cheryl stood on the step, hands on hips. "Mind if I come in?"

She was dressed for the beach: striped top, denim skirt, flip-flops she kicked off the second she was through the door. It suited her. I'd still rather have had Rosemary, but I wasn't a robot. Cheryl was blonde, slim and half my age. I can't say I was disappointed to see her, and yet there was that odd calculation about her still. Nothing I could put my finger on but something that made me uneasy.

"Day off is it?" I asked as I fished in my meagre crate of groceries for the teabags.

"That's right." She sat on the edge of the bed. "I worked all weekend so I wanted to do something fun today."

"That doesn't explain what you're doing here." I smiled at her and she relaxed.

"I wondered whether I could watch you paint again."

She tugged at the hemline of her skirt, pulling it half an inch further down her thigh. The part of me that appreciates the artistic beauty of the human body couldn't help assessing the smooth lines and tight curves, the curtain of hair so blonde it was almost yellow, but not brash – Jasmine yellow, Vanilla. The other part of me – the part that appreciates the human body for entirely different reasons – began to pay attention too. I turned back to the kettle.

"I don't know what I'm doing today," I said. "Nothing big. Maybe a small, quick painting – nothing more than a sketch. I don't know that it'll be very interesting."

"How about me?"

"You?" I handed her a mug. "You mean, paint you?"

"Why not?"

Indeed. Why not? Because when I was with her I was too much of man built from flesh and blood and hormones, and too little of an artist? Because I didn't understand why she was here? Because as a bachelor at 50 I knew all too well why I didn't discourage her visits?

"I could give it a go," I said. "Though it won't be very good."

"Oh well, we can think of it as practice – for when you introduce me to the glamorous world of modelling." She laughed and rolled her eyes as if carrying on a running joke between us. "You said you thought I could be a model, didn't you?"

"I did. I meant it." I opened the door to the studio. "I'm sure you'd be popular in London."

That's what they all wanted to hear wasn't it? And anyway, I had seen far worse-looking models than Cheryl. She proved to be an enthusiastic subject, draping herself to the chair I placed in front of the window. She crossed one leg over the other, skirt riding up again. Her back was arched, one arm resting on the back of the chair, opposite hand on her hip. It was a good pose. A challenging pose.

It was the greatest of the cubists, Picasso, who said, "Art is a lie that makes us realise the truth." And as I painted Cheryl, I finally got what he'd meant. The physical truth was obvious: the sun lighting up her hair, her face thrown into half shadow, the tiny mole at her hairline, the smudge of lipstick that had escaped the bow of her lips. But there was another truth as well, one that didn't appear until I started to paint.

I never painted in watercolours and I never painted things how they really looked, but with Cheryl I found myself doing both. It was a lie, of course – art always is. Every aspect of her became exaggerated, caught in one magnified moment of time. And through that magnification, reality appeared for what it was. By painting a lie, I realised the truth: Cheryl wasn't here for the art, she wasn't posing for the thrill of having her portrait painted; she was posing in order to make me look. The picture that appeared on my easel – the exaggerated Cheryl – was screaming for attention from every brush stroke. And it worked.

Artists are meant to sleep around. Everyone thinks artists can have whoever they want; they are irresistible. Before I knew any better, I thought so too. People assume that for every day an artist spends painting on the banks of the Seine, there must've been a night you're not telling them about. It almost certainly involved high-class courtesans in Can-Can dresses, and attic bedrooms with red velvet drapes and balconies overlooking the alleyways of Paris. It can be a self-fulfilling prophecy. Some artists I knew in London had girls throwing themselves at them only on the assumption that other girls threw themselves at them. It wasn't like that for me, and despite this false lure, I didn't get what Cheryl saw in me. She could surely have her pick of the young men in Lockhaven. I didn't dislike her interest – show me a man who would – but I didn't understand it. Or trust it.

I'd intended to paint for long enough to keep Cheryl on side and then make my excuses, but when I looked at my watch, nearly two hours had passed. Cheryl had been the perfect model – barely moving, not speaking.

"I'm pretty much done."

She made a show of stretching before walking round behind me to view her portrait. She brushed against me, standing so close I could feel every breath she took. And the thrilling discomfort made me step away.

"Wow! It's great," she said. "Loads different to your other stuff – I thought it'd be more abstract."

"It's just a quick sketch." I took my dirty brushes to the table and started to rearrange the paints how Rosemary liked them. "You can have it when it's dry."

"Don't you want to keep it? You can add it to your collection."

I didn't want to keep it. I didn't want it in my studio, keeping God at bay. I couldn't say so though. So I let the question hang and somehow in my silence I found myself having lunch with her on the beach, giving her my number, asking her to come back whenever she was next free. As I watched her disappear through the kissing gate back towards the bus stop, the possibilities of Cheryl's friendship occurred to me. I won't deny that. I realised then that if push came to desperate shove, having Cheryl might mean not needing Jenny.

The following morning as I lay looking at the Periwinkle sky, even the gulls couldn't drag my thoughts back to Cheryl. There were more important things to consider. I hauled myself into a sitting position to look at the beach properly. It wasn't even six o'clock yet, but a couple being walked by a black Labrador were already out on the sand. They paused at the edge of the incoming tide to greet another figure descending the steps. It was Rosemary.

Kicking myself free from the tangle of sheets, I grabbed the previous day's clothes. By the time I emerged on to the sand, Rosemary was standing in her familiar attitude, looking out to sea. I jogged over to join her. The chill of the night hadn't yet disappeared, but the smell of coming warmth rose from the rocks and the straggling seaweed. Each tongue of water ran up the sand and then withdrew, only to run a fraction further with the next wave.

"I'm afraid it doesn't look much like rain today."

Rosemary glanced sideways at me as I drew level. "No. That's the drawback of summer."

"*Non simper erit aestos*," I said. *It will not always be summer.*

"I suppose not." She looked up towards the black-timbered box of Mrs. Baxter's house and caravan park beyond. "They'll all have to go home sometime."

"If you wanted something to do while waiting for the foul weather to return, you're always welcome at the cottage. You could come along this afternoon."

"I could, yes."

"I thought I might've seen you on Monday, what with it being so disgustingly sunny."

"I'm busy Mondays."

"I'm dying to know what you get up to." I picked up a stone and made an unsuccessful attempt to skim it off the next wave. "Off you go on the bus and don't come back until late afternoon. What can you be doing?"

"What indeed?"

Rosemary stooped to pick up an empty juice carton, the resumed her walk along the sand.

"Perhaps Monday is your day for fighting crime? Are you busy busting human traffickers?" I hurried after her. "Or are you, in fact, a human trafficker yourself?"

"I probably wouldn't tell you if I was."

"Maybe it's something more wild then. Snake charming? Exotic dancing?"

Rosemary gave me a sharp look. "You need good knees and a strong back for that sort of thing. At my time of life, you're lucky to have either."

"I don't know – you look in pretty good shape to me."

She either didn't hear this comment or it was beneath her contempt.

"I know, I know." I held up my hands. "If you told me what you did on Mondays you'd have to kill me, right?"

"Something like that."

"Fine. I'll have to find out the hard way." I skipped ahead of her and then turned to walk backwards, forcing her to face me. "Come and paint this afternoon and then we'll see what secrets your picture reveals about you."

Not only did Rosemary turn up to start a new painting that afternoon, she also returned on Friday. I couldn't have been more surprised therefore, when I opened the door to her – still dressed in her oldest clothes – on Saturday as well. I didn't comment on it. Commenting on her sudden enthusiasm for painting would certainly have meant not seeing her again for weeks, but as she took her place in front of her easel, I couldn't help feeling smug.

When we'd painted for long enough to get stiff, I put my own palette down and joined Rosemary in front of her canvas. Blue arrows in various shades collided or shot away from each other across a field of black. The overall effect was order within chaos. Not bad for three afternoon's work.

"Remind me what it is again," I said.

"Newton's Third Law of Motion."

"Ah, yes." I made a study of the finer details while racking my brains. It was no good. "And remind me what that is again."

Rosemary tutted. "To every action there is always an equal and opposite reaction."

"Of course." I pointed at two curved arrows, twisting away from each other at the top of the canvas. "You've got a good eye for colour. The way the Steel blends into the Cornflower, is beautiful. I'd say it was a very good likeness of Newton's Law."

"Have I failed then?" Rosemary added a fleck of paint to the last pair of arrows. "I thought good paintings don't look like what they're meant to be."

I was about to launch into a practised speech on the nature of abstract art when I caught the expression on her face. If it wasn't impossible, I'd have said she was teasing me.

I returned to my own easel before asking, "What are you going to paint next?"

I waited for Rosemary to say she'd wasted enough time already, or that she disliked painting, or that she was only here to please that pen-pal of hers. The protests didn't come. She folded her arms and frowned. "Not sure. The other laws of motion aren't as inspiring."

"How about you leave Newton out of this next one then?" I added another twist of Amber to my picture. "Let your mind wander and see what comes out on canvas. Sometimes you don't know what something is until you've painted it. You have to approach it sideways – not really thinking about it at all."

"Is that what you're trying to do with God?"

I inspected my painting. It had gone well that week. Rosemary's presence had given me the space I needed to complete the waves and spirals, punctuated by the geometry of blues and greens. I was pleased with it. As with Rosemary's painting there was chaos and there was order, there was warmth and cold, hard edges and soft depths, gentleness and ferocity; it was everything a god should be, and yet still no God. My usual methodical approach had gone out the window. Instead of working on discrete sections in order, I'd found myself painting inwards. All the colours and lines, both rigid and freestyle, seemed to be reaching for the centre, racing to get there and yet dancing around it. Never quite touching.

"I can't quite make it work. It doesn't look right." Out of the corner of my eye I saw Rosemary opening her mouth. "And no, not in a good way!" She shut it again. "Maybe you were right, it was a mistake to try painting God."

"Don't be so defeatist." Rosemary marched over to my easel and glared at it. "It was ridiculous of you to start this painting, but it would be even more stupid to stop halfway. What if I'm wrong and you're right?"

"I hadn't realised that was an option."

"It's not likely, I'll admit." She smiled. "But what if God wants you to finish it so that people know what he looks like?"

I shook my head. "What have you done with the real Rosemary Blunt? The one who thinks God doesn't exist."

"When did I ever say that?"

"On that day when you flounced out of here."

"I didn't flounce." Rosemary blushed. I'd never seen her blush before. "I don't do flouncing."

"So you do believe in God then?"

"No. But I do think he exists." She began to clear away her brushes. "I think you exist too, but that's a very different thing to believing in you."

"So you're saying that I'm a bit like a god to you?"

Rosemary snorted and wandered over to the table. She muttered to herself as she began to sort clean from dirty, rags from Hobnob packets, empty tubes from full. I decided to leave her to it and returned to my own easel, only to have my attention caught by a figure on the beach, picking her way between towels and sandcastles. My heart sank as I remembered the text I'd got late last night – and the enthusiasm with which I'd responded. It had completely slipped my mind.

Jenny I could've dealt with. There was nothing embarrassing about Rosemary and Jenny meeting there. Cheryl was a different matter. I know I'd encouraged her to come, but it felt seedy to me – a woman half my age turning up in beachwear. I didn't want Rosemary to think I'd fallen for blond hair and curves – that I'd encouraged her to come. I didn't want it to be true.

Leaving Rosemary at the table, I got to the door just in time to stop Cheryl knocking.

"Cheryl – back so soon?"

"Am I disturbing you?"

"I was working on God."

"How's it going? Can I see?"

I tried to think of a way to put her off without it sounding like a dismissal. Right then, God and Rosemary's effect on him were all I cared about. The gap I left after her question stretched on a fraction too long.

"Sure." Defeated already, I gave her my best smile. "Why not?"

There was nothing for it. I had to take her through to the studio. Rosemary hadn't noticed I'd gone, and was halfway through saying something when I reluctantly said her name. She turned and the oddest look crossed her face at the sight of us. Before I could identify it, it vanished, but I found myself wishing more than ever that Cheryl hadn't come.

"Rosemary, I'd like to introduce you to somebody." I ushered Cheryl towards the table. "This is Cheryl. Cheryl, meet Dr. Rosemary Blunt."

ROSEMARY

Letter from Julia to Rosemary.

Thursday 19th July

Dear Rosemary,

The baby has arrived! Four days early but big enough already – 8lbs 11oz. And she's a girl. At last! The labour was so fast I knew nothing about it until it was over. Rory called as I was to going to bed and I didn't sleep a wink after that. I'm already halfway through my first pair of pink booties. They've named her Martha May which is very respectable – I'll be able to tell the ladies at Pilates without embarrassment. I went round to meet her first thing this morning and she's the most beautiful baby there's ever been – a head full of hair and the chubbiest cheeks you can imagine. Jake adores her already. I'll send photos with my next letter, whether you want me to or not.

I could ramble on about Martha for a good few more pages, but I'll spare you. Did you go back to paint with Ben in the end? Please say you did.

I won't have you talking that way about Michael. Of course leaving you was for the best. He was nothing but a waste of space. And if you think he treated you as he did because Grace died, that only makes him more of a... I don't know what. Do you really imagine if you'd produced children he would have been a different man?

I also won't have you saying that you're despicable. If you were then I'd have shaken you off years ago. I didn't and I won't now. I'm coming to visit in October, whatever you say.

Do you think Ben will still be there when I arrive? The thought of meeting a real artist who's travelled the world, is too thrilling. I shall warn

George that I might fall in love and never come back, though he'll just say, "Yes, Dear," and continue reading the sports' pages.

Do let me know what you're painting.

With love, Julia

Letter from Rosemary to Julia.

Friday 20th July

Dear Julia,

Congratulations on becoming a grandma again. Of course you must send me photos. Even I'm not mean enough to deny you a little boasting, and I need to keep my Braithwaite family album complete, don't I? Send Rory and Alison my love, and you can even give Martha a kiss from me if you want.

I did go to Ben's cottage (don't say I never do anything for you), and I even started a painting. It's not happiness, but it's the nearest thing I know – Newton's Third Law of Motion (no, don't roll your eyes like that – I know you did). It's actually rather fun. At the moment it's mostly black, but at least it's more interesting than trying to get the shadows on sand right.

I don't know if Ben will still be here in October. I think he said he was only renting for summer, but you never know with these artists. I can put in a request if you want, but better hold off telling George in case it comes to nothing.

Love, Rosemary

. . .

Losing Michael was a slower process than marrying him had been. In the weeks following the birth and death of our daughter, a forest of silence grew up between us, dark and full of thorns. In the years to come it became too easy to forget that Grace belonged to Michael too. Men weren't meant to be affected by such things. They were meant to shake their heads, say how unfortunate it all was, and then move on. I assumed that was how it was with Michael. Now, I wonder how much the death of Grace contributed to the death of the Michael I'd married and the birth of somebody new.

The pretence of our marriage couldn't be sustained for long. I tried to be a good wife – and Michael probably tried to be a good husband – at first, but night after night of stilted conversations over the dinner I'd had to learn to cook, killed off any chance we had of making a go of things. We both supposed that another child would fix us, but another child didn't come. There were one or two times when I was late, but within a day or two of beginning to wonder if the nausea was coming, my period would arrive – heavier than usual and more painful. We never got further than that.

My mother had near enough disowned me. I'd failed her. The baby that would've brought respectability back to her family and given her something to dote on, had been a monster to her – an abomination born to die. For the next few months she continued to call, and we'd make impersonal conversation for an hour while she criticised my housewifery with every sweep of her eyes around our home. Eventually, she stopped coming. If it'd been only her, I wouldn't have bothered going to my parents' house either, but I couldn't bear not to see Dad, so I'd walk the three miles there and back again, trying to eke out the housekeeping Michael had left for me that week.

The best times were when my mother happened to be out when I called. Dad would buy cakes from the baker on the corner and we'd chat as freely as if I was five again. He'd run me home in the car without my mother's knowledge and disapproval, and he'd squeeze me tight before I got out. And it'd be all I could do to hold in the tears until he'd disappeared round the corner again, waving at me all the way. Every time he returned to the house that still should've been my home too, it was a reminder of all I'd thrown away.

If it hadn't been for Julia, I might have gone mad sooner. Two or three times a week she'd come to the house after lessons and for the first time in my life I was desperate for gossip. I wanted to know who'd been to the pictures with who, and who'd got into trouble for rolling their skirt up at the waistband on their way home from school. The only thing I never asked about was the lessons themselves. I couldn't bear to think of them. Apart from that, Julia told me everything and I had nothing to tell her in return. Even when Michael started hitting me – six months or so after Julia had taken a job as a doctor's secretary – I didn't say a word.

The first time it happened was the key. I think I could've stopped it then. It was ridiculous; I hadn't been caught in adultery or threatened to leave him. I'd burned the dinner, that was all.

"What's this"? Michael poked at it with his fork.

"Shepherd's pie – it caught a bit on top." I took my seat opposite him. "I think it'll be alright if you just scrape away the top layer of potato."

"Rosie, I worked hard to pay for this food. I don't want to be scraping bits of it into the bin."

"I know. I'm sorry. I got distracted for a few minutes and forgot about it."

"Distracted? By what? What the hell do you have to be distracted by?"

It was then that I caught the whiff of alcohol on his breath that explained why he was so late home. He wasn't drunk – that took a bit of effort – but he was never at his best after a drink, even a single whisky.

"You don't have to do anything all bloody day." He pushed his plate away. "No children to look after, no office to go to. I work all day every day to keep you, and you can't even do the one thing you're good for without messing it up."

"I said I'm sorry."

"That doesn't make me less hungry."

I'd never heard him like that before. We may have fallen out of love, but he'd been brought up to be civil. We were strangers, not enemies. Even then I was aware of it being faintly absurd. The potato was slightly blackened; it was far from being ruined.

"Make me something else."

I stared at him, but he was serious. I took our plates to the sink. "Perhaps if you arrived home on time more than once a week it wouldn't be so hard to get your dinner right."

I said it under my breath, not sure whether I wanted him to hear me. He did hear. In a second he was on his feet as well. He swung me round, fingers digging into my arm, and slapped me across the face. It wasn't hard – if Michael had wanted to hurt me he could've broken my neck, the size he was – but the shock brought tears to my eyes.

Michael took a few paces away from me. "I'm sorry." He seemed almost as stunned as I was. "I didn't mean that, Rosie. It's been a long day. I didn't mean anything... I..."

If I'd put my foot down then – gone running to Dad, or told Michael I wouldn't stand for it – it would've been the last time as well as the first. Perhaps. But pride and some misguided sense of duty took control of my

19 year-old mind and I said nothing. When I returned to the kitchen – face washed, hair tidy – Michael was at the table, eating his shepherd's pie. My own plate was back on the table too and I sat, as if nothing had happened, and forced myself to eat. It wasn't until much later I realised that in that moment of silence, I'd given Michael all the permission he needed.

It didn't happen again for several months, but once it did, it became routine. Perhaps Michael found it easier after the second time. Maybe once you've realised that it wasn't a one-off – that you really are the kind of man who hits his wife – it gets easier.

Sometimes he'd apologise, and it was almost worth the humiliation and pain to hear him talk with tender words, to pour me a glass of wine, to soothe me with empty never-again promises. In those moments I would catch a glimpse of the man I had thought I'd loved and who'd tried to love me against the odds. Other times he hardly seemed to notice he'd done it; it was of no consequence. Those times, I only saw a bully and a brute. And, if I'd looked closer, a man who'd lost Grace just as completely as I had.

When I read stories now about women who put up with abusive husbands, I think they're fools. Why stay? Because of love? I wouldn't know about that. For the children? I wouldn't know about that either. Is it fear? Some women may fear what their husband would do to them if they left. Or they're frightened of what leaving would do to their reputation, or family, or bank balance. They stay because when somebody's hitting them, they're getting some sort of human contact; at least somebody has noticed they're alive. There's always some excuse, some reason to remain.

It only took a few months before my fear of disappointing Dad or finding myself homeless didn't matter. It wasn't why I remained. I didn't stay with Michael for some named fear, but because I didn't know how to be anybody other than the person Michael made me. If I stopped being Mrs. Blunt, I would have to go back to being Rosemary, and I didn't recognise her anymore. It was so much easier to imagine that without Michael I would have been somebody special. If I didn't have him, I would've been a successful academic, a cultured theatre-goer, a big name in any chosen sphere; I would have been a lady, a member of the intelligentsia; I would have run away to the circus, become an astronaut, a pirate on the high seas, a princess in her castle. In the end, it was less perilous to be the inadequate woman

Michael knew, believing I could have been more, than to risk finding out for certain that I couldn't.

So I hid the bruises. It was incredible how many doors I could walk into, stairs I could fall down and rugs I could trip over without questions being asked. People believe what they want to. Even Julia didn't suspect anything for a long time. It was only when she saw the bruises on my forearm – unmistakeably finger marks – that the light dawned on her.

Part of me wanted her to ask about it, even as I desperately tried to think of an excuse. What could I say? I nearly fell off a bridge and Michael caught me by the arm in an act of heroism? I did it to myself in my sleep? There was no plausible explanation; if she'd quizzed me, I would've confessed. She didn't. The shock on her face, turned into hurt and then sorrow, and the bigger part of me – the part that didn't want to talk – took over and I tugged my sleeve down again. Move along. Nothing to see here.

It must have been around that time when I learned the importance of compartments. When Michael shouted and lashed out, I'd wait until I was sure it was over and then I'd seal the memory of it away in a corner of my mind. I'd lock the door on it and carry on as before. Visiting my parents would go into another cubbyhole, seeing Julia in a third. Every part of my life was given its own label. Each bit could be filed away until it was needed: shopping, cleaning, fulfilling my wifely duties in the kitchen, fulfilling them in the bedroom – all separate.

It started as a way to protect myself. When I was occupied in one division of my mind, I didn't allow myself into another. If Julia asked a question about baking, or Dad asked how Michael was doing at work, I'd unlock the necessary compartment, extract the relevant bit of information or a well-crafted lie, and then lock it again. It became second-nature and I think I hid it well. The trouble with second-natures is that if you're not careful they become first-nature – they stop being a conscious choice. It took a while, but at some point between that first slap and the day Julia married Dr. George Braithwaite, on the eve of my 22nd birthday, I lost the ability to be only one person.

Sometimes Julia would ask what I'd done that morning, or how my parents were, and I would find that I didn't know. There would be a blank between breakfast and lunch, or I would struggle to recall my mother's face.

Perhaps those periods of nothingness in my memory should have disturbed me, but they didn't. They were my lifeline. The Rosemary doing the dusting didn't have to be the woman who stayed with a husband who hit her; she didn't have to be despicable. The Rosemary who silently submitted to Michael's rough advances when the lights were out, was somebody different to the woman who passed the time of day with the butcher. She didn't have to be me.

My capacity to be two or more different people, grew over the years, until each Rosemary was hardly even aware of the existence of the others. In some vague way, one Rosemary might be aware she'd talked that morning with somebody whose name hovered out of reach, but it was an awareness of shadows. Something not quite real and easily forgotten. It was a lesson that stayed with me long after I lost Michael for the first time, but to call it a skill would suggest I had a choice in the matter. I'm not sure I ever did.

CHERYL

I couldn't stop thinking about that painting. It was weird. When Ben painted me I expected to see a mess of shapes and colours – perhaps like one of those Picasso paintings with noses in the wrong places. Instead, he painted me as I was, and somehow more so. It was me and it was doubly me. It's not that I didn't like it, it just wasn't what I was expecting. Despite the fact Ben said almost nothing in two hours, I felt as if it had created a bond between us somehow – as if in painting me, he'd found something out about me that nobody else knew. I couldn't wait to see him again.

I wasn't meant to have another day off only four days later, but I'd worked too many Saturdays already that summer so when the schedule came out I was free again. Lauren had a spa day booked with her sister and I had nothing to do in Lockhaven – there was no reason not to go to Brackton. Ben had sort of led me to believe he wanted me to see him again anyway – it wasn't all one-sided. I still thought he was a bit too old, but that seemed to become less important every time we met. He was kind and funny, and not only did he think being a nurse was a good thing, he also didn't think it was so bad to be considering a career-change already. With Ben, I felt understood in a way I wasn't with my parents, or even with Lauren.

The beach was crowded by midday and it took me a few minutes to pick my way up it to the cottage. I glanced up as I drew nearer to see if Ben was in his studio. He was. He also wasn't alone. There was a woman in there with him and he was laughing as he turned away from her. Laughing until he spotted me coming, then the smile disappeared. It wasn't a good sign. Before I could reach the door, he had it open, his body blocking the entrance.

When I asked to go in, he hesitated a few seconds longer than I would've liked. I began to get nervous. I couldn't think of a reason he wouldn't want me to meet whoever was in the studio. Not a good reason anyway. But when I did finally get through the door, I relaxed. The woman inside had grey hair. The hand reaching out to take a biscuit from the packet on the table was wrinkled. She was old. Ben didn't need old women. Not when he could have someone like me. I was safe from her at least.

She didn't seem to have noticed our arrival and was saying something when Ben interrupted her. "Rosemary?"

She turned and stopped short when she saw me. Her eyes widened and then a strange blank look dropped over her face. It was Dr. Blunt.

It's funny when worlds collide. Only two days earlier I'd seen Dr. Blunt at her husband's bedside. She'd watched in silence as I'd washed and shaved him, in that unnerving way she had. She always unnerved me. Most relatives want to talk – to fill the silence their comatose husbands and daughters give them. Dr. Blunt never wanted to talk, though I wouldn't say that stopped me feeling sorry for her exactly. Her husband was in a coma and it didn't look as if that was going to change until she decided to pull the plug on him. That had to suck whoever you are. I never warmed to her though. She never appeared to me to be grieving, even after Dr. Richards had had The Chat with her. And there she was in the middle of this supposed trauma, hanging out with Ben, making him laugh in a way I hadn't seen before. Even before the truth came out about her, it seemed a bit sick to me. A little bit twisted.

If her behaviour at the hospital was odd, it was nothing to what came next. When Ben introduced us, she took a step towards me, hand outstretched, eyes locked on to mine.

"Hello Cheryl," she said. "I don't think we've met."

For a second I thought she was having a laugh, which was freaky enough. Then it crossed my mind that maybe I should be offended – could she have watched me wash her husband's private parts, clean out his tubes, cut his nails and god knows what else and not have noticed who I was? But it wasn't that either. She *had* recognised me. I'd seen it in her face. She knew who I was and then she didn't know. That sounds weird – it *was* weird – but it was exactly like that; one second she knew me, the next I was a stranger. She must've been acting, I suppose, and she was a darned good actor. It really was as if we'd never met. She was blind to me.

I could've corrected her. For some reason, I didn't want to. There was something eerie about that blankness in her face.

"Are you a friend from London?" she asked.

"No." I took her hand and shook it. "We met at the Brackton Show a few weeks ago."

"That's nice." Dr. Blunt put her biscuit down and turned to Ben. "Sorry to dash off, but I hadn't realised the time. I must go and leave you two to it."

"There's no need..." Ben began, but she was already out of the door.

I waited until she was halfway down the beach. "Who was that?"

"One of the locals." Ben offered me a biscuit. "She lives in that house at the top of the cliff steps. She comes down here to paint sometimes."

"Is she married?"

Ben gave me a strange look. "No. Why?"

"No reason. Thought I recognised her from somewhere, that's all."

If Ben hadn't been laughing like that when I'd first seen them together, or if he hadn't sounded so desperate to stop her leaving, I might've forgotten about it. It wasn't as if she was serious competition. She shouldn't have been anyway. I'm not the prettiest or wittiest person ever, but I like to think I could outshine a pensioner when it came to getting male attention. There was something in it though. Something I didn't like. Ben had never laughed with me as he'd laughed with her; he never sounded sad when I had to leave.

That must've been it then – the day I knew I did want Ben after all. And it *was* him I wanted. People can say I was only interested in his offers of finding me a job as a model, or in the thought he might take me with him when he next went travelling, but I'm not that kind of person. I liked Ben and I didn't like Ben liking Dr. Blunt. I wanted him to myself. That's not so bad, is it? It's not as if I went and threatened to kill Dr. Blunt or anything. I only wanted her to know he didn't have time for both of us. It had to be her or me.

It had to be me.

ROSEMARY

On the 12th October 1968 I was making bread. Michael was late again. A decade earlier, newly-married and beginning to waddle under the weight of Grace, I would've been worried. But not then. If I was lucky, Michael would come home only smelling of whisky. When he was that late however, he usually came home smelling of a cheap perfume I'd try not to recognise on the women I passed in the street the next day.

Our usual hour for dinner had come and gone, but I didn't dare eat. Michael wouldn't stand for that. All traces of the dashing young man in the old Austin had trickled away – abandoned in the dregs of a pint glass, belched out after too many chips at the football, snowed-in under piles of invoices at the office. He no longer read good books and listened to good music. As his waist expanded towards middle-age, his world shrank until it only encompassed him and his needs.

He must have been better at his job than at being a husband, because he'd been the manager of the department store for a year by then. We'd moved into a semi with a little garden I couldn't keep under control and couldn't fill with children. The money meant nothing to him, except making him that little bit more popular with publicans and bookies. He never had to pay for sex; a man with money doesn't. He has his wife when he doesn't want to make an effort and any number of other girls when he wants to feel young again. And. at 37, Michael needed to feel young again. It was an era where society had not stopped being shocked at promiscuity, and had not yet worked out the more shocked it was, the more promiscuous this new generation would be. Michael knew which halls were holding discos and which pubs to hang around in. He could fill the backseat of his Cortina with crocheted dresses and striped miniskirts three times over every night. But he usually limited himself to once or twice a week.

I was making bread for the next day, trying to distract myself from the hunger sharpened by the aroma of chicken in the oven. The physicality of kneading would keep me in my Good Housewife compartment until I heard Michael's key in the lock and had to shift into Submissive Spouse. The dough had turned out extra-elastic that night. I still remember how it felt as I folded it over, picked it up and slapped it on to the worktop, punching the air out of it with a sticky sigh. Fold, slap, punch. Fold, slap, punch.

By the time Michael rolled in, the chicken had dried out and I was knocking the dough back.

"Where have you been?"

I didn't usually bother asking. He never told me if I did.

"Seeing a friend." His words came out slurred.

"Oh yes?" Fold, slap. "What was her name?" Punch.

He didn't answer, only headed for the sideboard where we kept the brandy and poured himself a double. "Is my dinner ready?"

"It's quarter to 10. It was ready three hours ago."

I was feeling reckless. Talk like that could go any which way with Michael, especially if he was drinking. But I'd forgotten to care about being hit that night. I'd left a door open in my mind somewhere and one Rosemary – the brave, respectable Rosemary who nobody would dare lay a finger on – had got her wires crossed with Rosemary the cowed wife.

"Forget it. I've got a headache. I'm not hungry."

"There's a whole chicken in the oven."

"I said I'm not hungry."

"You should eat something, Michael."

"For Christ's sake, woman." Michael slammed his empty glass on to the table. "Stop nagging. It's bad enough being married to you – don't go on at me as well."

"Oh, because being married to me has been so terrible for you, hasn't it?" I rounded on him in a way he wasn't used to and surely wouldn't tolerate. "Having your shirts ironed and meals prepared while you philander your way about town must be so tedious."

I waited for the slap – even thought I deserved it. But Michael laughed. "You think you're a good wife?" He waved a hand around the kitchen. "Just look. Look at our healthy brood of children. Look at the effort you put into looking good so I can be proud of you. Listen to the sounds of our little ones laughing for joy." He snorted. "Jesus, Rosie, open your eyes."

I was suddenly aware of the smudges of flour dotting my skirt, the strand of loose hair in my face, the sweat patches staining my blouse. The silence of the empty house.

"At least I wasn't unfaithful." I returned to the bread dough. "At least I tried."

To my surprise, Michael's shoulders drooped. He leaned against the doorframe between the kitchen and hall and ran a hand through his thinning hair. "I never meant it to be like this, Rosie. I really didn't." He spoke quietly, without looking at me. "I thought I could make a go of marriage – I wanted to be a good husband. I suppose I'm just one of those men who can't be satisfied with one woman. It's not my fault. Perhaps if you'd managed to have children..."

I don't remember throwing it. One minute the dough was in my hand and then it was hitting the far wall, missing Michael's face by inches. For a second it clung to the plaster, before sliding its oily way down to the floor.

He didn't hit me. The only time I've ever wanted him to, he didn't. In that moment I wanted him to kill me; anything was better than indifference.

"Clean it up."

That couldn't be it. He had to say something – *do* something – more than that. I threw myself at him, scratching at his face, kicking at his shins. And it was pitifully easy for him to restrain me.

"For God's sake, Rosie!" He sounded disgusted. "You're a mess, woman. Is it any wonder I get what I want elsewhere?" He pushed me away from him, turned his back and headed for the stairs. "My head's killing me. I'm going to lie down. I expect the kitchen to be clean in the morning."

I watched him retreat down the hallway, clutching at the walls for support.

"I HATE YOU!"

He didn't even pause.

"I hate you I hate you I hate you I hate you."

On the third stair, Michael looked back. He winced and put a hand to his forehead.

"I wish you were DEAD."

"Then kill me, Rosie. Go on. I won't resist." He held his arms out wide, eyes fixed on my face. When I didn't move he smiled and dropped his arms again. "You couldn't kill me, Rosie. You don't have the guts. You never will."

"You don't know what I could do, Michael. You don't know me."

"Fine. Whatever you say." He began to climb again. "If you're going to kill me, you'd better make it quick though, because I'm leaving you tomorrow."

He reached the top and looked down at me in the hallway. The landing light fell on his face, catching those pale blue eyes that a lifetime ago had studied me from the other side of a linen cupboard.

"You think I need you, Rosie? I could replace you in a week." He pulled his tie over his head, tossing it on the floor. "I resigned from my job today. I'm going to Australia to start a new life." He began to unbutton his shirt. "And I'm not taking you with me."

...

"What do you think, Michael? Do you still know best? Still think I wouldn't be able to kill you?"

Your face is thinner. The wrinkled skin is grey now, clinging to your cheekbones, sagging round your chin. Your neck, sticking out from fresh pyjamas, looks thin enough to snap. To anyone else you might've been a corpse. I know better. If I look long enough, you'll flicker.

"You think I'm going to tell Dr. Richards I know you're awake, don't you?" I don't take my eyes from you as I sit down. "I haven't yet though, have I? A whole year and I've kept quiet, even though Dr. Richards can't wait to get rid of you. I don't have to tell him anything I don't want to."

The door clicks open and I don't have to look round. I know who it is. Without realising it, I've been expecting her. I'm not sure why. She walks round your bed and picks up your clipboard, records your pulse and blood pressure with deliberate slowness. In those minutes before she speaks, I wonder if you can tell who she is.

"Why did you tell Ben we don't know each other?"

I remember now. This was the reason I didn't want her to come. Because of this question; a question I don't understand; a question I don't have an answer for.

"I've been trying to think why you might not want Ben to know we've met." She runs one hand up and down your drip stand. "Here's what I reckon... If Ben knew we'd met, he'd want to know where, right? So you must not want him to know you come here. Why would you hide that? What's wrong with visiting your dying husband?" She pauses and, with the air of a detective making the final denouement, says, "Ben doesn't know about Michael, does he? He doesn't even know you're married."

"It's none of his business."

"Why lie about it though? Why *shouldn't* you tell him? He'd probably feel sorry for you."

I don't like this girl. I think I did like her once, I can't remember. She's dangerous now – that's what it feels like – and I can't quite get a grip on why that should be. How much does she know about you and me? How much has she guessed about Michael Blunt and his wife?

She sits on the edge of your bed as if you don't exist. "Are you sleeping with Ben?"

"Don't be ridiculous."

"Then perhaps you're in love with him. There's something going on, isn't there?" She examines one pink fingernail. "I can't work out how he hasn't found out about Michael yet. I'd have thought it would've come up in conversation with somebody else by now."

She looks at me, expecting an answer, and I scramble to find something to say; anything that won't make it worse. I don't think fast enough. A dangerous ray of light dawns on her face.

"Nobody knows, do they?" she says. "Michael was already in here when you moved to Brackton and you never told anyone about him."

Is that true? It can't be, surely. I've lived in Brackton for years.

I know I must say something. "Don't tell Ben." I didn't mean it to come out like that – desperate, pleading. I don't beg anymore, Michael. I haven't begged for over 50 years.

She looks at her feet. "Why shouldn't I tell Ben? Why don't you want him to know?"

"It's not about Ben."

"Then what is it?"

"I can't tell you." I don't know.

Cheryl looks at me, something like pity in her eyes. Pity mixed with the gaze of snake, trying to work out if its prey is too big to swallow. "I don't want to be nasty," she says and she even sounds as if she might mean it. "I really don't. I'm not going to say anything to Ben if I don't have to. It's your business. But I know he likes me and I want things to work out between us, so I'd appreciate it if you kept away from him for a while."

Is this blackmail? This gentle, persuasive apologetic thing – is it blackmail? Does Rosemary Blunt allow herself to be blackmailed?

"If you stay away from Ben, I don't see why I'd ever need to tell him about Michael." She smiles into my face. "It can be our secret. Ben need never know."

"It's important to me that you don't tell anybody about..." I look down at the bed. At you. "Very important."

"Then we have a deal? You'll stay away from Ben?"

"If that's what you think best."

Her smile broadens. "Cool. I'm glad we understand each other. I won't say a word to him, I promise." She makes it sound as if we have a cosy conspiracy. Bosom pals.

I'm not sure how long it takes me to breathe again after she shuts the door behind her, but at last I'm aware of my heart thumping, of your brooding body in front of me. And although it might appear as if your face hasn't changed, I know it has. I can see you laughing in there. I can see your withered, mocking expression that tells me exactly why I didn't tell Cheryl where she could stick her deal.

"You enjoyed that, didn't you? Well, you won't be laughing soon, I can tell you. Not when I sign those forms." I won't let you mock me. "Because I don't need you, Michael. I can do whatever I want with my life: go to India and sleep with men half my age and play with Ouija boards in motels and find God."

I grip your shoulders, and I hope it makes you jump. I hope you feel helpless. "I'm not afraid to do it. I'm going to be free of you at last. I'm going to tell Dr. Richards that I'll do it – I'll get rid of you. I'll tell him right now."

The weight of your body is hardly enough to disturb the pillow as I release you and grab my bag instead. I get almost to the door before turning back. "Tomorrow. I'll tell him tomorrow."

JENNY

When the door to the church squeaked open I was halfway through the final chorus of *Some Enchanted Evening*. I stopped singing at once. Ben stepped into the gloom.

"I thought I might find you here." He pushed the door shut behind him. "I've been listening to you from the porch. You're good."

It was embarrassing enough to have been caught singing, let alone something from a musical rather than a hymn. Not that I think God minded too much what I sang. I wasn't the best singer in the world but I could keep a tune and it was one of my biggest joys. To me, singing was a moment when I could forget who I was. I never expected – or wanted – an audience. It's why I restricted my singing to Mondays.

Monday afternoons were my favourite time of the week. Vicar was off on house calls and the devout people of Brackton – of which there were about a dozen – were unlikely to pop in the day after the main communion service, so I had the church to myself. It's silly, but it felt as if I had God to myself then too. Other people might've found the echoing building with its funny shadows creepy. I found it comforting. Even the saints staring down from the stained glass windows were friends watching over me as I hunted down dropped hymn books and replaced hassocks on hooks.

"I like to sing." I gathered the stack of books and carried them to the back, where Ben was standing. "I get it from my mum."

"She was obviously a talented lady." He helped me unload. "I've missed you these last few days. Haven't seen you since Thursday. I'd been hoping you would consent to dinner again sometime, but perhaps you've been avoiding me?"

Perhaps I had. Not purposefully – there had been extra shifts to cover at the post office and Dad had had a cold – but deep down I think I hadn't wanted to see Ben too much. After our dinner together the previous week-end, it almost felt too good to be true. When he'd talked about cubism, when he'd insisted on staying to drink coffee together after pudding, when he'd walked me home, when he'd kissed my cheek on the doorstep before disappearing into the night – it had been too perfect. I hadn't wanted to ruin the memory with reality. Even Dad had understood, without me having to say a word, and had hardly asked me anything about our not-a-date dinner. I'd spent a week trying to make that evening nothing more than it had been, only seeing Ben once in all that time. And now he had undone all my good work with one smile.

"Dinner would be lovely," I said. "I enjoyed it so much last time."

"Wonderful." He waved a hand at the empty nave. "I can see you must be busy, so I won't keep you now. I'll save the pleasure of your company for dinner – say, tomorrow night, same time?"

I didn't know how to say that I wanted him to keep me. That as far as I was concerned the hassocks could look after themselves for one day. So instead, I smiled and said, "Tomorrow would be fine."

He clapped his hands, the echo fluttering round the high stone walls. "Perfect. What a wonderful thought to keep me going for the next 24 hours." He leant in to kiss my cheek in that familiar way of his that was so unfamiliar to me. "I'll let you get on. Don't want to get on the wrong side of the vicar by distracting his most trusted advisor, do I? This church would fall down if you weren't here."

If only he hadn't said that.

I'm a firm believer that you shouldn't need gratitude to do your bit for the world. Knowing that God sees what you do should be enough. Only sometimes it isn't. Sometimes, I wanted to know that somebody thought what I did was worthwhile, even if it was only mending prayer books and polishing the altar rail, and not curing cancer or running mara-thons. I suppose I did know that Vicar and all the others were grateful, but I wanted them to say it. In actual words. I didn't realise how much I wanted it, until Ben said that. He'd noticed me. Asking me out to dinner, telling me he'd missed me – that was all lovely. The fact that he'd noticed me and what I did, that was what got me. That was when love became a dangerous possibility.

For several minutes after he'd departed, I stood looking at the door he'd left open, and for the first time in goodness knows how long, I began to get this funny feeling: maybe life didn't have to be the same way forever, after all.

I couldn't go back to tidying. I made a start with rearranging the drooping flowers, but I couldn't concentrate. Suddenly it didn't seem to matter; nobody was going to notice anyway. The only time the church needed more than two pews was at weddings and funerals, though the number of the former had been slowly replaced with more of the latter in recent years. None of the regular gathering looked up from their order of service for long enough to care if the flowers were fresh or the lectern was gleaming. It could all wait. I wandered up to the altar, ran one hand along the polished surface, then knelt the wrong side of the rail, facing down the length of the nave.

The church had changed very little since the days when I'd first taken to slipping inside when it was empty. In those days, when I would sit and talk to God about Tom, the embroidery on the hassocks hadn't faded and there'd been pictures done by the Sunday School on the wall at the back, but it was still the same old place underneath: high coloured windows, huge oak beams, the solemn dark wood of the pulpit and choir stalls, and that same sense of expectation, as if in the shadows God was listening.

"Dear God, thank-you for sending Ben to Brackton. Thank-you for him asking me to dinner again."

I stopped, already lost for words. What should I pray for? Romance? Hope? To pull myself together? My eyes strayed from the dusty cushion under my knees to the aisle stretching away to the door. Ever eager to show me up in front of God, my mind began to wander. Imagine coming in through that door with all eyes on you. Imagine being the one gliding down the aisle on your father's arm, clutching a posy of roses. Imagine not being one of the crowd, watching somebody else's biggest day. Imagine being more than just Jenny for one afternoon.

I shook my head, shifted my gaze back to the pulpit and the cross above it. Childish fairytales were not why I'd come.

"Please look after Ben and help him to find you in his painting. Help me not to get carried away. Help me not to think too highly of myself or to hope too much. Help me to do the right thing for once." I squeezed my eyes shut,

125

trying to keep the unwelcome-welcome thoughts at bay. "Please God, could you... I mean, if it's alright with you, might we..." I bit my lip. I hadn't found it so hard to pray for over 20 years. "I like him, God. You know that already. And you know about Tom and... well, you know everything and..." My fingernails dug into the worm-eaten wood of the altar rail. "Please God. That's all. Just... Please. Thanks for listening. Amen."

"I do hope I'm not disturbing you."

I jumped up so fast I nearly catapulted myself over the rail. "Mrs. Baxter — I didn't hear you come in."

She was already halfway down the aisle, soft shoes soundless on the tiled floor. I hurried down to meet her.

"How nice to see somebody in this heathen place at their prayers. Who were you praying for, Jenny?"

"Some of the people in the village."

"My tenant, for example?"

Her aim was perfect.

"He was one of the people, yes."

Mrs. Baxter slid into a pew and, feeling foolish, I joined her. We both sat looking straight ahead at the figure of Jesus.

"You like Mr. Summers, don't you?"

"He's a very nice man."

I felt her knowing smile, rather than saw it.

"I'm glad to hear it. You never know with artists, do you? Though I took references of course. It's wonderful that you're praying for his welfare." She let the silence trickle on for another few seconds before adding with a tone of casual interest, "I wonder if that young lady of his prays for him? I doubt it somehow."

Her words took a minute to sink in. And when they did, they landed with a thump. The cavern of the church crowded in on me.

"She's pretty of course." Mrs. Baxter looked at me. "But I'm sure he can't be involved with her. She can't be half his age and no respectable man would chase after a girl who's barely out of school." She smiled. "I'm sure there must be some innocent explanation as to why she keeps shutting herself away in that cottage of his for hours on end."

Something in my face must have satisfied Mrs. Baxter because I didn't need to meet her gaze before she changed the subject.

"I came to give you this." She opened her handbag and took a 20 pence coin from her purse. "For the collection. I was sorry not to make communion yesterday. My mother had one of her turns and the home asked me to pop in."

"Thank-you, Mrs. Baxter," I said automatically. "I'll pray for your mother. It was very kind of you to come by."

"One must do one's Christian duty."

She left again as silently as she'd come. I didn't walk her to the door. All I could think was that she should have come sooner. If only she'd got to me before Ben. If only I'd spoken to her before he'd asked me to dinner again, before he smiled at me, before he'd made me feel human. There was no going back now. It was too late not to care.

ROSEMARY

Letter from Julia to Rosemary.

Friday 27th July

Dear Rosemary,

It's been over a week now since I last heard from you. Are you OK? I'm beginning to worry. If I don't hear from you by Monday evening then I'm getting a train down to Lockhaven tomorrow and I'll walk from there to Brackton if I have to.

Even George has noticed the absence of letters. George! It took him three days to notice when I had my hair dyed chestnut and cut into a bob and yet, over breakfast this morning he asked why I hadn't had any letters from you this week, and I had to admit I didn't know. I do wish you'd get a house phone, or at least switch on your mobile from time to time. What's the point in having one if nobody can call you? And an e-mail address wouldn't go amiss either. It's not all spam about Viagra.

Write back, Rosemary please. I won't tell you any more about Martha than necessary (though she is the dearest little thing and definitely smiles at me, whether or not she's meant to be able to at this age). If I've annoyed you I'll say sorry as many times as you want.

Lots of love, Julia

Letter from Rosemary to Julia.

Saturday 28th July

Dear Julia,

Cancel the train tickets and stay right where you are. I'm perfectly alright and not in the least bit annoyed with you, except for getting yourself in a flap. I was a bit under the weather for a few days and hadn't got round to sorting my post, that was all. It wasn't anything much – a summer cold I expect. At any rate, I'm fine now, though the interval between my letters doesn't mean I have any more news than usual. No spate of crime while I was shut away indoors as far as I know.

When you do come to visit, I don't recommend walking from Lockhaven station – it's nine miles along hilly lanes. There's a bus that only takes 45 minutes and I promise I'll keep my phone on me all day so that you can give me unnecessarily frequent updates on your progress. But I draw the line at e-mail. I had to have one for the last few years at the university and it drove me mad. Why on earth should I want to make it easier for people to contact me?

Give my regards to George and see if you can coax a smile out of Martha for me. Oh, and tell Jacob I found a toad in my garden yesterday, but it hopped away before I could get its legs into the cauldron. Or is it only frogs that can be used for such things?

With love, Rosemary

Letter from Julia to Rosemary.

Monday 30th July

Dear Rosemary,

You never get ill. You were always disgustingly healthy and wouldn't even pretend to be sick to get out of games, even though you hated the mud and rain as much as the rest of us. In the entire history of St. Boniface, you're probably the only person never to have missed lacrosse. I don't suppose you've told an untruth in your life, have you? You're incapable of it.

You must have been spitting to be confined to bed during all that awful weather last week. What a terribly wet summer we're having. Still, at least it isn't sunny again yet – every cloud has a silver lining. Or, in your case, every cloud is a silver lining. You're the only person in England who retires to the seaside and prays for bad weather. And I love you for it, of course.

I gave George your regards and he said, "Send them back," over his paper. I'm sure he meant me to send his and not return yours as unwanted, dear. I didn't tell Jacob about the toad's legs because he's gone off magic and is now into animal welfare. He was vegetarian for a few hours until the rest of us had sausages for lunch. Now he'll eat what he's given as long as you tell him it's organic. He doesn't think you're a witch anymore, but you could gain extra credit by inventing an eco-warrior past next time you come to visit. (Yes, that is a hint – it's been nearly two years since you last came, and you need to meet Martha).

Now that I know you're alright, I can resume bullying you for news. How did your painting of Newton go? Did you ask Ben to stay until October?

Love, Julia

PS: I'm working on a surprise for you. I hope to have it ready by the time I come to Brackton!

. . .

I couldn't tell you what I did, or who I saw in the last week of July that summer. Time has obscured what was already a hazy, ill-defined period of my life. For the first time since my 20s, I wasn't looking for ways to fill up the empty hours of the day. Instead, I climbed into bed each night hardly aware that time had passed since climbing out of it. The comforting blankness of my life between getting on the bus to Lockhaven and getting off it again some hours later had spread into other days. A veil drew itself over every compartment whether I wanted it to or not, and that unsettled me – all the more so because I didn't understand it. I knew I couldn't see Ben and I knew it was something to do with my trips to Lockhaven, but the logic of it – the precise mechanism of my isolation – escaped me. Sometimes I'd be halfway down the cliff steps in my paint-smattered shirt before I remembered there was something wrong.

If I'd known mentioning my visits to Cheryl was the last thing Ben would've done, I might have been bolder. But I had no reason to suppose at the time Ben wouldn't tell her in passing, in their everyday casual conversation. And that would've been a disaster. I was aware of that at least. And, as with all disasters in my life, I knew this one was connected with Michael.

When Michael had left me for the first time, I was too shocked to feel much. In the weeks following his emigration to Australia I learned to be ashamed of my new status of Abandoned Wife. In those first few days I was too busy rebuilding and relabeling the structures in my mind to be anything but numb. I didn't even tell anyone for three days. If rumours of Michael's absence hadn't reached my father, I don't know how long I would've sat alone in the ashes of our 10-year marriage, not answering the door.

It was easiest to tell people he'd given me a divorce. Even Julia believed it and, unlike my mother, saw less shame in that than in staying married to a monster. Only Dad knew the truth. Although my mother grudgingly let me into the house, she hardly spoke to me again. A divorced daughter with no children was the worst thing imaginable to her in an era when she so wanted to join the condemnation of the youth she saw around her. She'd have let me sit in the silence of my childhood bedroom forever; a defiled Miss Havisham surrounded by teddy bears still propped where they'd been laid to rest on the wedding day. Dad, however, only gave me a month before coming to drag me out of myself.

"You're 28 Rosemary." He sat on the bed, fiddling with the edge of the crocheted blanket that had been mine since birth. "That's not old. You can still do anything you want with life. There's nothing to stop you marrying again."

"I'm still married, Dad."

"We can sort that out if need be."

"I don't want to marry again. I never want to see another man."

"Good." Dad put an arm around me. "You're too good for marriage."

He stood up and pulled a box from the shelf above my bed. It hadn't been opened for a decade. After a bit of rummaging, he found what he wanted and set it down on the bed beside me. It had been his present to me – much to my mother's disgust – on my 11th birthday.

"You used to look at insects under this and tell me how you were going to be a famous scientist one day." He ran a finger over the dusty microscope lens. "You still could be."

It took me a couple more days to realise he was right. Somewhere deep down I remembered I'd thought I could be anything once. My mother no longer cared what I did – I would always be a ruined woman in her eyes. In a way that made me more free than ever; she had no illusions for me to shatter anymore. So with Dad's help I enrolled in night classes to do the A-levels Michael's Austin had interrupted. And without any help at all, I applied to university and got myself accepted by Cambridge – as a widow, of course. Three years after Michael disappeared, I found myself pedalling along by the Cam at last.

For somebody who wanted nothing to do with men, physics might have seemed an odd choice. Really it was a logical one. I wanted a subject that only required me to think, not to feel; something that would make sense of a world that had stopped making sense to me. It was pioneering and exciting, but relentlessly sensible. I was the only woman reading physics and that in itself was a challenge. The other students – most of whom were a decade younger than me – didn't know what to think of women. And I preferred them not to think of me as a woman at all. The tradition of banging on desks whenever a woman walked into the room was abandoned in the first week, and grudgingly at first, but later with more enthusiasm, they came to treat me as one of them.

I rather fancied myself as an academic and assumed the people at home would feel the same. I felt as if I could hold my head up high again; I was doing something worthwhile with my life. I wasn't expecting a ticker tape parade or the keys to the town, just a smile in the street and a friendly word. I was naive. To the women who'd shared Michael's bed, or pitied me from afar, I would always be Abandoned Wife. Quoting Latin or knowing how the planets stayed in orbit didn't impress them. The whispers and the giggles didn't stop. So when Julia and Dad started coming up to Cambridge to see me, I stopped going home altogether. I thought I'd cut all the ties.

When I earned my doctorate, I should have reverted to my maiden name. I'd been back in education almost as long as I'd been a housewife by that point, and I could have chosen to be Dr. Shelley without too much difficulty. Nobody asked why I kept my married name and I was glad of that because it meant I neither had to lie, nor admit to something that no true woman of the 70s ever would've done. The truth was Michael still owned me.

On my 39th birthday I was officially made a doctor and already had a lectureship at a red brick lined up for the autumn. To all appearances I was the woman I should have been 10 years earlier. 10 years earlier I would have become a doctor for the love of learning only. Now, that was secondary. My real reason for becoming a doctor was because it was the last thing Michael would've wanted.

It's a curious thing – to spend years trying to be everything someone wants you to be, without success, and then when you're finally free of them, to spend the remainder of your life trying to be everything they wouldn't want you to be. It's a kind of madness: grey, creeping, invisible. I didn't have time to do anything except be the kind of person Michael would hate. My career was a success by anybody standards, but I wasn't a high achiever for the sake of furthering human knowledge, nor even for personal glory. I only wanted to wound the ghost that lingered at my shoulder.

With only my work to focus on, the compartments in my mind grew distorted. One of them had grown monstrous, pushing the others back, squeezing them into smaller and smaller spaces until they were insignificant blots on my consciousness. None of them mattered. I continued to feed myself and do the laundry, write to Julia and to Dad until he died, but they were minor distractions. The only one I cared about was the compartment I thought of as 'Work'. If I'd looked closely I'd have seen the label really read, 'Getting Back at Michael'.

The irony was that I believed I was free. No more ironing and cleaning, slapping and pushing and shouting. I was free of him. It wasn't until later – decades later – when the past came back to haunt me, I realised how stupid I'd been. I was never free of him. My liberty weighed on me as heavily as my captivity had done. Michael had dictated every move I ever made, as easily as if he was still sharing my bed. I thought I'd cut the strings, but while he'd made a new life for himself on the other side of the world, he'd remained the puppet master. And I'd danced to his tune all along.

BEN

The one thing you learn when you move into a small community is that there are some things you'll never learn. By the end of July, I knew who the movers and shakers were in Brackton and what I had to say to keep on the right side of them, but there were some things that would remain a mystery to me if I'd lived there forever. The foremost of these things was Rosemary's whim.

You'd have thought I would've been used to her turning up unannounced some afternoons and then disappearing for days on end, but I wasn't. I was certain that if Cheryl hadn't disturbed us that Saturday, Rosemary would've started a new painting – she'd been almost keen. But by the middle of the following week I was beginning to lose hope that I'd ever see her again.

I was getting on with God the best I could, considering Rosemary's absence, but the nagging space in the centre of the canvas still prodded at me as I dabbled with this and that. There was no spark; I didn't feel connected to it. With each passing day I was becoming more aware of time ticking down and the absence of God. I felt that if I could find him – if I could finish the painting – it would all be alright. Other people might have said that it was too late to make everything OK again – I should've made my plans months before then, maybe even years. I still had hope though. If Rosemary would come back so I could finish God, he would rescue me. But she didn't, and I had a horrible feeling that it was something to do with Cheryl.

I know what I would've thought if I was Rosemary. A young woman wearing less than might have been expected had turned up without warning as if she had some right to me. I could tell what that must have looked like. Surely though, Rosemary couldn't have been so disgusted she didn't even want to paint anymore? I intended to put her straight about Cheryl as soon as

I saw her again. Or did I? No, maybe I didn't intend to tell her the real truth. I certainly had no plans to confirm the stereotype of Ageing Man Meets Busty Blonde, and I don't suppose I was really going to tell Rosemary why I allowed Cheryl to keep coming back, but I could've told her that I felt nothing for Cheryl – nothing emotional. That *was* the truth. Part of it, anyway.

I hadn't expected to see Rosemary on Monday because of her mysterious trips to Lockhaven. I'd had high hopes for Tuesday though. When I finally had to admit she wasn't coming, it was getting late and I had to run for my date with Jenny. Even so, I couldn't resist stopping by The Lookout on my way to the pub, scanning the windows for signs of life. Nothing.

I arrived at The Oak five minutes late and in a bad mood – not the gentlemanly face I'd hoped to show Jenny that night. It would've been even less gentlemanly to enquire after Rosemary, so I was glad when Jenny mentioned her first.

"Dr. Blunt was telling me your painting of God is nearly finished."

"Was she?" I tried not to sound too interested. "I haven't seen Rosemary for days. I thought she might be ill."

"She seemed fine this morning. Said you'd be finished soon."

"I don't know about that. Another couple of weeks at least, I'd say."

Rosemary being ill or away was my last hope. Apparently she wasn't either. She probably wasn't even actively avoiding me this time. My bet was that she'd found something better to do and I'd slipped her mind. I won't pretend I wasn't offended at the thought.

"I've been thinking of popping back to London," I said. "I need to get a few of my smaller paintings into the galleries. Most of my current ones have sold." I raised my glass to her. "You'll have to come to the cottage and tell me which ones I should sell. I'm sure you'd know best."

I waited for the embarrassed smile and flustered protest. Neither came. And it was only then I realised something was wrong. Jenny wasn't the world's greatest conversationalist, but she wasn't this quiet. Not this subdued.

"How was your day?" I struggled to remember something about her. "Were you at the church today?"

"No, I was at the post office."

"Are you OK? You seem quiet tonight. I'm sorry if I've been distracted – my painting isn't going as well as I'd like."

She did smile then, but it was a pathetic little thing, hardly worthy of the name. After another few seconds of awkward silence, she said, "Mrs. Baxter happened to mention in passing that you have a lady friend. I was wondering whether this lady would mind us having dinner like this."

Bloody Mrs. Baxter. She must've been watching the beach like a hawk to spot Cheryl coming and going. And now she was going to ruin everything, just when I was about to get to the point with Jenny.

"A lady friend?" I made a show of thinking. "She means Cheryl, I suppose. But there's been a misunderstanding. Cheryl is definitely not my lady friend or any other euphemism." I suppose that wasn't a lie, though I took no comfort from it. "She's somebody I met at the Show. She's studying art at Lockhaven College, so I said she could come to see my paintings. She's a bright kid, but she's young enough to be my daughter."

Jenny looked down at her paper napkin for confirmation of my story. I could feel how much she wanted to believe me. I took her hand, pressing home my advantage.

"I prefer women, Jenny. They're so much more interesting than girls." I squeezed her fingers. "I wouldn't have asked you to dinner if there was another woman in my life. You do believe that, don't you?"

Some of the people at the bar were looking at us by then. Jenny's hand twitched under mine, itching to pull away from the scrutiny. For another second she frowned at our fingers, then she lifted her head. "I knew Mrs. Baxter must've been mistaken." She smiled right at me for once. "Sorry for asking."

"That's fine." It was all I could do not to look away. "I can see it must have seemed odd. I'd hate you to think badly of me."

I released her as the waitress arrived with loaded plates. I resolved to give Jenny my full attention for the rest of the meal – no more thinking about Rosemary, God or Cheryl. It was the least I could do.

"What would you like to do most in the world?" I asked her. "If money was no object, what would you do?"

She didn't answer at once and the blush that had only just died away, came flooding back. She shook her head, as if to rid it of some troublesome thought, and I would've loved to know what it was, because I'm pretty sure it wasn't the answer she came up with.

"I'd like to take Dad to see the pyramids. He's always wanted to go."

"You always want to do something for other people." I felt a sudden burst of affection for her. "What about something *you'd* like to do?"

"That *is* what I'd like to do." She sounded surprised. "I'm sure the pyramids would be lovely and – well – don't you think seeing other people happy because of something you've done is one of the nicest things there is?"

"I like watching people open the birthday presents I've got them, if that counts? But I don't think I'm selfless enough to waste my one wish from a genie on taking somebody to see the pyramids."

"I've expect you've seen them already, haven't you? You've probably painted them."

"I haven't actually, but my parents have. Dad's oils of the atmosphere you get inside the tombs are incredible. And Mum's watercolours of the Nile..." I gave what I hoped was a modest laugh. "I couldn't compete with that."

"But you've been there?"

"Oh, yes. They're amazing – so much bigger than you'd think. Did you know the Great Pyramid at Giza was the tallest man-made structure for nearly 4000 years? It was only beaten in the end by Lincoln Cathedral."

"You're so clever." Jenny looked suitably impressed. "I don't know how you remember all the things you do. I'm sure you know something about everywhere in the world by now."

"Comes from having a good education."

I topped up our wine. Jenny giggled. "I don't usually have more than one small glass."

"We're celebrating."

"Celebrating what?"

"Good company." I chinked my glass against hers. "And good conversation. I'm already finding out more about you."

"Only that I want to visit the pyramids."

"Ah, but that might prove to be the vital piece of information that provides the key to your whole personality." She was laughing now and I liked that. "Where you want to go says as much about you as where you've been." I sat back in my chair. "Where *have* you been? Travelled much?"

"Not at all. A school exchange to Germany and family holidays to the Isle of Man – they're the only times I've been on a plane."

"I suppose travel is pretty expensive. I worked my way around the world, but most people can't do that of course. If you don't have much money..." I trailed off and watched Jenny's face.

"There's that." She dabbed at her mouth with her napkin. "Though we were never short of money. Dad's not super-rich, but he's always done alright for himself. We're just not the sort of people who travel much. Foreign holidays seem rather a faff. We're slow kind of people. Not made for adventure." She looked away. "I suppose that seems silly to you."

"Actually, I think it's rather charming. The world could do with more people like you."

I meant it.

"We shouldn't be talking about me." Jenny turned her attention to her potatoes. "You're meant to be teaching me what came after cubism."

"I'm meant to be," I said. "I don't want to though. Not tonight. Tonight I was going to tell you about corruption and war and all sorts of other nasty things. And I don't want to ruin our evening with such crudity." I attacked my steak again, one eye still on Jenny's face. "I want to hear more about you."

When we reached Jenny's front door, it opened before she could retrieve her key. Mr. Gribble stood in the doorway. "So you're the man who's had the pleasure of wining and dining my daughter?"

"I'm the lucky one."

He beamed at me, chest puffing out with pride. The light from the hallway spilled down the path and I stepped into it so he could see me, though heaven knows it was the last thing I wanted.

"Would you like to come in for a nightcap?"

Did I want to sit in this man's front room pretending to be the kind of person he'd want for his daughter? Not really. There was something a bit weird about it. Jenny was my age for goodness sake; it was the 21st century, not the 1950s. And Mr. Gribble was looking at me with such determined friendliness I was embarrassed even to be there.

"I think I'd better be calling it a night," I said. "Some other time though?"

I kissed Jenny's cheek, trying to ignore her dad. I'd just reached the gate again when he called after me. "You're welcome here any time, Ben. Any time at all."

The sun sank below the horizon as I walked down the cliff steps and along the beach. I stood outside the cottage for a few minutes, inhaling the still twilight, replaying the evening's conversation in my head: ambitions, dreams, exotic places. Money. Christ, how I hated money. That moment, more than any other I hated it. And needed it. The foolish, flightless thought I'd had when I first arrived in Brackton – that money could be the cure for my ills as well as the disease itself – had grown wings. But for the idea to fly, I needed to get hold of cash.

I'd had some money of course. Thank God I'd been paranoid enough to build up a stash at home under the mattress. It was enough to pay Mrs. Baxter for the first three months at the cottage and keep myself in paint. Not enough for everything. I couldn't fund many more meals at The Oak, and the train ticket to London was something I could've done without. The trickle of money coming in meant I could eat, but not much more. My cash was running out as fast as my options.

I closed my eyes against the fading light and tried not to picture Jenny's face, smiling shyly at me from across a table. And before I went inside, I offered up a silent prayer to the god who brooded just out of reach. *Find some other way. Help me find some other way.*

...

It hadn't been chivalry or laziness that stopped me wanting to teach Jenny about suprematism over dinner that night. I'd meant what I said – I didn't want to talk about dark things then and there. I knew I'd have to tell her eventually though. If I wanted her to understand – to look back on that summer and understand, I had to tell her about Malevich.

It was inevitable really. Once Picasso and friends started messing with shapes, total abstraction was within touching distance. And the suprematists were the masters at removing the real world completely. To Malevich, his *Black Square* – simply that, a black square on a white background – was the logical conclusion to all the art that had gone on before him.

Scandalous as it is to admit, suprematism does nothing for me. Squares and circles and crosses in limited colours – I don't find it inspiring. I do, however, appreciate what they were getting at. The suprematists wanted to find zero-degree art – the last point at which something can be called art. They wanted to see how far you can travel from reality, before reality ceases to exist and you are left with nothing. I can sympathise with that.

I was trying to tell Jenny about it the day after our meal, sitting on the Green with her before her afternoon shift. I'd barely got to the start of the Great War though, when the bus from Lockhaven pulled to a stop across the road. Cheryl got out. She bounced across the grass towards us, her eyes taking in and dismissing Jenny in the few seconds it took her to cross the Green. After the work I'd done convincing Jenny the previous night, Cheryl was the last person I needed to see. Cheryl and Jenny were two worlds not meant to meet.

I rose to greet her, thinking fast. "You should text when you're coming." I tried to laugh. "I'm not always home and I'd hate you to come all this way for nothing."

"It's no bother. I like the bus ride anyway."

Jenny got to her feet beside us, smiling at Cheryl and looking sideways at me.

"Jenny, meet Cheryl." I flapped a hand in the space between them. "I was telling you about her the other day – the one who likes art."

Cheryl beamed, partly at Jenny, mostly at me.

"And Cheryl, meet Jenny, who has been providing me with cakes and soup in abundance since I arrived here."

I was pleased with that introduction. Both women flattered, neither suspicious of the other. I hoped. I wasn't prepared to let it go any further though. Danger signs were clanging all round.

"I'm afraid I'm busy today," I said to Cheryl. "I'm off for a walk to clear my head. If you want to come and watch me paint another day, you're welcome."

"Great." She nodded. "I'll text you later in the week."

With the politest, least flustered goodbyes I could manage, I headed for the cliff path, not daring to look back. My head was bursting with Cheryl and Jenny and money and the continued absence of Rosemary.

Never before had I understood the suprematists as I did in that moment, walking away from the mess – the potential chaos – of Cheryl and Jenny and all the implications they held for me in London. I completely understood why the suprematists did what they did. When they'd started painting their pure shapes, World War One was kicking off. They too knew what impending chaos looked like. The world they knew was crazy with destruction; life had changed, broken beyond repair. It wasn't a world they wanted to record. To remove the insanity of the war-torn world by painting over it with sharp purity – there was something noble in that. When life is ugly – when the real story is one of corruption and regret – why not paint over it with something entirely other? When the truth is rotten, perhaps creating our own reality is the only sane thing to do.

ROSEMARY

The doorbell rang for the third time. I watched the figure below take a couple of steps backward, waiting for an answer. When he didn't get one, he disappeared again and I heard the clack of the letterbox being pushed open.

"Rosemary?" Ben's voice echoed through the hall. "Are you home?"

The letterbox snapped shut and I stepped behind the curtain as Ben craned his neck to look up at the house.

"Is something wrong?" Jenny was at the front gate. The hem of her skirt was damp with dew.

"You haven't seen Rosemary, have you?" Ben hurried back up the path to meet her. "I haven't seen her for well over a week now and she's not answering the door. I put a note through on Saturday, but she hasn't replied."

Jenny frowned and glanced up at my window. "I saw her on Friday, but not since. Do you think she's alright?"

"That's what I'm wondering. If nobody's seen her since Friday she could have been ill for four days by now and we wouldn't know."

"Come to think of it, she did look a bit funny all last week." Through the gauze I could make out Jenny's silly face, wrinkled in concern. "She was very pale and nearly jumped out of her skin when I said hello."

"I'm going to give the doorbell one more try." Ben's voice got louder as he turned towards the house. "If she doesn't answer it then I'm going to see if there's a window open round the back."

"Do you think you should?"

"What if she's ill? She could be dying in there for all we know."

The screech of the gate was followed by two pairs of footsteps on the path. He'd got me. I couldn't very well let Ben break into the house in an act of heroism to find me here in perfect health.

In the hall mirror, I caught sight of my face for the first time in days. A week of little sleep or fresh air had done nothing for me. I looked as old I was.

The bell rang again, accompanied by a hearty pounding on the front door.

"ROSEMARY! ROSEMA..."

I threw open the door and glared at the two would-be intruders. "Can a woman not have some peace?"

"I thought you were dead!" Ben's voice was high – panicked even.

"I've been busy."

"Didn't you get my note?"

"Yes. What of it?"

In the briefest second before the grin slotted into place, a strange, hurt expression crossed Ben's face. "Don't tell me, you've been tied up with all that human trafficking and exotic dancing again?"

The look on Jenny's face was quite something.

"It's alright, Jenny," I said. "He's being flippant. I'm neither a slave trader nor a gentleman's entertainer."

"No, of course not." Jenny blushed. "I...I would never have thought for a moment that..."

"Not anymore anyway." I stepped backwards. "I suppose you'd both better come in, now you're here."

Ben was across the threshold before Jenny was even halfway through her polite protests. They followed me down the hall and into the kitchen.

"Nice place." Ben stood at the head of the oak dining table and ran his eye over the room. "Kind of quirky, isn't it?"

I'd never thought of it as quirky. I'd never thought I had any sort of style in fact. But I suppose he was right. Besides the table that was far too big for me, there were work surfaces running round the edge of the kitchen, covered in the mismatched assortment of utensils I'd picked up along the way. I'd never been one for going to John Lewis and buying a set of anything. I picked up things I saw in markets and didn't consider whether they matched what I already had. Giant grocer's scales took up one corner – though I rarely did any baking – and on two of the walls a row of hooks held the sort of jugs and tools that could've belonged in a forge rather than a kitchen.

"I was expecting it to be more clinical, or something." Ben flopped down on to one of the chairs and began to rifle through the pile of magazines on the table. "I thought you'd have it all kitted out in stainless steel and granite."

"I can't think of anything more vulgar. I like chaos, so long as it's organised properly. It's why I became a physicist."

Jenny was hovering by the table.

"Make yourself at home, Jenny." I flicked the switch on the kettle. "I see Ben already has."

Ben didn't look up from the three-month old copy of *National Geographic*. He wasn't reading it, just flicking through the pictures.

"You've got a lovely view, Dr. Blunt." Jenny was staring out of the window, at the endless stretch of sea beyond the back fence.

"It's why I bought the house – to look at the sea." For a moment I forgot who I was talking to. "There's something unnerving about it; something exciting about not knowing what's on the other side."

When I tugged my gaze from the window, I felt foolish. Ben was staring at me thoughtfully.

"It's France, isn't it?" Jenny said. ""My geography isn't very good, but," she frowned, "I'm pretty sure it's France."

She didn't see Ben roll his eyes and return to the magazine.

"I suppose you're right." I poured the water into the cafetière. "I suppose it is France."

"Ben would know more about that then we would." Jenny turned to look at him, face glowing. "You must have been to France."

For once, Ben seemed reluctant to show off. "What? Oh... yes... I've been to France lots of times. My parents took me all over Europe – Paris, Vienna, Rome..."

"Had a penchant for capital cities, did they?" I dumped a tray full of mugs on to the table. "That must have been handy for home-school geography lessons."

The grandfather clock in the hall struck the hour and Jenny leapt from her chair. "The mobile library! I'd forgotten. I'm going to be late. Do excuse me, Dr. Blunt."

After a great deal of flapping and kerfuffle, Jenny made it to the front door, accompanied by Ben. I could hear them saying their goodbyes in the hall.

"Such a shame you have to go," Ben was saying. "Please come and see me again soon."

"If you'd like me to..."

"I'd *love* you to."

This brought on a fresh burst of wittering from Jenny, but eventually the door clicked shut and Ben reappeared in the kitchen.

"I can go too if you want." He leant against the doorframe. "I don't want to force my company on you when you're gone to great lengths to avoid it for the last 10 days."

What did he expect me to say to that?

After a few seconds of silence, he asked, "*Do* you want me to go?"

"No." I forgot to lie. "Though you probably should."

"Why?" Ben resumed his seat. "You afraid people will talk about us?"

"Don't be silly. I don't care about idle gossip. I just don't want to cause... friction."

"I'm no physicist, but I don't understand how two people and two cups of coffee could cause friction."

"A certain person might be unhappy about you being here alone..."

Ben laughed and pressed the cafetière plunger. "The mystery deepens. Who is this suspicious character?"

The conversation had gone too far already. I didn't know how to change track now.

"Oh, God!" Ben laughed. "It's Jenny isn't it? You think that something's going on between us?"

I didn't really – not on his side, anyway – but it was safer to agree. "Isn't there?"

"Hell no."

"The village grapevine says differently. You've taken her to dinner twice – does *she* think there's nothing going on?"

I was expecting a glib reply – something reasonable about dinner not meaning anything these days. But Ben wasn't glib. He didn't answer at all. Instead, he sat, staring out of the window. "I liked what you said about the sea earlier. About not knowing what's on the other side."

"I was being stupid," I said. "Jenny's right. It's just France."

"It's not *just* anything. Even if you end up on French soil, you still don't know what's on the other side. Adventure? The start of a journey? Romance? God?"

"She's falling in love with you, you know."

Ben didn't take his eyes from the window. "Jenny?"

"It's obvious to everybody who sees you together." I didn't know why I was bothering to say it. It was none of my business. And besides, it would do Jenny good to fall in love and be heartbroken. Shouldn't that sort of thing happen to every woman before a certain age? "If you don't feel anything for her then go carefully, Ben."

In the silence that followed, a sudden madness gripped at me. Not slow insanity but wild impulse. I wanted to tell him everything: all about Michael and Grace and the life I'd left behind; losing God and trying to find him again. And I wanted to tell him about Mondays and Thursdays and terrible secrets that I only half-knew. I wanted him to tell me what to do. In that instant he had a quality about him, as if he wasn't quite real. If I reached out to touch him, my fingers would brush through air. He wasn't flesh and blood, only colour and shape – a painting that had come to life. I knew I could tell him everything that had ever happened to me – everything I'd forgotten – and it would be like whispering to the wind. Secrets would never escape him because he wasn't real; he was an imitation of reality, a child's sketch of a man.

Even as that strange magnetism pulsing from Ben began to drag the words and confessions from somewhere inside me, he turned to look at me. And I had the unsettling feeling that those grey eyes saw more than I knew, without me having to say a word.

I began to stack the scattering of magazines into piles according to publication. Ben helped, not needing to be told to order them by date. We worked in silence until he said, "I'm going away for a couple of days. Back to London. I'm leaving tonight."

"I'm impressed you made it this long before getting bored of us."

"I'm not bored. I need to sort out a couple of things. I'll be back at the weekend and when I am, I want to go painting somewhere different. I was thinking of going along the cliff path for a day and finding a sheltered spot out there." He neatened the edges of his pile. "I was wondering whether you'd come?"

I picked up my stack and carried it through to the bookcases that lined the hall. Ben followed me with his. "I was thinking of going on Monday."

He crouched to slide his pile on to the shelf with the other *New Scientists*. "How about it?"

"You know I can't do Mondays."

My way back to the kitchen was blocked by Ben's folded arms.

"It's none of my business what you get up to on Mondays – or any other day of the week – but can I ask you something?" He didn't wait for consent. "Would you enjoy painting with me more than you'd enjoy whatever you'd normally do on a Monday?"

To answer Ben's question would involve knowing what I did on Mondays. And I had no intention of knowing. That compartment stayed locked while I was in Brackton. It was so far removed from my standing-in-the-hall-with-Ben compartment, I couldn't possibly consider opening it to find an answer inside. But as hard as I tried, I also couldn't stop the odd image from floating into my consciousness: a blue blanket, a fragile hand, a man.

"Are you alright, Rosemary?"

"It's not as easy as you think."

"Is it not? Can you really not change your plans for a single week? Tell me there's no way and I won't ask again, I promise."

My mistake was in looking at Ben's face. For a second, when my eyes met his, it was as if a grey veil had been drawn back. I could see in colour for the first time. The world was not black and white. I knew instinctively that colour would be dangerous, but also that a world of colour had more possibility than a world without.

"I suppose I could come with you." I nodded slowly. "Just this once."

...

Letter from Rosemary to Julia.

Wednesday 1st August

Dear Julia,

I haven't yet asked Ben if he'll change his life plans to fit in with you, but we've arranged to go painting on Monday, so I'll ask him then. Anything else while I'm at it? Shoe size? Favourite colour? You'll have to be patient until next week as he's skipped back to London for the time being and left Brackton bereft of his presence. Well, Jenny will be bereft anyway.

My Newton painting wasn't the prettiest thing you've ever seen, but I was quite pleased with it in the end. My next challenge apparently, is to paint a picture without any preconceived ideas. I'll let you know how that goes too. I admit I'm apprehensive. Ben seems to be trying to turn me into a real artist with the airs and graces to match. You won't recognise me when you visit – I'll be wearing a beret by then and calling everyone 'dahling'. Not that Ben does either of those things, though I wouldn't put it past him.

You must know I don't like surprises, Julia. I shall be in a state of nerves until I see what you've got in store for me. Why don't you tell me now?

With love, Rosemary

PS: Emma Jolly finally caught Martin in the act of letting his beast foul the green. She took a video for the dog warden who gave Martin a fine. Did you know dog wardens even existed anymore? I didn't.

Letter from Julia to Rosemary.

Friday 3rd August

Dear Rosemary,

I shan't tell you my surprise, so there! You'll have to wait. It's not ready yet anyway – I'm waiting for an e-mail before I can tell you what it is. Until then I'm not even sure myself. Is that cryptic enough for you?

Going painting with Ben, are you? Very nice. I think you're taking quite a shine to our young artist, however much you ridicule him. Sounds as if you haven't entirely put him off your company either, despite your best efforts. You can find out his favourite colour for me – he's bound to know what our favourite colour ought to be – only, don't let it be mauve, dear. I can't stand mauve – it's my last defence against old age. Not so bothered by shoe size, but if he can tell you anything about the Canary Islands let me know. George is thinking of them for our holiday next year. I expect they're far too commercial for a seasoned traveller like Ben, but you never know.

I can picture you on the beach now, windswept and moody, pining for the absent artist. And Jenny will be doing much the same by the side of the duck pond, or in the deserted graveyard – how romantic life in Brackton is!

We're up to our eyeballs in wedding planning here (and I'm making Martha the sweetest dress), but it's still not half as romantic as your life.

Lots of love, Julia

PS: Hooray for Mrs. Jolly. At least somebody in the village is taking her Miss Marple duties seriously.

Letter from Rosemary to Julia.

Saturday 4th August

Julia,

You are an idiot. Brackton is only romantic because you choose to make it so. Nobody else finds it in the least romantic. Certainly not me.

For your information, I haven't taken a shine to Ben, though heaven knows he could do with a polish. His company is merely not entirely unpleasant to me. For all his pretentions, he's likeable enough. When he's not trying to impress me he almost seems a real person instead of a grotesque caricature. I've certainly not been pining for him though. I don't think I've even been particularly moody. Windswept I will admit to.

We're well into the school holidays now and the forecast is for sunshine for nearly a week. How hideous. At least on Monday we're going along the cliffs, so I won't have to witness the destruction of the beach at the hands of hordes of horrible children. I'm sure summer holidays are longer now than they were in our day.

I'll quiz Ben on the Canary Islands and mauve and report back on Tuesday.

With love, Rosemary

JENNY

Dad noticed the two mugs on the draining board as soon as he walked through the door, hands muddy from the allotment.

"Had a visitor?"

"Ben popped in to say goodbye on his way to the station."

It's only been a few hours since I'd left Ben at Dr. Blunt's house, so I'd been surprised to see him again before he'd left. With only 20 minutes until his bus was due he'd accepted my offer of tea and nearly ended up missing it after all. I don't think anybody had nearly missed a bus for me before.

"He's not gone, is he?" Dad said. "Not left for good."

"He'll be back soon. He's popped to London for a few days."

"Rather him than me. Wouldn't catch me anywhere near London at the moment. Brackton gets crowded enough this time of year."

"I expect he's used to crowds," I said. "Some of the cities in India and China must be worse than London."

Dad raised his eyebrows as if he couldn't imagine anywhere being more crowded than London. "Still, shouldn't complain. All those extra tourists taking up space gives him an excuse to come back as soon as possible, doesn't it?" He winked at me and before I could protest, said, "Put the kettle on. I'll be in the front room."

While I made the tea I wondered how much I should say to Dad. I'd always told him everything, but this was different. I knew he was getting his hopes up and it wasn't fair. It wasn't fair on him and it certainly wasn't fair on Ben. He'd taken me out to dinner, he'd kissed my cheek and been nice to me, but he hadn't said anything definite. So was I going to tell Dad about the way Ben had pressed my hand as he'd left, and the way he'd lingered on the doorstep even though the bus had already pulled into the stop on the opposite side of the Green?

Dad was sitting in his usual chair when I carried the tray through, but for once, he wasn't doing anything. He was one of those people who had to have something in his hands – a newspaper or crossword book. If he was sitting without anything to entertain him, that meant he was brooding. I'd only seen it a few times before: after Mum's funeral, on the eve of my 18th birthday, and on that day 21 years earlier when I'd come home from the wedding, still dressed in my Sunday best. He'd been sitting in exactly the same position that day too, staring out of the window.

I pushed the memory out of my head and put the tray on the table. Dad looked round at the clatter.

"I was just thinking about Tom."

He never said Tom's name. And I was so surprised to hear it drop from his lips, I didn't check myself in time to stop myself saying, "Me too."

I sat in the chair in the opposite corner of the bay window and we looked out at the Green together. Tom's name hung over us, eager to be said again. It wasn't a name we ever mentioned, not because I was still in love with Tom, but because of the frailty of Tom's love for me. I didn't cry myself to sleep over his photo every night, more than 20 years on from when I'd last seen him. Most days – most days until Ben came to Brackton anyway – I didn't think of Tom at all. My love for him had been no uncompromising love 'til death; it was only the death of love.

I thought I was the only person who knew the truth of why Tom had done what Tom had done. And although that truth bubbled up as Dad and I sat in silence, wanting to be told, I still couldn't betray him. The whys and hows of what happened didn't matter, so long as Dad knew the one important thing I'd clung to ever since Tom had left Brackton.

"Tom did love me you know."

"I know." Dad took my hand. "I could never doubt anybody loved you."

"I'm serious. He did love me. He didn't love Shirley more. That's not why."

"I'm serious too." He gave my hand a squeeze. "I know that Shirley didn't mean half as much to him as you did. It was obvious."

Dad looked at me. There wasn't sadness or pity in that look. Only truth. And I realised then I'd been foolish to ever think Tom's secret had been a burden only I carried.

"I know why he married that girl," Dad said. "And I suppose it shows he was a man of honour. Even though I had other names for him at the time."

That wasn't quite true. Dad had had no names or words for Tom, or about Tom then. From the day he came to see me in that same front room for the last time, it was as if his name had been struck from Dad's vocabulary.

Tom hadn't looked like a man who'd got engaged to his sweetheart that day. He hadn't looked excited and in love. He'd been crying. I hadn't let him tell me he still loved me; there was no honour in marrying somebody and telling another woman you loved her. Whether or not you had the affair, the words – the thought – was bad enough. And I didn't want to remember Tom as a bad man. He was never that. Even when he was telling me the words that stopped time, I loved him. He was flawed, he was human, he wasn't perfect, but he was good. I refused to forget that, no matter whose bed he'd spend his life returning to at night, and who held the right to call themselves by his name.

I did go to the wedding, despite Dad's pleas. I wore the same blue dress I wore to all weddings and I complimented Shirley on her white one. I smiled as she walked down the aisle past me, and when I returned home to find Dad sitting alone and silent in the gloom of the front room, the two of us had cried together.

The clock on the mantelpiece stopped that day. Not the day Tom told me what he'd done, but day he married somebody who wasn't me. Dad couldn't work out why he couldn't fix it – he'd always been good with things like that. To me though, it made perfect sense. If it had stopped at the moment they were taking their vows it would've been a romantic tragedy. But not even that one day of my life could be romantic. Instead it stopped at no particular time at all, when the world was going about its business in the usual way; life hanging itself in limbo.

"Jenny, about Ben..." Dad began.

I stopped him. "Don't. I know you want there to be something between us, but I can't believe it. Not yet."

Even that was an admission of sorts. Not yet. Maybe some other time. Maybe some other time I would be able to believe there was something between Ben and me. Was that so stupid? Yes - he'd only taken me to dinner, he'd only come to see me when he was going away, he'd only tried to find out all he could about me. But he'd taken me to dinner, he'd come to see me when he was going away, he'd tried to find out all he could about me.

"I wasn't going to say that." Dad sighed. "I wasn't going to talk about marriage or silly things of that sort. You're barely halfway through your life yet, there's still plenty of time – you're still young." He smiled at me as if he knew exactly what I thought of that. "Besides, no man on earth's good enough for you."

He was silent for so long then, I thought he must've finished.

"What *were* you going to say then, Dad?"

"I was going to say that Tom took away your chance of happiness with him. He doesn't have to have taken away your chance of happiness with everybody else." He turned his attention back to the window. "If there's a chance you could be happy with this Ben chap – even if it's only a bit of fun and not forever – then don't let what happened with Tom scare you off. Lightning doesn't strike twice." He patted my hand and released it. "Take a chance. Don't miss out."

BEN

My hasty trip to London did nothing to cheer me up. If I'd expected to find a means of escape there, I was disappointed. I was unable to get hold of any more money, unable to sell any more of my few remaining bits of furniture to raise funds. I was out of options. The only solution was what it had always been – somebody needed to find the cash for me. And it wasn't until London was speeding away from me again, a diminishing grey mass, I finally admitted the truth.

Cheryl was a slim chance – I'd never seen a tabloid headline about how nurses were overpaid. However, I preferred to bet on Cheryl having money, than to ask Jenny for it. I might've managed to extract from Jenny that her dad was well-off during our last date – and I felt bad enough for that piece of sleuthing – but I couldn't bring myself to go any further. Not until I'd explored the possibilities of Cheryl fully anyway.

If I'd been a professional conman Jenny would've been a dream. Naive, honest, trusting and never selfish. She'd fallen for me – oh yes, I did know it, even if I pretended to myself otherwise – without me even having to try. And those very reasons she should've been perfect, were the same reasons I couldn't bear to use her. She trusted me. She was socially awkward, easily flustered and impossible to take seriously; she was the best person I'd ever met. She's the best damned person I've met since for that matter, not that that's saying much. The thought of leading Jenny on further made me feel sick. Not sick enough to rule it out altogether though.

As the train flashed onwards towards Lockhaven, I made the only decision I thought I could make at the time. We'd passed Hayward's Heath and were gunning for the coast before I settled on Cheryl. I needed to find out if she had any money. If she did, then I would forget any thoughts of using

Jenny – put a stop to my fooling before I did any real harm. My only question was how I was going to get Cheryl to trust me. She already liked me, but liking somebody was a long way from telling them about your finances and handing over a bundle of cash without suspicion.

The answer, when it came, was obvious. Cheryl wanted adventure and a change of scene. She was one of those girls who couldn't be content with having anything tomorrow – it always had to be yesterday. If I could promise her the world I'd told her about – modelling, travel, a job away from home – then she would give me what she had. She just needed to believe I serious about her. And with mere days left on my clock, there was only one way I could think of to persuade her. Sex. I was disgusted with myself for thinking of sleeping with her – truly, I was. I won't lie though; I was excited too.

I didn't have the nerve to text Cheryl on Friday evening when I first arrived back at Anchor Cottage. I didn't sleep either. All night I sat in front of my painting of not-yet God, staring at the blank patch of canvas, willing something to appear in the middle distance. I knew if I finished it, God would come. The world might swallow me up, a thunderbolt could come down to smite me – I didn't care how God did it, he just needed to do something. I didn't – couldn't – finish him though. And nothing happened.

On Saturday morning I picked up my phone and put it down a dozen times before selecting Cheryl's number, and another dozen before pressing send.

Back in Brackton. Do you want to come over this evening? We could get a take-away or something. B xxx

I bought enough wine to get half the village tipsy, and Cheryl brought even more. She showed up at eight, bottles clinking in her bag. She looked good. Her dress was dark blue with a low neckline and cutaway slash along the side to show-off the smooth curve where her tiny waist widened into hips. Somehow it wasn't trashy. Under normal circumstances I wouldn't even have needed one pint.

These weren't normal circumstances.

I wanted to pace my drinking, but Cheryl kept filling our glasses with cheap white wine not made to go with our curry, and I kept knocking it back. Neither of us ate much. By the time we stumbled out of the cottage on to the moonlit sand for a paddle, it seemed a good idea. And when we rolled back in, laughing and shushing each other, it was out of my hands completely. It was Cheryl who steered us towards the bed. What could I do? I was an artist after all.

"I really like you, Ben. Do you like me?"

It was Cheryl who flipped back the covers with a too-practised sweep.

"Course I like you. You're beautiful."

It was Cheryl who unzipped her dress and stepped out of it, held out her hands to beckon me closer. I only obeyed.

If I'm honest, I don't remember the nitty-gritty of the next hour. Which probably makes me a bastard despite the excuse of three empty bottles of wine. I do remember that Cheryl was surprisingly demanding. I hadn't expected her to be shy and virginal about the whole thing, but she was the first woman who put my hands where she wanted them, rather than waiting for me to strike lucky. And I do remember that she looked as good out of her dress as she had done in it. Other than that, the night is a fog – a series of images, whispered words and the strangest feeling that I was doing something I both wanted and would regret before it was even over.

When I'd woken, it'd taken me a minute to remember why I was on the floor. The narrow bed had served its purpose, but it didn't sleep two. Cheryl lay curled under the sheets, blonde hair spread in a tangle on the pillow. There was something about the smudge of mascara under her eyes and the last traces of lipstick clinging to her mouth, that made her look young. As young as she was. And I had the absurd idea I wanted to paint her like that – vulnerable and dreaming. So I left the cottage.

The tide was beginning to turn when I sat down on the rocks. The cool early-morning light illuminated a world stretching out the stiffness of sleep. Far out in the bay, the sun that had barely cleared the horizon caught the surface of the calm sea with its dusting of pink-gold – Tea Rose and Coral. Red sky in the morning.

In the stillness of that Sunday dawn, it felt for a moment as if I had the world to myself. As if all the circular thoughts and impossible plans were somewhere out there, floating their way to whatever lay on the other side of the sea. France and all the rest of it.

"God? Are you there?"

He didn't answer me. At least, not in a language I could understand.

"I could do with some help here."

A wave lapped at the edge of the rock, retreating to leave a slash of Carmine seaweed draped across it, as if the rock was bleeding.

"I know it's all my fault. I've done some pretty crappy stuff lately and I'm not proud of it. But I can't go back now, God. I can't undo it all. So I need you to help, OK?"

There had been times in London when I'd thought I might stay to face the music, rather than skulking back to Brackton. I hadn't been brave enough. Now, I wasn't brave enough to be back in Brackton either.

My head was thumping as much as I deserved, but the sea breeze began to clear my thoughts. A few blurred memories of the previous night drifted into focus. We hadn't slept straight after sex; Cheryl had been in a talkative mood. I hadn't intended to quiz her on anything then – not half-drunk and off my guard – but I hadn't needed to. She'd giggled and hiccupped and clung to the arm I'd thrown around her shoulders as we lay crushed together. She'd told me all about her ambitions for life – vague and ill-formed as they were. She told me she was destined to do something big and bold with her life – if not to be famous then at least to have the kind of life other people wanted to hear about at parties. And she told me the only thing holding her back was money. She didn't have enough money to do anything – no savings, no inheritance no rich relatives. She had nothing but a junior nurse's salary. It had all been for nothing. I didn't need her.

"It's all down to Jenny now, God." I threw an empty limpet shell as far as I could, losing the quiet plop under the screech of a waking gull. "And I don't want that. I'm not that kind of person. Why don't you find me another way out? If you show me another way to get the money, I promise I won't go near Jenny again. I don't *want* to hurt her." I looked up at the clear sky, on the off-chance he was up there. "Once I'm clear of here I'll work like I've never worked before. I'll pay it all back – every penny."

Nothing. Just the shushing of the water on the rocks.

"With interest?"

But God wasn't there.

CHERYL

I needed Ben.

He was what I'd been waiting for – excitement, drama, the kind of person you'd never meet in Lockhaven. He wasn't my Prince Charming, my happy ending, or anything soft like that. Not that I would've said no if he had proven to be a fairytale. For me though, he was my next thing – if not Mr. Right, then Mr. Now. I liked him. I just didn't know whether he liked me in that way too. Until I got his text.

There were no buses after eight from Brackton, so inviting me over for the evening was the same as inviting me over for the night. That was fine by me. Until then he'd been hot and cold – always friendly and welcoming, but sometimes looking at me as if there was something he couldn't work out, something not quite nice. That day though, it was pretty clear what he wanted.

The last time I'd seen him before that evening hadn't been a success. I'd wanted to surprise him at his cottage, only to find on arriving in Brackton that he wasn't there. Instead he was talking to another woman on the Green. It wasn't Dr. Blunt this time – someone younger, more like Ben's age. That might've made me wary, but to be honest, I could see from the start I wasn't in danger. Partly it was the way she dressed. The only fashionable thing about her was her baggy knitted cardi, and it didn't suit her. It wasn't only the clothes though. As I drew closer to them I could see the way she was looking at Ben, all smiley and shiny. It was impossible to doubt what she thought of him. But I could also see the way he was looking at her. She was no competition for me.

After the briefest introductions Ben scampered away on his own, leaving Jenny and me standing around like lemons. I was about to leave to – hoping to find somewhere to read the latest *Cosmopolitan* until the bus was due back to Lockhaven – when I caught sight of something on the bench. Ben had left his phone behind. I picked it up. The message icon was flashing.

"Oh dear, he'll miss that," Jenny said. "He doesn't go anywhere without it. I could pop it down to his cottage later maybe."

"Sure." I pressed a couple of buttons. "That'd probably be best."

I handed the mobile over to Jenny, but not before I'd had the chance to peek at the message in the inbox.

Where the hell are you? This isn't a game, Ben.

I avoided talking to Lauren about Ben as much as I could, but when his text came through the following weekend, I knew I couldn't keep the news to myself. I called her at work as soon as I'd replied to Ben.

"This is IT!" Lauren was as over-excited as I'd suspected she would be. "Properly 100% IT."

"He's only asked me over for a takeaway. Doesn't mean anything's going to happen."

"I suppose you're going to spend an entire evening sitting two metres apart, before retiring to separate beds, are you?"

I giggled. "Might do."

"Bullshit." Lauren snorted. "What are you going to wear?"

I rifled through my wardrobe. "That red dress I wore out for Michaela's birthday?"

"Too tarty."

"The skirt you got me from Top Shop last Christmas then?"

"Not tarty enough."

I ran through another handful of options. Lauren wasn't impressed.

"Look, you'd better get round here at lunchtime and I'll see what I can do." I heard her flipping through the pages of the appointment book. "Do you need to book in at the salon this afternoon?"

"Don't think so."

"All tidy down there? No emergency waxing needed? I could get you a discount."

"I think I'm good."

"Cool, then I'll see you in an hour or so." She gave a little squeal. "This is so exciting. I can't believe you are actually going out with an artist. You've got yourself a sugar-daddy."

"He's hardly a millionaire."

"I bet he is. Did you hear how much he said his paintings sold for? He just doesn't care about the money. Which is even better – all the more for you. Just promise me you won't forget me when you're a model in London."

"Don't be an idiot."

Lauren huffed. "I won't be an idiot if *you* don't ruin your chances of something exciting happening by playing all hard to get. Don't be a prude and don't get too drunk."

I wasn't intending to get drunk. Tipsy maybe, but not hammered. It was Ben who kept the wine flowing. I only had to take two sips before he was topping me up again. It was nice stuff though – cheap but kind of spicy. I don't usually drink much, but by the time we'd eaten the food a couple of bottles seemed to have disappeared and things were moving on.

"I think you're beautiful." Ben's word came out slurred. "Couldn't believe it when you turned up at my cottage that first time."

We were sitting on the floor, backs against the bed. He leaned in closer, and I could smell alcohol and garlic, mixed with an aftershave I'd never smelled on him before.

"I liked you as soon as I saw you." I leaned in to meet him, our eyes bridging the remaining few inches between us. "I thought I'd be too young for you."

"And I thought I'd be too old for you."

"When you're good-looking, age doesn't matter."

"You don't think so?" Ben's hand crept along the back of my neck and into my hair. "I'm glad."

"Look at paintings," I said. "Loads of old ones are still beautiful aren't they?"

For once, Ben didn't seem to want to talk about art. I glanced away for a second and when I turned back, he was too close not to kiss. Without breaking stride he pulled me to my feet, one hand tugging the sheets and blanket down the bed, the other fumbling for the zip of my dress.

He knew what he was doing. It didn't last long – ten minutes at the most – but I didn't have to do much other than lie back and let Ben do what he wanted. I shouldn't have been surprised. He'd probably had sex with a woman in pretty much every country of the world by then. He should know his way round one. He was enjoying himself, I could tell. Even half-drunk it was obvious. Some guys might be able to fake it, but he wasn't one of them. He also wasn't one of those guys who's asleep by the time you're back from the bathroom – unlike my last boyfriend. I don't remember much, but I think we talked for a while. I remember his arm around my shoulder, my head on his chest. It was comfortable, easy, and I didn't feel as if I was using him. I felt happy. In that moment I wanted to be with him, whether or not he could make me a model, or take me travelling.

When I woke in the morning, the front door was opening and Ben was coming back in, accompanied by the racket of seagulls. I sat up and pulled the sheets around me, hoping I didn't look too morning-after, wishing I'd woken earlier and fixed my make-up as Lauren had told me to. Ben came over to the bed, knelt down next to it, finally lifted his head to meet my gaze. And the smile I'd prepared for him died away as I saw the expression on his face. My stomach tightened. Something was wrong. This wasn't how he was meant to look in the morning. This wasn't right at all.

JENNY

I needed Ben.

Dad was right. He wasn't right to keep the money – not to assume that one day I'd be walking down the aisle in a Hollywood dream – but he was right in saying I couldn't let Tom take away everything forever. I had to stop thinking of Tom as my lost life: The One That Got Away. I needed to live as if Dad's money might be needed one day. I needed Ben.

He'd given me his mobile number before going back to London, but I was too much of a coward to use it. Not having a precise day for his return to Brackton I decided to leave it until Sunday morning before going down to the beach again. When Sunday came I was far too eager. Shamefully eager. I got to the sand too early for social calls. There was nothing for it – I'd have to go for a walk first and look in on my way back. If Ben was up I'd invite him for Sunday lunch after church. Maybe I'd even invite him to the church service as well.

There were no curtains at Anchor Cottage and it cheered me to see the easels and canvases standing around inside the studio as I tramped up the deserted sand in the morning sunlight. It was all so familiar, so Ben, and for the first time I realised I thought of it as Ben's cottage now, not Tom's. I'd only taken another few steps when I saw through the other window. I wish – even now – I hadn't looked.

She was in his bed. Her shoulders were bare, the sheet tucked under her arms. Ben was kneeling on the floor next to her, back to the window. I can see it as a photograph: one of her hands in his, her face tilted down, his tilted up.

When I'd first met Ben, I'd been so conscious of the weight of history. Everything – every contrast, every similarity – seemed sharp. A man smiling at me in that cottage. A man asking me out to dinner on that front step. Tom. Ben. History repeating. So I should've expected it, shouldn't I?

I should've known Dad wasn't right about everything. Lightning can strike twice.

I backed away from the cottage — the only thing that could possibly make it worse would be if Ben or Cheryl saw me. The humiliation would've killed me. Yet, I couldn't go home; I couldn't walk away from the beach. I stood at the edge of the sea, waiting for the numbness to wear off, the resignation to hit me. Life to return.

"Jenny? Are you quite well?"

I was only vaguely aware of Dr. Blunt walking towards me along the edge of the water. She stopped next to me, arms folded, hands clamped in her armpits.

"It's happened again," I said, as if she should've known it all. "Tom. The cottage. All of it has happened again."

She didn't sound patient. "What are you talking about?"

"He told me she was a student, but she's there, in the cottage." I glanced back up the beach. "In his bed."

"Who is? Who's in there?" Dr. Blunt's voice was sharp now — not impatient, anxious.

"This young woman he knows. They're talking about something and looking so serious." I looked at my feet, damp from the incoming tide. "And she's very young and blonde and everything I'm not, and I've been so stupid." I couldn't bring myself to look at Dr. Blunt. "He never said anything, you know. He never said it. But I was stupid enough to think... to think...."

"Come on Jenny." She pulled me away from the encroaching water. "You need a cup of tea. Come with me."

Although she hurried me up the cliff steps with more speed than care, I was touched at her brusque concern. At the top of the steps I looked back across the bay and caught the twitch of a net curtain up on the opposite headland. And I could feel a pair of dark eyes watching us disappear into Dr. Blunt's house, with a satisfied smirk.

BEN

Cheryl followed the line of my gaze out across the beach to the cliff steps.

"It was that cow who was here last week, wasn't it?" She drew her knees up to her chin. "She put you up to this. She told you to get rid of me."

"Of course she didn't. Why would she?" The conversation was turning out every bit as badly as I'd feared. "This isn't about anybody else – just you and me. And it isn't going to work between us."

"So you keep saying."

I resisted the urge to watch Rosemary and Jenny's progress up the cliff. Why had they both been on the beach so early on a Sunday? And why were they leaving so suddenly and together? They hadn't been out there 10 minutes ago when I'd come back in. I didn't like it.

"Cheryl, I'm twice your age. That's far too old. You should be going after younger men."

"You weren't too old last night, were you?"

"We were both drunk last night." She flinched and I cursed myself. "Not that I wouldn't have wanted to if I'd been sober," I added, too late. "But I would've stopped myself if I hadn't been drunk, because I know it won't work between us."

"It could." She looked down at where I knelt beside the bed from behind those dark rings of mascara. "I love your art and we get on so well and... and I thought you liked me. Why else did you send that text?"

Crap. She was going to cry. I'm no good with crying. And she was trying to hold back the tears which made it even worse.

"I do like you." I patted her knee. "You understand my work more than anybody else down here. I like chatting to you."

"But not sleeping with me?"

"Of course I liked that." I was pretty sure it wasn't a lie. "That doesn't mean it was right. I don't think you should come here anymore – I don't want to hurt your feelings again."

"We don't have to sleep together. We could carry on as before for now – hanging out and stuff." The first tear trickled down her cheek. "Please."

I'd expected her to be angry, not this upset. She hadn't seemed the crying type. She must've liked me more than I'd realised, and, even in that awkward silence, my stupid ego gave a little kick of pleasure.

"I don't think it's a good idea," I said.

She dropped my hand and threw back the covers. For one second I thought she was offering herself to me. I felt an involuntary rush. But she got up and stooped to grab her knickers from the floor. Now she really was angry.

"It *was* her, wasn't it? Dr. Blunt." She spat the name across the room. "She told you to get rid of me, and you had to take what you could get from me first."

If I'd had any decency, I'd have looked away as she pulled on her clothes, but it didn't even occur to me.

"What's the deal with Rosemary? Why should she have anything to do with this?"

"Perhaps you should ask *her* that." Cheryl wriggled into the tight dress and somehow it didn't have the appeal of the previous night. "Why don't you ask her why she doesn't want me around? Why don't you ask her about her husband?"

"She doesn't have a husband. She's not the marrying type."

"That's what *you* think. But when did she move here, tell me that." Cheryl struggled with the zip for a moment before reluctantly allowing me to do it up for her. She spun round and backed away from me as soon as I let go. "I bet it was within the last year, wasn't it?"

"No, she's been here about six years I think."

Cheryl snorted. "She told you that, did she?"

"Probably. But other people have said something similar." I still couldn't see where this had come from, or where it was going. "She's been here for six years and never had a husband – not in all that time, anyway. You must've got her confused with somebody else."

Cheryl's face changed. Her eyes flicked to the window and the cliff again. She frowned, shook her head, looked at her feet. Something wasn't right.

"You're lying," she said at last. "You're just like all the others." She blinked back a fresh supply of tears. "If I'd wanted to hook up with a bastard, I could've done it in Lockhaven. I didn't have to come all the way here for you."

I shrunk to about three inches tall. She was right.

"Cheryl," I reached out to her, "I really am sorry. I don't usually sleep with people and then ask them to leave. I really don't. You're a nice girl and I never should've..."

Cheryl snatched her arm away from me and pushed past to the door. "Whatever." She pulled her coat around her shoulders. "You're an artist, aren't you? I should've guessed what you'd be like." She scanned the debris of the room: foil trays still half-full of rice, empty wine bottles, used condom. Her eyes rested on this last item for a few seconds. "I suppose I should be grateful you haven't given me some disease you picked up while you were shagging your way round India."

"I'm not like that."

She took a step towards me and I thought I was in for a slap – it might've made me feel better if I had been. Instead, she kissed me. I was so surprised I forgot to not kiss back. When she released me, her face had set into a hard look: angry, triumphant. Before I could excuse myself – before I could say anything at all – she'd slammed out of the cottage and was tottering as fast as she could down the beach.

I sank on to the rumpled bed. What a mess. I'd sent Cheryl away for good – slept with her and dismissed her. I was a man who'd had sex with someone and dumped them. I could never not be that man again. And what for?

In the quiet of the empty cottage my mind turned to Jenny. She must've seen Cheryl. Fate couldn't have arranged it any other way. The very moment I needed Jenny to trust me, it was all ruined. What had she been doing on the beach at that early hour? And Rosemary? If Jenny had seen Cheryl, Rosemary almost certainly had too, and for some reason that disturbed me even more. Why had Cheryl been obsessed with Rosemary? Rosemary had no motive – other than common decency – to stop me seeing Cheryl. Not one that I knew of. But then, I was learning there were many things I still didn't know about Rosemary Blunt.

I flopped back on the pillow and tried to think. Cheryl had been my Plan B and she had come to nothing. Jenny – Plan C – was almost certainly ruined now too. I hadn't got as far as Plan D. I needed a miracle, but miracles require bravery and I wasn't brave. So instead, I needed somebody to think of a way I could escape from my mess for me. The things was, nobody else knew anything about me in Brackton. If I wanted help, I had to confide in someone.

It came to me then, lying on my bed, what I had to do. There was only one person in the world I still trusted. Rosemary probably didn't ever want to see me again after knowing what happened last night, but she was my only chance. If I could get her to trust me, then I'd know for sure that she too could be trusted. I'd tell her everything. If she didn't slam the door in my face the following morning, then we'd go painting as planned and I'd ask her one last time what she did on Mondays and Thursdays. If she told me the truth – and I knew I'd know the truth if I heard it – then I'd trust her. I'd confess the whole damned thing and beg her to help me think of a way out. It wasn't much of a Plan D, but it was all I had left.

ROSEMARY

I couldn't go painting with Ben. Despite telling Julia about our planned expedition, I knew it was impossible. If Cheryl found out I had not only seen Ben again but actually gone on a day-trip with him, it would be the end of everything. I knew that, without knowing how I knew. The only way to stop her, would be to get there first.

I don't suppose I could've told Ben everything really. Not then. It was still all beyond my grasp – too many patches of fog in my memory. I could've told him something though. I could've tried to explain whatever was in my power to explain, before Cheryl got there. Why I should've chosen Ben as my confidant rather than Julia or even one of the counsellors I found listed on a shredded piece of pink paper at the bottom of my bag, I don't know. For some reason, Ben was the person I wanted to tell. Perhaps I recognised in him somebody else who was haunted by the past.

I tried to speak to him early on Sunday morning – the day before we were due to go painting. I never made it. After meeting Jenny on the beach and putting two and two together, I knew it was too late. Cheryl was in his house and they were talking. That was enough to bring a sense of peril – of grey uncertainty – sweeping over me. When I finally ushered Jenny out of my house, I sat on the window-seat in my bedroom, looking down at the beach below and wondering what Ben was thinking. The sun grew hot and high, and began to sink again, and the door to his cottage remained shut.

The following morning was as sunny as that Sunday had been and I should've got the bus into Lockhaven as I always did. I wasn't expecting Ben to turn up – not after what Cheryl must've told him. I didn't go though. It was the first Monday I'd not caught the bus in a year, and for the first time I think I had an idea of why I usually did catch it. Not a clear idea; a tentative one. The sort of idea that lingers in your peripheral thoughts, disappearing when you try to drag it into the light.

I didn't want breakfast. Instead, I drank back-to-back coffees and read old magazines, not taking in anything. It was half past nine before I heard the tinny ring-ding from outside. It sounded over and over again until I went to the door.

Ben was at the gate, straddling a bicycle with a ridiculous trailer hooked up behind. Along with a couple of folded easels and two cases, there was an enormous wrapped rectangle, which could only have been his painting of God. Propped against the fence next to him was another bike. His face broke into that annoying grin as soon as he saw me.

"You hadn't forgotten our date, had you?"

Either from surprise or relief I didn't bother squashing his ego. "Of course not." I walked down the path to join him. "Why on earth are you lugging that monstrosity with you?"

"God only works when you're around. I'm not wasting the opportunity to spend a whole day on him."

I studied his face. His smile was masking something. It didn't look like the disgust or confusion I was expecting. It was something more like anxiety. Even as I finished scanning him, I caught his eye and realised I wasn't the only one trying to read minds.

"I took the liberty of hiring you a bike," he said. "You can ride, I suppose?"

"I haven't since I was a girl."

"You'll remember quickly enough." He flapped a hand. "Nobody ever forgets. It's like..." he smiled again, "... well, it's like riding a bicycle."

I examined the contraption he'd brought me. It looked identical to the one I'd ridden in the early 50s, complete with bell, basket and rickety frame.

"I'm not sure I agreed to this."

"You'll be fine."

"It doesn't look very safe."

"For God's sake, Rosemary. Go and grab your stuff and get on the bloody bike, would you? It's perfectly safe."

For once, the wind was coming from inland instead of blowing off the sea. We were able to find a spot near the cliff edge that had both uninterrupted views of the English Channel and was sheltered by a copse of trees. To our left, the crooked line of cliffs stretched away into the distance, their chalk faces plummeting down towards water rippling with light as the sun met the wind-worried waves. To our right, the expanse of grassland we'd puffed across, lay empty. Although we were barely three miles from Brackton, it felt as if we had settled in a different world.

"Remember," Ben said as he secured a blank canvas to my easel, "don't try to paint anything specific. Just start and see what happens."

From the cases, Ben produced the usual paraphernalia that was spread about his cottage: boxes of paint, brushes and palettes. Within five minutes he was busy with his canvas, humming to himself as he worked. I watched him for a while as he added bold black lines over the painting: train tracks running down from the top of the canvas to the bottom, other lines intersecting them at strange angles or bisecting smooth black arcs that swept across the right-hand side of the picture. There was still a gap in the middle.

"When are you going to finish? It's been weeks now."

Ben came out of his reverie and frowned, first at the canvas and then at me. "I know. Won't be long – another two or three sessions, maybe. I'm still waiting for that special... something."

"Like God?"

"That would help."

"I never understood why you were so keen to capture him anyway."

"That's because you never wanted to understand." Ben unscrewed a new tube of paint and squeezed some on to his palette. "I think it's natural to want to know what more there is to this world. We all want that, deep down. I used to see people walk past the office and I'd wonder if they were happy." He gave an embarrassed laugh. "That sounds stupid, but in London I reckon one in 100 people are actually happy. They just don't have time to realise it. Too busy making money."

"Is religion the answer?" I began to rummage in the box of paints, unsure what I was looking for. "All those unhappy people – do you really think they need religion?"

"God no." Ben wrinkled his nose. "They need faith. It's not the same thing at all. Religion's only the fear there might be something more to our faith than we understand. It's faith in a box. Look at those few people who actually make a difference. They might be Christian or Muslims, but they're not *only* religious are they? They're faithful. They believe what they're saying. Going to church or whatever if only part of it – it's not 'it' on its own." He glanced at me. "But you think that's rubbish, right? Who needs faith when you've got physics?"

"That's a sentiment some of my old colleagues would have approved of, certainly."

"Not the types who were painting God at the weekend then?"

"I think I worked with two Christians and one Jew in my entire career."

"I'm amazed it was even that many." Ben poured himself some coffee from one of the thermoses. "I would've thought the supernatural was taboo in your line of work. Adds another uncontrolled variable."

I found another mug and held it out to him. It was bound to taste atrocious but it was all he was offering.

"Not all scientists limit their interest in the world to the things they can see or measure," I said. "It's just not the sort of thing that was discussed in the office. Not by me, anyway."

"You weren't interested in all that?"

"Not really."

I should've said, "Not publically." In public I stayed as far from God as possible. I didn't deride those of my colleagues who dared couple a career in science with a faith in God, but I didn't understand their confidence, and I didn't stick up for them when others ridiculed them. If the subject came up during a coffee break, or while we were waiting for an experiment to run its course, I maintained my distance. Why should I want to talk about nonsense? After Michael left, completing my quartet of desertion – Love, Grace, God, Michael – I wasn't interested in finding faith for a long time. Somewhere though, I think faith might have been trying to find me.

I blame my upbringing. If I'd been brought up in a good unbelieving home maybe I wouldn't have felt God's absence so keenly. Maybe I wouldn't have gone looking for him again when that deep down whisper began to nag at me. In those long, solitary evenings at my flat, more than a decade into a career that had not needed God, maybe I wouldn't have allowed myself to get drawn in.

Finding something divine seemed too remote and ridiculous at first. So in true 1980s fashion, I settled for finding myself. I'd work as late as possible at the university and then sit up half the night reading the legendary self-help manuals of the time. I was quarter of a century too late to join the *I'm OK, You're OK* frenzy, but I read it anyway. In fact, I read them all. I learned how to win friends and influence people, without doing either; developed the seven habits of highly effective people, and remained ineffective; I forced myself to embrace the power of positive thinking, without ever feeling positive; I felt the fear and did it anyway, only to feel the fear again. If I'd been hunting a few years later I'm sure I even would've asked who'd moved my cheese. None of it helped. None of it scratched the itch. So I moved on to the harder stuff: religion and psychology – individually and combined.

I tried pretty much everything going – church services, weekend retreats, study classes. I watched businessmen pretending chairs were their mothers and shouting at them until they cried. I fasted until I fainted. No good. I found neither myself, nor God. So in the end I allowed him to desert me for the second time. And I told myself that it was a phase – a throwback to a childhood dominated by a fanatical mother – which I had got out of my system for life at last. And I think I believed it, right up until I saw Ben's painting.

Ben was watching me. He slurped a mouthful of coffee before saying, "So you weren't brought up to believe then?"

"Protestant parents, Catholic school. Enough to put anyone off for life, I'd say."

"And did it? Or did it just put you off Sunday-morning Christianity? Did you look elsewhere?"

"Perhaps." I wasn't committing to more than that. I don't know why I was letting him ask me such personal questions at all. Nobody else got away with it.

"Did you find what you were looking for?" Ben asked.

"Does it look like I found what I was looking for?"

Ben made a non-committal noise, studying his painting with deliberate concentration.

"I looked hard." I turned back to my own blank canvas. "I never found it."

"What?" Ben tilted his head to one side. "What's 'it'?"

"You know... It. Me. God. I couldn't find any of us. People promised all sorts of things if I jumped through their particular hoop. However many hoops I jumped through, I didn't find anything useful. And so I stopped looking. I settled for a smaller life."

"Maybe you don't need God to lead a big life."

"You need something," I said. "If not God, then what? Love? Hope? Ambition? I might've worked hard but I didn't have any of those things that make life big – all those... those..."

"Thousand-word things?" Ben suggested.

"Exactly."

Ben sighed, and in that sigh I recognised something surprising: the same crushing liberty I'd carried since Michael left; the same weight of the invisible expectations of freedom. Ben – carefree, bohemian Ben – was worried.

"You've led a big life, haven't you?" For the first time since we'd met, I was the one trying to force eye contact. "You've been everywhere and done everything. You've played with a Ouija board in Arizona for heaven's sake. I've never even played darts in a pub."

Ben shrugged and said, "Leading a big life hasn't done a lot for me. I'm no more sure of who I am and who God is than you are."

"You still hope to be sure, don't you?" I pressed. "You must do, or you'd never have started this painting. That's the difference between us."

"It doesn't mean anything unless I succeed." He shook his head at his unfinished picture. "And what are the chances of that now?"

I was glad he didn't wait for an answer – I had none to give. Instead, he gave himself a shake and switched his attention to my easel. "You haven't even started yet! Here, take these." He scooped a handful of tubes from the box. "Get a wriggle on or it'll be dark before I've got anything to psychoanalyse."

It was a joke – at least, I thought so – but an uncomfortable one. Could a painting really tell you about an artist? I snuck another peek at Ben's canvas – bold and daring and incomplete; it was full of life, but had lost its way.

For a few more minutes, I continued to stare at the blank canvas. What should I paint? Was it safe to let my subconscious take over? I picked up my brush and painted a tentative streak of brown, ruining the cool cleanness of the canvas forever. It was ugly and freeing.

Without warning an image flickered into my mind and hung there for a second before being extinguished. A man. A man in a bed. A motionless man in a bed, in a white room. A man who – No. I knew there was a good reason not to think of him, and a good reason not to remember what that reason was. I would be safe if I didn't remember. I shook my head, erasing the etch-a-sketch image, and replacing it with one of Julia. I could think of Julia and the sea and my ugly house overlooking the beach and a dozen other safe things. Concentrating hard, I drew another line. And the battle began.

The colours Ben had handed me were mostly dark: Forest Green and Midnight Blue, Eggplant and Rosewood. Only Crimson stuck out like a wound. Each image I brought to the front of my mind, grew twisted and distorted, overlaid with snapshots that were nothing to do with me – nothing to do with that Rosemary. A ticking clock, a frail hand resting on a blue blanket, a skeletal face. I painted without knowing I was painting, pushing the unwanted images away, only to be replaced with others: a mouth twisted into a sneer, a raised fist, an arm swinging back, taking aim. I slammed doors in my mind, turned keys, leaned against them, panting for breath. But as memory after memory smashed against them from the other side, the walls began to give way.

Minutes ticked by and joined forces to form hours, filled with swirls of colour and darkness. I would turn my thoughts towards Dad and university, graduation and school. And my brush would think instead of a little girl without a brain, a beautiful freak of nature, a monster. My daughter. With the thinnest brush I could find I attacked the dark mess of the canvas with crimson, tracing lines of memories that were filed and done with years ago: spoiled dinners and violent words.

I kept painting until Ben's voice made me jump. "Check you out! I thought you said you didn't paint."

I looked at my picture for the first time. It glowered at me from the easel, uneasy and unforgiving. Ben, new flecks of paint on his shirt, had left his own work to study mine.

"That is epic." He peered closer. "I would *love* to know what you were thinking of when you painted this. Or *who* you were thinking of. I hope it wasn't me."

And there was the moment – the tiniest window of time – when I could have told him. This time there'd be no Cheryl in his bed to stop me. If only he would stay quiet for a minute, I would gather my thoughts and take the plunge. I'd tell all. I'd ask him what to do about Michael; what to do about the man in the bed, who I shouldn't have been thinking about there – the one who belonged to a different Rosemary, a bolder, braver, stronger Rosemary. If only he'd wait, hold back, let me break the silence. I'd smash it with the truth.

But he didn't. He spoke first. "Rosemary, what do you do on Mondays? Please tell me."

When I answered, the words came from somewhere far away from us – from a different world. "I go to Lockhaven. I visit someone in a private hospital there."

BEN

She was lying. I asked her and she lied. Almost anything she could have said would've been more believable. She wasn't some sort of bloody Florence Nightingale. I was insulted she thought I didn't know her any better than that. She couldn't even look at me when she said it.

So that was that. The deal I'd made with myself was off. If she didn't trust me enough to tell the truth, then I couldn't trust her either. For all I knew she'd have been on the phone to the police before I had the chance to explain myself properly. I was back to where I was before – up a creek with a conspicuous absence of paddles.

Rosemary was still staring at her canvas. Spiteful red lines tore the darkness into fragments. It spoke of fear and anger and something wild – a caged animal that had been let loose to hunt for itself. Was Rosemary a wild animal? It didn't seem likely.

But she might be rich.

I tried to banish the thought from my head as soon as it entered. It refused to be shaken. Why hadn't I considered Rosemary before? She owned a big house in a prime location, didn't appear to have a taste for expensive furniture or fancy clothes, and had no obvious dependents. She probably had a fortune squirreled away somewhere. I'd been so brutal in trying to snare Cheryl and, to some extent, Jenny too. Why not Rosemary?

The obvious answer was that Rosemary had my card marked from the start. Pulling the wool over her eyes would've been impossible. And hadn't that been why I'd liked her – because she didn't give a toss who I was, but took me at face value every day? Wasn't that why my painting of God had flourished in her company? Because I could paint it as myself. She wouldn't have been fooled into thinking I loved her. If I'd told her that I thought more highly of her than any other woman I'd met for as long as I could remember, I couldn't have persuaded her it was true.

Only, of course, it *was* true. That was the not-obvious answer that came to me as we stood on the clifftop. It wasn't respect for her acid intelligence that made me unable to try manipulating her; it was simply that I couldn't bring myself to do it. I didn't *want* to use Cheryl or Jenny, but when thoughts of the future had loomed over me, I'd been able to do it. With Rosemary it was different. I won't insult her by saying I loved her, there was certainly no romance between us. She was the same age as my mother, irritable, brusque and didn't suffer fools for a minute – hardly Juliet material. But there was more to her than that. There was a wistful look at the sea beyond her windows; there were mysterious trips to Lockhaven; there was an anger bubbling below the surface; there was a big life trapped in a small one.

All that time – while I'd been trying to ingratiate myself with two other women in a quest for money – I'd not seen and never suspected the person I needed was right there in front of me. And it didn't matter because I couldn't use her – because I felt something for her that wasn't love. Something much more important than that. She was my muse.

"We've been painting for hours." I shook out the picnic blanket. "It's almost tea-time and we haven't had lunch."

We sat in the shadows of our paintings, eating scotch eggs and soggy sausage rolls. And I couldn't help but feel God was cutting it a bit fine to make his appearance. The vacant patch of canvas had shrunk again, so that barely two inches square remained untouched. I still didn't know which colours would fill it. What shape would God take? What if I was painting in the wrong style? Maybe God wouldn't show up because he wasn't an abstract expressionist but a fauvist or cubist, or even a neo-plasticist.

After lunch, Rosemary didn't return to her violent painting. She didn't even seem to want to look at it. Instead, she sat on the grass, looking out to sea, hands idly covering page after page in the sketchbook with the recognisable – a wave caught by the wind, a seagull diving for fish – and the speculative.

Despite the nagging space, I enjoyed that afternoon's work. The finer lines and paths laid over the blocks and swirls were soothing to paint. Instead of concentrating on where each stroke went, my mind wandered far and wide, leaving my hands to seek God alone. Maybe if I'd concentrated,

God would've shown up that afternoon. I doubt it somehow. To picture him, I had to paint him; to paint him, I had to picture him.

Rosemary didn't look up all afternoon. Sometimes she'd acknowledge the biscuit or coffee I settled in the grass by her side; often she wouldn't notice. I wanted to understand what was going on in her head but didn't dare ask. Was she still trying imagine what might be on the other side of the sea?

I like to think now that she'd guessed everything, and that moment alone together contained no secrets. The memory of that afternoon doesn't have to be tainted with lies. I know it's not true though. I let the chance for honesty slip by. So when I do think of that day it is a sepia memory, a faded photograph. And I try not to remember the vicious voice that crept into the edges of my consciousness as I watched Rosemary watching the sea.

Why not use Rosemary? I bet she's rolling in it. She could spare the money. Hell – you don't even have to lie to her. You do like her, don't you? How hard could it be to get her to trust you, like you did with Jenny? A lonely woman who's never married. In a few days she could be practically begging to help you out, if you play it right.

In my defence, I know – whatever anybody else believes about me – that I didn't ever have any intention of playing that game. I wasn't going to use Rosemary. I wouldn't say one word that might tempt me to cheat her, or manipulate her when the crucial moment came. But however firmly my mind was made up, it didn't stop the voice. And it didn't stop me wondering if the voice was right.

ROSEMARY

We painted until the shadows had grown long, until the thermoses were dry and the biscuit packet empty and we were in danger of having to pedal back to Brackton in the dark. As we packed everything into the trailer, I remembered Julia.

"Do you like mauve?"

"Mauve?" Ben raised an eyebrow. "What sort of question is that?"

"Julia wants to know."

"That friend of yours wants to know some very odd things. No, I'm not a huge fan of mauve."

"What is your favourite colour then?"

Ben laughed and dug me in the ribs. "I think this Julia of yours doesn't exist and you use her as an excuse to ask me questions without having to appear as if you care."

"You'll be wishing that's true if you're still here in October. She's coming to visit and is dying to meet you. She's besotted with you already."

"Hmmm... now I'm interested." He winked. "Is she pretty?"

"She's my age."

"The two things aren't mutually exclusive." He bent to gather the last stray tubes scattered on the grass. "As well you must know."

We pushed the bikes for a while, until the stiffness in our legs eased. We talked of Julia and the people of Brackton as we ambled towards the village and it was all very safe and comfortable until Ben suddenly said, "I told Cheryl not to come to see me anymore." He hesitated before adding, "I wanted you to know that."

Cheryl's name brought an end to the sunshine of the day.

"It's really none of my business."

"You did see us though, didn't you?" He kept his eyes on his shoes. "At the cottage, yesterday morning."

"No. But Jenny did."

"I thought as much."

I swung a leg over the crossbar and strained to get the pedals moving. "As I said – none of my business, and unless you told Jenny you'd marry her or something ridiculous like that, it's not hers either."

With a dangerous wobble, I finally got the bike going. Grunting with effort, Ben did the same.

"I probably owe Jenny an apology," he said. "I told her that nothing was going on between Cheryl and me. There isn't, of course. But it must have looked... bad."

"If having a naked woman in your bed constitutes nothing going on, I dread to think what Jenny might have seen if there *had* been something between you."

Even in the failing light I saw him flinch. And for the first time, the full implication of what Jenny had seen, hit me. I'd been too worried about what Cheryl might have told him to think about much else, but as we pedalled along the cliff path, I realised that he really had had sex with her. There, in the cottage on the beach where I'd painted Newton and he'd painted God, he had done what I should have known, and never really believed he would do. Despite his idiotic showing-off, he hadn't fitted my stereotype of an artist and I was disappointed in him for falling for a river of blonde hair and a pair of painted lips. Maybe I'd thought more of him than I'd realised or he'd deserved.

. . .

Letter from Rosemary to Julia.

Tuesday 7th August

Dear Julia,

You can relax, Ben doesn't like mauve. He likes Sunglow and Harlequin Green apparently. He's such a show-off. You were right about the Canary Islands being too touristy for him. He's not been, but says he's heard that La Gomera is nicer than some of the bigger islands.

You're not the only one who can ask questions. Ben was asking me about you – asked if you were pretty, if you please! Perhaps he'll stay around to find out for himself. He didn't mention leaving when I said you were coming, so you might be in luck. If you're planning on eloping though, best not to tell George until the day before, otherwise he'll only forget and you'll have to explain all over again later. Dear George.

The painting expedition was wonderful. Marvellous weather – and I mean sunshine for once. I can't say that I surpassed myself artistically, but it was a pleasure to be away from civilisation for a bit – Ben doesn't count, he's not in the least bit civilised. He was working on his painting of God and dragged it in his bike trailer all the way along the cliffs. You should have seen the colour of his face when we stopped. For all that I disapprove, I'm beginning to think his painting is good. I wouldn't go so far as to say it looked like any sort of god to me, but there's something rather splendid about it.

Ben was behaving most peculiarly on the way home. Kept opening his mouth to speak and then shutting it again and sighing. When he did speak it was banal and incoherent – quite unlike him. If there's one thing that man can do, it's talk. When he left me at my front door he hung around for ages, looking for all the world as if he was about to ask me something terribly serious. In the end he muttered a goodbye and disappeared. Most odd. Mind you, we'd just been talking about your visit, so perhaps he was just bowled over by the thought of meeting you at last. Either that, or he's plotting his escape from Brackton before October.

How are the wedding plans coming along?

Love, Rosemary

Letter from Julia to Rosemary.

Wednesday 8th August

Dear Rosemary,

Can it really be you? In your letter you not only used the word wonderful, but also marvellous and splendid. If this is what painting does to you then I fully approve. I suspect it's not just the art though. Do you really not hold a candle for Ben? Not even one of those tea-lights you put in oil burners?

If you do like him, I promise I won't elope. I'll do no more than let him whisk me off somewhere exotic for a week. That way I'll be back before George notices and you can disappear on some terrific adventure with Ben and we'll all be satisfied.

Even if you won't admit you like him, it sounds as if he rather fancies you. (And don't tell me you're too old for that!) He invited you – only you – on a day-trip and then got all tongue-tied on the way home. If you weren't so sharp with people he'd probably have proposed by now.

Alison is lamenting the difficulties of finding a wedding dress while still carrying some baby weight. Trouble is, if she leaves it any later it'll cost twice as much. She's determined to have the fairytale wedding, even if it does mean re-mortgaging. All her flapping has got me worried about what I'm going to wear too. It's so hard to be glamorous at our age without looking like the Madame of a house of ill-repute. I shall look for a dress in Sunglow or Harlequin Green and if George asks why (he won't, of course) I shall give a knowing smile. I shall also tell him that we must go to La Gomera next summer. I won't hear of us going anywhere else.

With love, Julia

Letter from Rosemary to Julia.

Friday 10th August

Dear Julia,

However much you bully me, I shan't be declaring undying love for Ben. Even if I had any notions of romance – which I most definitely do not – it would be absurd. I'm far too old to have butterflies when the doorbell rings, especially on account of a man who thinks he can paint God. I mean, really! It's pathetic enough for Jenny to be silly over him and they are at least the same generation.

I like Ben. I'll admit that. He's irritating beyond belief but there's something about him that's different from anyone else I know. I think of him differently. But to pretend that's romance would be no less ludicrous that saying that you and I are romantically involved because I feel differently towards you than I do to anybody else. He entertains me, and his conversation can be half-decent. He has a way of looking at things that is so alien it's almost fascinating. That's as far as I would go. It's all irrelevant anyway. He'll be going back to London soon, and then I'll never see him again.

As it happens I haven't seen him properly since our expedition. I popped by to say hello on Tuesday evening and he looked atrocious. I've never seen anybody so pale. He said he had some sort of stomach bug and didn't want to ask me in, in case he was infectious. I'm sure he'll let me know when he's better.

Tell Alison she'd look splendid in a sack, so she needn't worry about finding the right dress. The same goes for you too.

With love, Rosemary

JENNY

My footsteps echoed to the rafters as I walked the aisle between empty pews.
If I closed my eyes I could almost hear the sound of the organ, feel the hundred pairs of smiling eyes on me, smell the bouquet of roses in my hand. I
slid into the front pew. Despite the bright day outside, the only ray of sunlight that made it through the windows at that time of the morning fell on
to the pulpit, catching the toes of Jesus in its glow. My gaze followed the line
of the cross, up from the sunlit base to the shadows of his face.

"You promised."

He didn't say anything, only hung there, pale and bleeding, a sliver of
paint missing where the nail was piercing his right hand. It might not have
been strictly true – God hadn't given me a rainbow as a sign of his faithful-
ness, nor written his words on stone tablets – but as far as I was concerned, he
had promised Tom wouldn't happen again. By letting me sit in the front pew
on a Sunday, by giving me a hundred small jobs to do around the church, by
bringing Ben to Brackton, he'd promised.

"You PROMISED."

It'd been three days since I'd seen Ben and Cheryl in the cottage on the
beach. I hadn't been into the church since. When Vicar called to see why I
hadn't been at the Sunday morning service and, more importantly, why the
flowers hadn't been done, I'd told Dad to tell him I was ill. I must've looked
the part, as not even Dad questioned it. I hadn't been able to face anybody,
much less God – first out of shame, and then out of anger.

It wasn't Ben's fault. He hadn't asked me to love him. Not in words.
And perhaps I hadn't loved him. But I'd allowed myself the possibility of
love. Mrs. Baxter had tried to warn me, and I'd dismissed her warning for
Ben's version of events only because I wanted to. Hadn't I been on the shelf

long enough to know better than that? I only had myself to blame. And God.

"We would've been alright." I kept my eyes fixed on his face. "Dad and I would've been fine if Ben hadn't come here. And now I've got to tell Dad to stop hoping all over again."

It was a small mercy that Dad hadn't realised Ben was back from London. He hadn't tried to get me to go to the beach, or offered to go down to tell Ben I was ill. It'd given me time to pull myself together. But however hard I tried – however many times I reminded myself that I must be forgiving, that God was good, that in the grand scale of eternity none of it mattered – I couldn't make it not matter, and I couldn't make God good again. The sharp pain that had hit me full in the chest on the beach that Sunday morning, would only subside as far as a dull throb somewhere in the space Tom had left.

"Why couldn't you have left us alone?" I walked over to the pulpit. "I know sometimes I wished I wasn't so silly – that I understood the world as other people understand it. But you're God aren't you? You're meant to know which prayers to answer." I paused at the bottom of the steps. "You should've ignored me – left me as the silly woman I was."

That was the worst of it. The one glimpse through the cottage windows had not only taken Ben from me, but had taken me from me too. All the suspicion, the cattiness, the gossip that riddled the village – I could understand it. I understood why people wanted to know everything, and why they always doubted everybody else's motives. I understood why it's less painful to think badly of people, than to have your illusions shattered. And more than anything else, I wished I didn't understand. I wished I knew nothing again.

I climbed the steps, reached out a hand to the plaster Jesus, more paint crumbling from him at my touch. "I thought you said you'd look after me."

The church door creaked.

"Jenny?" Ben stood in the entrance, hands in pockets. "I thought I might find you here. Can we talk?"

We closed in on each other from opposite ends of the aisle. I kept my eyes on the tiles, cracked and familiar. Even when he chose a pew and I took the one across from it, I only lifted my gaze as far as the goosebumps on his folded arms.

"I know you saw me in the cottage with Cheryl on Sunday." Ben spoke softly. Churches had that effect on people. "And I wanted to say sorry."

"You don't need to apologise to me. It's not my business who you see. I'm sure she's a very nice girl."

"No. I mean... she is, but not like that... I mean, I don't feel anything for her."

"You don't have to tell me what you feel."

"I told you there was nothing going on between us and then you saw... that." Ben sighed. "I want to apologise for that at the very least."

I did look at him then, just a quick glance. And I was shocked. Those grey eyes that had sparkled at me all summer, were dull and surrounded by dark circles. He was thinner than before he went to London and the hand he ran through his hair wasn't entirely steady.

"You don't look well."

"I'm OK. Not sleeping properly, that's all." He hesitated before adding, "I miss you."

I shifted my gaze back to Jesus. Was this meant to be some kind of joke? Or a peace offering?

"I meant what I said – there's nothing going on between Cheryl and me. I know it looks bad – and I'm not going to deny we slept together – but that was all it was."

Of course. Hadn't I known it was only sex? Wasn't that what history demanded?

"You slept with her, but you don't love her?"

"No." Ben rested his arms on the pew in front. "I suppose that makes me the worst kind of man in your eyes, but please try to understand – it's a different world. Among the people I grew up around it's normal to have... to have..."

I wasn't sure whether it was me or the church that was making 'sex' so hard to say.

"It's normal to have a physical relationship without feelings. You don't jump into bed with people you respect. You take them for dinner."

"You've never taken her for dinner?"

"Not once. And I don't want to. And I've told her not to come back. I've realised what's important to me – *who's* important to me."

I didn't trust myself to say anything, nor even think anything. The person I had been, believed him. The person I had become, couldn't.

"I don't expect you to excuse my appalling behaviour." Ben shuffled round to face me. "But I couldn't bear to think I'd upset you and not apologised. If you could ever find it in your heart to forgive me, it would be more than I deserve."

My heart. I pressed a hand to my chest, surprised to feel something thumping away inside. "I can forgive you," I heard myself saying. "There's nothing to forgive."

I don't think I sounded convincing – not to my ears anyway – but Ben was willing to be convinced. He hung his head, as if exhausted by the battle I hadn't made him fight. "I'm so sorry," he said again. "Sometime – when you can stand my company again – perhaps I might take you to dinner, to show you how sorry I am? We can go into Lockhaven – somewhere nice."

He didn't wait for my answer. In another minute he'd disappeared into the sunshine. There was a pause, then the fading scrunch of feet on gravel and the squeak of the lych-gate. I breathed again. Every inch of me wanted to believe he was genuine, yet it was no longer that simple. Wanting to believe isn't the same as believing. Out of instinct, I looked to the cross for guidance. And then I remembered – we weren't talking, were we?

I shook my head at the man hanging from it. "You can't even let me hate you, can you?"

But yet again, he didn't reply.

ROSEMARY

Letter from Julia to Rosemary.

Saturday 11th August

Dearest Rosemary,

I don't care what you say, I shan't ever believe that you don't feel something for Ben now. There was more in that last letter than you want to admit. I know you too well. I feel as if I'm not being told some juicy piece of gossip – promise to tell me when he asks you out for dinner? I'm even more excited to meet him now. Heaven knows what might have happened by October. He does like you Rosemary, I know he does. Has he recovered from his bug yet?

Tell me if I'm talking out of turn here, but don't you think letting yourself get a bit carried away with Ben might not be such a bad thing? At least admit that you might like it if he <u>does</u> ask you to dinner. Even if he goes back to London in the end, perhaps enjoying his company until then is just what you need in order to let the memories of Michael go at last. Don't be cross with me for saying so. I only want to see you happy.

Give my love to Ben when you next see him. Tell him to get better soon so his painting of God is finished by the time I arrive for a viewing. I had no idea one painting could take so long.

Lots of love, Julia

Letter from Rosemary to Julia.

Monday 13th August

Dear Julia,

I'm not sure which letter you read, but it can't possibly have been the one I sent if you found some reason to believe that Ben would ask me out to dinner, or that I would wish to accept such an invitation. It doesn't matter anyway, I have news that will shatter all your illusions. Ben is quite well again, Julia. And he didn't bother to tell me. There. Now how smitten do you think he is?

I saw Jenny coming out of his cottage on Friday. I assumed she was doing her ministering angel bit, but I saw them again on Saturday. They were having lunch on the beach. Ben was wearing his painting clothes and they were laughing away, having a fine old time. Jenny looked up at my house at one point and must've seen me in the window because she waved, and do you know what? Ben made this little movement as if trying to stop her. He didn't want me to see them. He must've told me he was ill so that he was free to chase after Jenny. I shouldn't be surprised. I'm only baffled as to why he bothered spending a whole day painting with me in the first place.

For your information, I don't need male company to forget Michael. Besides, it's not as if Ben's the first man I've spoken to since Michael left. I didn't work with another woman for the first 15 years of my career. One of my colleagues even proposed to me once. I didn't tell you that, did I? The summer of 1988 it was. We'd been working on a project together all through the university holidays. At the end of it he got down on one knee, there in the lab. It was quite ridiculous. We'd never even seen each other outside the university and our conversations had been limited to work and the small talk of people who have nothing in common. And there he was, saying he loved me.

I tried to let him down gently – went for the line about not feeling that way about him. It was all quite tactful until he asked whether I didn't think it was possible I could come to love him in time. I laughed. And once I started laughing I couldn't stop, even when he got up from the floor. I didn't mean to be cruel and I did apologise later, but I still feel bad about it. I wasn't laughing at the thought of somebody loving him; I was laughing that a man approaching 50 could still believe in the myth of love being a feeling floating around in the air, waiting to connect two people. Love isn't a feeling. It's something physical. You have it, or you don't. I didn't. And I still don't.

So you can stop all your silly talk about Ben now. He apparently has other fish to fry.

Rosemary

PS: I'm opening this letter again to add this twist in the tale for you. On my way to the post box I found a note pushed through my door. It's from Ben. In the true spirit of girlish confidences, I'll copy it out for you.

'Dear Rosemary, I've been an idiot. You won't believe me, but I've missed you. To tell the truth, I <u>have</u> been avoiding you as you probably suspect, but only because I've been afraid. I don't want to ask you for something that you can't – and shouldn't – give me. I don't want to put you in that position.

I can't explain myself more than that and I can't excuse myself. Ben.'

What do you make of that? I should tear it up. He's probably dropped a collection of hand-written love poetry though Jenny's door this very day. But somehow I don't want to tear it up. I'm clearly turning into one of those tragic old ladies who takes every scrap of human kindness she can get.

You have my permission to give me a hearty slap when you arrive.

Rosemary

. . .

No matter what I did to distract myself, I couldn't stop thinking about Ben: Ben and Cheryl, Ben and Jenny, Ben and the note he'd put through my door. I'm as convinced now as I was then, that it wasn't some embarrassing infatuation. There was more to it than that. Julia might've fallen for the guff the media peddle about love, but I didn't. Love isn't the only intensity that can hold two people together. There are other more powerful, more terrible things than love. And whatever that thing was, it was what made Ben look at my painting as if he understood it. The picture was Michael and Lockhaven and creeping grey shadows, and without knowing about any of those things, Ben knew me by looking at it. Worst of all, I knew me too. The blank spaces were slipping away. It was no longer easy to ignore the strange voicemails on my phone from a Dr. Richards, or to forget what I'd done. It took effort.

Oddly enough, I felt no panic. The prospect of losing Michael for the third time didn't only concern Lockhaven Rosemary anymore – the rest of us were implicated too – but I still felt safe. I'd lasted over a year by then, and the world was still holding together. If I'd thought about it long enough, I suppose the fullness of what I'd done and what I still had to do would've made me mad – or made me sane. So I didn't think about it. I thought of Ben instead.

The only thing that hadn't changed was the time I spent in the hospital itself. I suppose the compartment walls that encircled that white room with its grisly occupant, were thicker than most. I'm not a psychologist or a psychiatrist, all I know is that while the reason for my visits to Lockhaven were flickering into focus, the visits themselves were still blank. I could remember walking up to the hospital – sometimes even talking to the woman on reception – and I could remember closing the gate behind me on my way back to the bus stop, but nothing in between.

I don't think I thought of Cheryl much in those days. I have no idea if she was on duty at the hospital when I was there, but at home she didn't cross my mind. I'd almost forgotten her – I must've believed Ben when he said he'd sent her away. Why she hadn't told him about Michael, I didn't know and didn't want to know. The air over Brackton was already threatening enough without her presence. The promised rain hadn't come and the closeness of the atmosphere gave those days a dream-like quality. As I sat at my bedroom window, watching the beach below, the air hung heavy with static; expectant – as if a single spark might make the whole world explode.

BEN

If I had to choose one hero from the history of art, it wouldn't be Edvard Munch, much as I love him. It'd be Piet Mondrian. He's one of those artists who everybody knows, without knowing they do. You'll have seen something of his, I'm sure – one of his white canvases, separated into neat squares and rectangles with perfect black lines, a few of the squares filled in with bright primary colours. But the simplicity and ubiquity of his work are not why I admire him. The way he adapted and grew, but knew where his boundaries were – that's what I really respect.

As a Dutch school teacher he was more of an impressionist than anything, but when abstract art developed, he went with it. His natural tendencies towards the bright colours of fauvism took him to France where he found himself among cubists, and his paintings became a mass of interlocking planes and strange lines.

When war began to tear at Europe and the suprematists like Malevich retreated into their black squares and circles, Mondrian adapted again. Just as a fragile peace was being declared, he was beginning to work on those grids – the paintings that would define him. He could no longer be held by any definition that had gone before him and so he invented his own movement: neoplasticism. Over the years as he played with the thickness, colour and number of his lines and blocks, he couldn't constrain himself to canvas. He covered the white walls of his studio with placards and paper in the same bright colours of his paintings. He created a moveable work of art, interspersing periods of painting with periods of rearranging the colours on his walls to inspire him. In the age of jazz he was the master of improvisation. Every master has his limits.

You'd think that a man who had zipped from painting Dutch canals to the vibrant humour of his masterpiece, *Broadway Boogie-Woogie*, via everything in between, would be loose and liberal with his ideas. Not a bit of it. The line that Mondrian refused to cross was diagonal. He could cope with hanging paintings at an angle, so that the lines of the grid *looked* diagonal, but painting a diagonal itself was out of the question. This was no casual fancy; so strongly did he object to the concept, he stopped talking to Theo van Doesburg for five years. Imagine falling out with a friend over diagonal lines. He was a true artist.

Piet Mondrian was the history of abstract art personified. As time went on – both for Piet and for art as a whole – it marched side by side with abstraction. The stories being laid down on canvas, drifted further and further from physical reality and became abstract truths instead. That doesn't mean Mondrian, or any of the others, were slapdash. Their paintings were as meticulous as the realistic ones that had gone before. To be truly abstract requires boldness and discipline, audacity and selfishness. Each decision is important. One idea, one choice of direction and everything could change: a friendship ends, a new art movement created, an old one abandoned.

If we knew how every detail of our lives – from where we go to dinner to what time we leave the office – might change our whole future, make or break us, we would be paralysed by what-ifs. And so we don't know it. We are wilfully blind to it. Like Mondrian, we adapt and we change, toss the coin, roll the dice. We trust ourselves to the bravery of miracles. And we try to forget that after a lifetime of striving to beat the world at its own game, the important thing might turn out to be a line, an angle, the angle of a line. It's diagonal or it isn't. You falsify the paperwork or you don't. God shows up or you have to do without him.

I want it to be noted that I did try to do without God. I tried to keep Rosemary away from me. If nothing else, credit me with that. It was a stupid idea to put that note through her letterbox – defeating the whole agony of the previous week. It wasn't evil though. It wasn't calculating. Once I knew she'd seen me with Jenny again – that I'd lied about being ill – that should have been the end of the matter. I'd wanted her to stay away so I couldn't do anything despicable, and now surely she would. Only, I couldn't bear it. I couldn't bear to think that's how she'd remember me when I left Brackton. So I wrote the note. As if that could excuse anything.

Other stupid ideas I had at the same time included going to see Jenny again. Not because it wasn't worth a final shot – though even that's debateable – but because it was my last chance to look back at the summer I spent in Brackton and not feel ashamed. To try to patch things up with Jenny after all that had happened, to play on her feelings intentionally with no pretence of only wanting friendship – that was far lower than anything else I did.

I have a suspicion I missed a trick with Jenny. If, instead of trying to win her trust again, I'd confessed everything to her, she would've understood more than I gave her credit for. She might have been my saviour. I'll never know, because I'd fallen into the same trap as everybody else; I'd assumed Jenny was too innocent to understand anything of the real world.

After our chat in the church, I didn't know if I'd see her again – if she'd forgiven me. She didn't appear at Anchor Cottage the next day and in a way I was glad. I knew what a wretch I was. I knew if she came offering friendship, I'd take it and bleed it dry. And, sure enough, the day after that down she came, bearing bread and a fixed smile. That she was quiet and didn't stay long was irrelevant; the battle had been over whether she could forgive me enough to come at all. And she had. It was written all over her face – she'd fought and she'd won. Or maybe she'd lost. She looking battle-weary and tired. She looked like everybody else.

It was all pointless anyway. I didn't have time to make up lost ground with Jenny. I knew when my deadline was and two days was not enough. I either had to face the music, or find a way to silence it and, short of finding a gun and robbing the village store – which I drew the line at mostly out of cowardice – I was out of time. And suddenly it was hard to care. I was sick of it all: the accusations and meetings, the constant feeling that however many times I checked the stable door, I was too late, there was no horse inside. Hadn't I known, if I'd been honest with myself, it would all end that way? Maybe not at first, but at some point over the previous decade, I must have realised. I'd gambled. I'd lost. I wanted it to be over.

Those final few days, it felt as if the whole world was waiting for the end. The air held its breath, building up to some great exhalation. It ballooned through the sleepless Monday night and hung over Tuesday with sticky menace. Even the children on the beach were quiet, stifled by the thick sky. And there was nothing for me to do except sit by my unfinished god and wait for the break to come.

ROSEMARY

Another rumble of thunder, louder than the one that had woken me, came close on the tail of the lightning. I rolled over and looked at the clock. Bright red digits blinked relentlessly: 01:03, 01:03, 01:03, 01:04.

My slippers were nowhere to be found. In the clammy heat of the evening I hadn't needed them, but now the storm had finally torn the air open, there was a draught whistling through the gap in the sash window. I pulled the blanket from the bed and padded over to the window seat, wrapping myself up to watch the storm. I loved to watch – waiting at the glass, staring out into the fierce blackness for that one second where a sheet of lightning would illuminate the angry waves smashing against the beach.

Another flash, another rumble and the storm was nearly on top of us. The steady percussion of rain against the window increased in volume with a sudden rage. The next thunderclap was longer – loud and long, an end-of-the-world roar of divine disapproval. And, still half-asleep, I wondered if that wasn't exactly what it was. Maybe, after all my fruitless searching for God, God had found me instead. He'd walked back into my life and seen what I was doing.

A sudden flare of lightning lit up the beach and the sea attacking it. I recognised the shape of the opposite cliffs: Mrs. Baxter's house perched on top, jagged teeth of rocks snarling at the bottom. And there was something I didn't recognise too. A swooping, twisting shape, soared across the illuminated scene as if a giant bird had taken flight.

I fixed my eyes on the spot where I'd seen it, and waited. I didn't have to wait long. The next flash came 20 seconds from the previous one and was accompanied by the shattering roar of God as the storm loomed overhead. The light gave me enough time to see it wasn't a bird down there. It was a kite. A dark figure was standing alone in the middle of the sand, only feet away from the waves that ran ahead of the wind across the cove. The figure was trying to keep his grip on the kite as it spun and twisted in the tempest. And in that instant of time, as he skidded and jumped, trying to keep his feet on the sand, he looked just like a puppet, helpless under the jerk of the strings.

Could I have recognised Ben in the split second he was illuminated? Probably not. But I knew it was him – not because he was the most logical person to be on the beach at night, but by some strange instinct. Was he sleep-walking? Or mad? No sane person would fly a kite in a storm. Perhaps that's how I knew.

Flicking the lights on as I went, I ran through the house. At the front door I paused only long enough to pull on a coat and wellies over my pyjamas, before dashing out into the night. The wind was fierce. It tugged at me, ripping at my sleeves, battering against me with a vengeance I didn't know if I deserved. By the time I was through the kissing gate, the water had soaked through the pyjamas exposed between the hem of my coat and the tops of my boots. My hood whipped back, refusing to shelter me from the onslaught. Water ran down over the steps, making them more treacherous than ever. My torch beam barely broke the darkness. More than once on my way down I thought I would be blown off the cliff altogether. At last, I saw the sand. Even there, in the relative shelter of the cove, the wind was deafening.

"BEN!" I could hardly hear myself. "BEN!"

Now I was closer, I could see that he too had a torch, but it was no more use than mine was. It dangled from his wrist, his hands too occupied with the lines of the kite. I was almost on top of him before I could make him hear. The expression he turned on me was one of wonder, grey eyes squinting into the light I shone at his face. I clicked the torch into darkness.

"What the hell are you playing at?" Another flash of lightning forked over the sea. "You'll get yourself killed!"

"Nah, I'll be fine." Ben staggered as a stronger gust caught at the kite. "With these cliffs around, I'm nowhere near the tallest thing."

"It doesn't always work like that." His insane nonchalance startled and irritated me. "And put that bloody torch out. There could be a ship in trouble out there and you're flashing lights around like nobody's business."

I knew it was illogical. The feeble beam of Ben's torch wasn't going to cause a wreck – not with lighthouses all the way along the coast – but I needed a reason to be angry. I was soaked-through and frightened. Actually *frightened*. For the first time in decades I was feeling something more than the weariness of the end of a day, or the dull satisfaction of a completed task. I was frightened of the storm and the sea. And I was frightened of the overwhelming fear that had struck at me when I'd seen Ben's danger from my bedroom window.

Ben's torch went dark. In the sudden pitch black, I found myself taking a step in his direction, reaching for his arm. "Please, Ben. It's dangerous. Go back inside."

"What's life without a little danger? I thought you wanted to lead a bigger life, Rosie?"

I hadn't heard that name in a long time.

Before I could find his arm, his hands had found mine. "Come on then. Now's your chance."

He pulled me in front of him, so we were both facing towards the dark water. The lines of the kite were in my hands, the terrifying tug of the strings jerking my arms. I tried to protest, but Ben's hands closed round mine as well, and the feel of them – the strength of his grip – made me suddenly reckless. I pulled on the lines and felt the kite buck and swoop in the void about us. I forgot everything I knew about electricity and playing safe and living a small life. When the next flash came, I found that I was laughing.

I don't know how long we stayed there. All at once, the thunder had stopped, the rain had died to its steady thrum and we were falling in through the doorway to the cottage.

"I can't believe you did that." I pulled off my sopping coat and boots, only then remembering I was in my pyjamas. "You must be mad."

"You did it too."

I flopped down on the bed and wiped water from my eyes. Ben grabbed his towel from its usual place on the floor and offered it to me. I dried my face then pulled clips from my hair, squeezing water into a pool beside me.

"Forgive me, but I have to get out of these things." Ben pulled his jumper and shirt over his head and started unbuttoning his trousers. "I'm freezing."

I turned my back, though I'm not sure either of us was embarrassed.

"We could've been killed, you know." I said. "Really."

"I know." Ben's voice was muffled as he pulled dry clothes over his head. "In my case, that might not have been such a bad thing." He didn't wait for me to comment. "OK – I'm decent." He flipped the kettle on. "No coffee I'm afraid. You'll have to make do with cheap instant hot chocolate."

While the kettle got up steam, Ben sank down next to me on the crumpled bedclothes. "You took a bigger risk than me," he said. "It was a miracle you didn't fall from the cliff steps. What made you come out in weather like that?"

I opened my mouth to say, "Because somebody had to stop you killing yourself." Instead I heard the words, "Because I missed you."

"I missed you too." Ben leaned against the wall. "I'm sorry I've been such a... such a..."

"Liar? Idiot? Scoundrel?"

"All of the above." He laughed. "You've probably realised by now that I'm not such a nice person after all."

"It's OK, I never thought you were."

Our eyes met.

"You're a dangerous woman, Rosemary. You're the only person who seems to know exactly what I'm like."

"And yet, I keep feeling a strange compulsion to see you again. Perhaps that says something for you."

"Rosemary Blunt, was that a compliment?"

I was saved by the whistle of the kettle. Ben busied himself with the hot chocolate, then held out a hand. "Come on."

I allowed him to pull me to my feet.

"Where are we going?"

"To paint of course. I haven't been able to even look at God without you. I intend to make the most of every minute you're here."

"Ben, it's..." I checked the clock, "... nearly two o'clock in the morning."

"So I'm guessing you don't have a bus to catch?" When I didn't make a move towards him, he dropped my hand and gave me a stern look. "Rosemary, you have run around in the rain in your pyjamas and flown a kite in a thunderstorm. Surely you can stretch to painting in the small hours of the morning? It's the sort of thing big-life Rosemary is meant to do."

"Who says I'm going to live a big life?"

"I do." Ben unfolded his arms and pulled me with him into the studio. "You're going to do things you've never done and paint pictures of things you can't take photographs of and... and..." He grabbed my shoulders and looked me straight in the eye. "And I'm going to take you to India."

I searched his face for the tell-tale twinkle that appeared whenever he mocked me. It wasn't there. He meant it. For some bizarre and inexplicable reason, he really did mean to take me to India. He had taken it upon himself to make me live the life I couldn't. I was a project for him, a mission. And with a sense of curiosity, I realised that I wanted him to mean it. I wanted to go away; away from the mess of Brackton and Lockhaven and questions that I didn't even want to hear, let alone answer. This third time, I wanted it to be me who left Michael, not the other way round. And I wanted this strange man who had turned up uninvited into my life, to be the one to make it all disappear, simply because he knew nothing about me and understood everything.

"I'm going to take you to India," Ben repeated. He ran to the trestle table, grabbing at tubes and brushes with mad urgency. "As soon as I've finished my painting, we'll go."

"What if you finish tonight?"

"Then we'll go tomorrow."

He twitched the sheet that covered his painting into a heap on the floor and began to mix paint. He jerked his head at the smaller easel – my easel – a blank canvas sitting expectantly on it.

"Paint something, Rosie." That name again. "Paint something you can't describe. Paint anything that says something about how you feel. Or how you want to feel."

The song on Ben's lips as he prepared his palette, died away the second he put brush to canvas. Normally, I would have watched him work for a while before starting my own painting, but not that night.

The minutes ticked on towards dawn and the rain lessened, then died. We stood side-by-side painting our indescribable things. Ben painted his God: Burnt Amber, Cyan, Cobalt and Pistachio; geometric patterns and undefined swirls; all creeping towards the middle distance, the place where God would appear. And I painted something other. Something that was red. But it wasn't just red; it was Scarlet and Candy Apple, Amaranth and Vermilion, Crimson, Lava and Flame. It was wild shapes and soft corners, spikes and tangles. And as I painted, all thoughts of hospitals and husbands, angry pictures and dying men fled from my mind. There was only us and the paintings and the promise of India.

The sun was well-risen by the time Ben came to look. He stood behind me as he'd done when we'd flown the kite only hours before.

"I love it. It's one of the best paintings I've ever seen."

I glanced at his canvas my eyes following the shapes to the centre. I walked over to it and ran a finger over the tiny bare patch, half an inch square.

"You're not finished yet."

"Not yet. Nearly." His fingers joined mine at the canvas. "Soon."

Beyond the window the long shadows of the cliffs fell on the wreckage from the storm. Seaweed and driftwood scattered the whole lower half of the beach and strange drifts of sand wiggled their way to the water's edge in a reminder of all that had gone on the night before. And I was smiling.

"I should go."

It was the best night of my life.

BEN

The sudden break in the atmosphere had done nothing to lift the feeling of suffocation hanging over me as my time in Brackton came to an end. Rosemary would say I was being melodramatic, but I felt as if I was in a kind of non-existence. I had nothing except the dread of waiting. Two days to go. When I went out in the storm it wasn't an inept suicide attempt. It was a last bid to feel free.

Rosemary appeared as an apparition before me: wild hair, face contorted into a scream. In the violence of the world around us, there was something vulnerable about her; something frail, despite her anger. *Because* of her anger. Here was the one moment we'd both been waiting for without knowing it. In our hands were the lines of a kite and an instant in time. An instant where Rosemary could be dragged on the tail of a storm into a different kind of life. And my life, tangled with hers, either had to go with it, or be torn apart.

When I promised her India, I meant it. I've never been more serious about anything in my life. The reality of the next day, the hopelessness of everything, had evaporated. I was going to take Rosemary to India. I had no idea how any of it would work. We would drive each other crazy within a week. People would think she was my mother, or that I was her toy-boy, and we'd never be able to explain that our friendship was more important than either of those things. We'd never be able to make them understand that romance or sex or having the same genes didn't mean anything compared to the intense, corrupt purity of what we had. An artist. A muse. Two people as fatally dissimilar as they could be. Blood may be thicker than water, but paint was thicker than both. I'd always wanted to go to India and when I said those words to Rosemary, I believed them. The look on her face was so unexpectedly wonderful, it felt as everything had to be possible after all.

That night, for the first time in weeks – perhaps for the first time ever – I was a painter. I'd trodden the path of all those painters who'd gone before me for so long, the reality of everyday had become blurred. I'd gone to Brackton intending to express myself in bold colours that would provoke reaction and emotion. I'd been foolish to think it could stop there. For art could never have stopped at fauvism. It never stops moving on. And so I too had to become a distortion, a trick of the light, a picture viewed from all angles and none. I had to become more and more abstract until I was close to zero-degree: the point where I stopped being me. And it all converged to that night, when the life I'd been leading – from Munch to Mondrian – flowed out of me on to the canvas. I was no longer aware of myself, only the brush strokes. I was an artist. It was the best night of my life.

Until Rosemary left.

"I should go."

She wandered into the living area and bundled her soaking coat under her arm. She slipped her feet into her wellies and clipped her hair back in place. But she seemed reluctant to take those final two steps to the door.

"That note you put through my letterbox..." she began, but stopped.

"You got it then?"

"What did you mean when you said you were afraid you'd ask me for something I couldn't give?"

Had I wanted her to ask me that? Yes, I suppose I had. I wanted her to ask because it gave me one last chance to be honest. And all of a sudden I felt brave. We'd painted through the night together, risked our lives in a storm. There should have been nothing left to get in the way. No secrets. She would understand. I knew she would. Maybe she would even help.

"It must have meant something."

"I've not been honest with you." My voice came out husky, nervous. I cleared my throat. "About my paintings, I mean."

"Don't tell me. Hugh Grant doesn't really have one in his bedroom?"

"Nope. Neither has Madonna."

"Didn't think so."

That was the first time it occurred to me to wonder how much of what I'd said she'd believed. I knew she disapproved of pretty much everything I'd told her, but it hadn't crossed my mind she might not have thought it was the truth. I was offended. I was relieved.

"It's alright." She was smiling at me in that knowing way of hers. "There's something rather noble about a struggling artist, even one who tells little white lies to make themselves look good – and especially ones who really are rather good when it comes to it." She didn't give me time to dwell on the compliment. "What did you want to ask me?"

It was easier to keep going, now that I'd started. "I'm in a spot of trouble – financial trouble. I don't have much money and I owe some people. Big time. Really big time, actually."

I waited for Rosemary to speak, but she continued to look expectantly at me. After a while she frowned. "Is that it? You're worried about money?" She laughed. "You avoided me because you've got money troubles? Were you going to ask to borrow some?"

It was going better than I'd dared hope. Far too well to risk speaking. I nodded.

"Then why didn't you? I've got plenty of money. Of course I'll lend you some until you sell your next painting. How much do you need?"

And suddenly I wasn't sure if I wanted it to be going well. I didn't know if I wanted to be having this conversation at all. But when I tried to speak, the words got stuck somewhere beyond the reach of my tongue.

"Your paintings sell for about 5000 pounds did you say?" Rosemary answered her own question. "Then that's what you shall have, if that's enough? I'll get it to you by the end of the day."

"Rosemary, I couldn't..."

"Rubbish. You can and you shall."

And that was the end of the conversation. Easy. Just like that.

She marched to the door and flung it open. Out on the beach she lifted her face to the sky. "What a beautiful day."

"Beautiful." I looked up at the cliffs either side of the bay. "Although I fear I've tarnished your reputation forever."

Rosemary followed my gaze to Mrs. Baxter's house. "She's up early."

"More to the point," I said, "you're leaving my cottage first thing in the morning, dressed in your pyjamas. What *will* she think of us?"

"Who cares?"

"Don't you?"

"Not in the slightest." Rosemary waved up at the house as the curtains fell back into place. "She thinks what she likes of me anyway, so it won't make a blind bit of difference." She surveyed me critically. "You look exhausted. You should get some sleep."

"So should you."

"I have to go to Lockhaven."

"But it's Wednesday."

"Maybe I'm feeling reckless today." She laughed in a way I'd never heard before. "Besides, I get the feeling I won't be going there many more times."

"Will you ever tell me what you do in Lockhaven?"

"Of course." She turned her back on me, calling over her shoulder, "When we're in India. I'll tell you everything in India."

CHERYL

I didn't go back to Brackton for a long time after Ben kicked me out of his cottage. I was humiliated. I wasn't the sort of person who sleeps around and breaks hearts, but I also wasn't the sort of person who gets dumped the morning after.

I had to tell Lauren of course. And for a few days I was content to agree with her that Ben was a dick who didn't deserve a second-chance. We dissected him over the phone every night for three nights – his looks, his too-posh voice, his sexual performance. Then Lauren got bored of it. And I was sick of lying to her. So we moved on to other topics and I kept my thoughts to myself.

It wasn't that I was funny over Ben. I was angry at how he'd treated me, and I hadn't exactly been head-over-heels in the first place. It was more that I still had a feeling there was more to him than there was to anyone I was ever likely to meet in my narrow life in Lockhaven. I felt as if he was my chance still – whatever he'd said. There would be other chances maybe – I'd gradually build up some savings, I might get a better nursing job, I'd meet other men – but I didn't know where any of that would come from. Ben was right there in front of me. As I went back to the daily routine of nursing people who weren't going to live long or be grateful for the attention, I was deflated not to have something more exciting to think of just a bus ride away. My life and the lives in the magazines I read on my lunch-break were so far apart. I decided I couldn't give up on him yet. When Ben went back to London I'd wash my hands of him – until then, he was still fair game.

I knew he'd wanted to sleep with me, and I was pretty sure I could make him want to again. If I could get him out from the influence of Dr. Blunt, I could get him back. We'd sleep together again and he wouldn't dump me twice.

I'm not spiteful. I don't set people against each other for fun. Ben only needed to turn against Dr. Blunt enough to understand that her opinion on me was based on something selfish, not objective judgment. She was afraid of me, even though I had tried to come to a friendly arrangement with her. And she'd made him get rid of me – I was sure that must be why he'd done it. She'd ruined everything. Her with her fancy title and big house. I bet she'd never had a hard day in her life, yet she still couldn't let me be happy. She was one of those bitter old people who don't like to see young people having something that they'd never had or couldn't have again.

A week or so after I'd left Brackton on the Sunday bus, looking an idiot in my dress from the previous night, I decided to tell Ben the truth. I'd tried to tell him before – about Dr. Blunt's husband and her behaviour while he lay dying – and he hadn't listened. There was nothing to say he'd listen if I tried again, of course. After all he'd said, it didn't look as if a cosy chat was on the cards any time soon. It would be better if the truth came from somebody else entirely.

The only other person I'd met in Brackton was Jenny – the mousey woman who'd blatantly fancied Ben when I'd seen them together on the Green. If I could tell her about Dr. Blunt, I reckoned she'd jump at the chance to tell Ben. After all, if he realised what Dr. Blunt was like, he wouldn't want to spend so much time with her. That would leave more time for Jenny. That's what she'd think anyway. And then Ben would know Dr. Blunt was a liar. He'd know anything she'd said about me could be a lie too. He'd want to see me again and I couldn't see Jenny being much of a match for me in that case. I doubted Ben was sleeping with her. Jenny could get Dr. Blunt off the scene and then I could get Ben's attention away from Jenny.

OK, it wasn't foolproof, but it wasn't a bad plan: go to Brackton; find Jenny; tell Jenny the truth; wait for Ben to call. It could've worked. Maybe, given another few weeks, it would've worked too. I guess time wasn't on anybody's side that summer.

ROSEMARY

Your room is always spotless. It's how I'll remember it: pristine and clinical, gleaming windows and polished floor, crisp sheets tucked round your tidy body. No doubt I'll look back one day and wonder why I spent a fortune every month keeping you in immaculate luxury, instead of letting the NHS do their job. But perhaps we both know the answer to that one.

When I look at you today, I can only think of the first time I saw you. It's been a long time. I'm tired.

"I've told Dr. Richards that I'm going to let you die."

I thought I'd feel triumphant when I told you the news. Even as I walked the corridor from Dr. Richard's office, I imagined it would feel different to this. I'm not triumphant. I'm distant from it, as if reading a script for a play I have no part in. The curtain came down years ago, and the final scene wasn't played out in a sterile white room with old actors past their prime, but in a kitchen with a young wife and her husband, trapped together in a mistaken marriage.

"I don't need you anymore, Michael. I'm letting you go."

Today, when I wonder what you're thinking, I find that I don't want to know. I'm not looking for a flicker. I'm drawn instead to the shafts of sunlight spilling through the window. Outside, despite all the odds, the world is still spinning.

"I've found someone else. He's taking me away. India first, then the rest of the world. Maybe even Australia. We're going to live the life you don't want me to live: big, full of adventure. And it won't be because you would've hated it. Not anymore. It'll be because I want it. Nothing else."

I hold my breath. And in the silence I might have heard the smallest sound on earth – the flicker of an eyelid, the twitch of a finger. Perhaps you're finally ready to talk. Maybe you've realised that I'm not bluffing this time. Or maybe, there was nothing but silence after all. It's too late, anyway.

"Do you know what you did to me?" I wait for your answer out of habit. "I don't mean when we were married – we both know that. I mean everything afterwards. Do you know who you left behind?

"I spent my whole life trying not to be the Rosemary you knew. I thought that would make me free of you. How stupid I've been. All that time I was waiting for you to come back and see who I wasn't. And it's taken me this long – 40 years, Michael – to realise, I never was the Rosemary you thought I was anyway. She was never me."

I return to your bed. But I can't look at your face anymore. It's changed. I take your hand, tracing the lines of the veins through the wrinkled skin with one finger.

"I could've killed you. That night when you lay on the floor at my feet, I could've finished you off. I already had the knife in my hands, didn't I? You were helpless against me. But I'd already lost Michael Blunt twice. The end couldn't be that easy."

The clatter and chatter of nurses spilling from the staff room, means we have 10 minutes before we're interrupted. I don't need that long.

"Even though your face was distorted – twisted and drooping and pathetic – it made no difference. I could still see the face of the man who'd left me behind and who I couldn't let go." I release your hand for the last time. "I'm letting you go now."

The clock on the wall marks off another minute of the familiar vigil I'd never meant to start.

"I shan't visit you. There'll be no point, you'll be sedated. And I'm glad. I'm glad you won't feel pain after all. At last, I want something more than to prove I'm not the woman my husband thought I was."

I want India and Ben and everything that's indescribable.

"I'm going now." You don't flicker when I get up, and I'm glad of that too. "I'm not coming back again. Not ever. Goodbye, Michael."

At the door I can't resist one last look at you. And for the first time since the stroke, I can see you clearly. I can see your face for what it really is. Not the face of a monster, but the face of an old man: frail, gaunt, helpless. It is the face of a stranger.

"I'm sorry." I owe you that at least. "I really am sorry."

JENNY

The rumble of the engine as the bus crept past made the windows of the church rattle. By the time it had pulled into the stop on the opposite side of the Green, I was waiting in the porch. It was the last bus from Lockhaven that day. I knew she had to be on it.

The first thing I noticed as she appeared round the side of the bus was her hair. In six years I'd never known her to change her hairstyle, nor wear new clothes. Yet there she was with a Debenhams bag, and soft waves of grey framing the odd smile with which she surveyed the empty Green. Somehow it confirmed everything.

"Dr. Blunt." I hurried over the wet grass. "May I speak to you a moment?"

"Can't it wait, Jenny?"

"No. It can't."

I didn't wait to see if she would argue, but turned back to the church, giving her no option other than to follow or to walk off. I wasn't sure which I'd prefer. In the long hours of the afternoon, as I'd sat in the dim nave waiting for her to return, I'd wondered what to say. It all seemed absurd. It was frighteningly plausible.

The church had become home to me again. God and I had come to an uneasy truce. After Ben's apology, we had thrashed it out between us for hours in that dark space and I was beginning to understand. Or at least, I was beginning to accept. My anger at God, confusion about Ben and uncertainty of myself had been soothed by the familiar place, the sense of God-in-the-shadows. I didn't know which of us needed forgiving or whether I could forgive any of us. I knew I wanted to try.

I couldn't go back to believing love was unselfish, or that God would intervene only because I'd asked him to. And when the grief of losing myself wore off, I knew I didn't want to go back. Going back would mean a return to bumbling along – being me only because I didn't know how to be anybody else; life by default. I didn't have to think the worst of people, I didn't have to blame God for the imperfections of life, I didn't have to be cynical or bitter, but if I wanted to be the old me again, I had to choose it. I had to accept a fiercely incomprehensible God, a tough world, flawed people; I had to choose to be content with my eyes open, instead of choosing to be blind. Faith is only faith if it has battled doubt. I was only me if I'd faced reality and chosen to see the best in it anyway.

When I'd decided to visit Ben again, it was easier than I'd expected. We'd eaten together on the beach, talking about art and the world as if nothing had happened. And I knew that even if nothing ever did happen, I wouldn't be sorry Ben had come to Brackton. In the aftermath of his departure I know some people pitied me, but there was no need. I have no regrets.

A few days after our reconciliation there was a storm fit to wake the dead. All night as it flashed and roared, I worried about Anchor Cottage and about Ben. In the morning I decided to go down to the beach after breakfast to check everything was still intact, but I never got there. The minute I left my house, a figure hurried over to me. I recognised her at once.

"Jenny?" She stuck out a hand. "I'm Cheryl – we met once before, do you remember? I was hoping I could have a quick word with you. It's about Dr. Blunt."

My first instinct was to walk away. It would've been childish. I should've pitied the girl Ben had led on, not resented her for seducing him. All the same, I didn't fancy talking to her in front of the prying eyes of Brackton or the curiosity of Dad. I led her to the church.

I needn't have worried about finding words to say to Cheryl – she did enough talking for both of us. The stream of vitriol against Dr. Blunt – accusations of infidelity, mad stories of dying husbands – poured out of her as if she'd been practising. And I waited until the stream dried up before saying a word.

"I don't know why you think I might be interested." I tried to sound dignified. It had never come naturally. "Why are you telling me this?"

"Ben deserves to be told the woman he's carrying on with is already married. It's not fair for her to lie to him like this. I'd tell him myself, but I don't think he'd believe me." Her smile was bright. Too bright. "I could see how much he likes you when we met, so I thought you should be the one to tell him. You could make him believe you. And then he wouldn't want to spend time with Dr. Blunt anymore." She glanced sideways at me. "He'd have more time for other people."

It didn't make sense. Cheryl's description of Dr. Blunt as 'the woman he's carrying on with' was absurd. It was her, Cheryl, who had been in Ben's bed.

"This is none of my business." I kept my eyes on the pulpit. "Dr. Blunt is a friend of mine. I've no reason to believe she's anything you say she is."

"You haven't heard about last night then?" Cheryl's voice was low. "I've only been here an hour and I've heard. It's all the way round Brackton – Dr. Blunt was seen coming out of Ben's cottage this morning." She leaned closer. "In her pyjamas. Is that what a married woman should be doing?"

Cheryl sat back in the pew, watching my face. "Think about it. Isn't it time Ben knew the truth about Dr. Rosemary Blunt?"

Long after the clopping of Cheryl's heels on the tiles had died away, I remained in my seat. It couldn't be true. I thought of the time I'd seen Dr. Blunt and Ben walking along the cliff path, and the day I left them in her house together. I remembered how I'd walked into his cottage one afternoon with a Victoria Sponge to find them laughing about something as they painted. No, it couldn't be true.

So why did it seem so possible?

"What's this about, Jenny?" Dr. Blunt sat down beside me, bag rustling.

I didn't work my way round to the subject slowly. If I didn't ask her straight away, I wouldn't ask her at all. "Why do you go to Lockhaven so often?"

I wanted her to give me a straight, easy answer. One to neutralise all of Cheryl's poison. I wanted to believe the best in her. In the past I would have done. I didn't know what to make of her silence.

"Did you know Cheryl came to see me today?" I said.

She shrank away from me, as if I'd raised a fist instead of a question. She looked at me and then at the floor.

"She told me you had a husband in the private hospital where she works. She must've been mistaken because you don't have a husband, do you?"

More silence. This time I didn't break it. I watched Dr. Blunt struggle with herself. After several minutes she looked up at me again, scanning my face before she spoke.

"I did have a husband, a long time ago. I suppose I still do. He ran off 10 years after we married. He didn't have the decency to divorce me first."

"I'm sorry."

"I don't want pity."

"I don't understand." I turned my eyes away. "Cheryl wasn't talking about something that happened long ago. She said your husband was in Lockhaven now. She said you had to choose whether he lives or dies."

I didn't add that she'd had some choice words to say on the matter of Dr. Blunt's behaviour while her husband was dying. I didn't need to. I'm sure Dr. Blunt could've guessed.

"She's right. Michael is in hospital."

"How can he be your husband? Cheryl said he'd only been there a year, but you've been here for at least five, haven't you? Where was he before he had his stroke last summer?"

Even as I asked the question, I knew. Last summer. What was the one bit of excitement that had rocked the village the previous year? There *had* been a man at Dr. Blunt's house. A man who'd shaken her in a way nothing else had.

"The homeless gentleman – the one who had a heart attack outside your house..."

Dr. Blunt nodded slowly.

"He wasn't a stranger, was he? And it wasn't a heart attack. He was your husband? And he had a stroke? He didn't die?"

She looked at me with a queer expression, as if trying to work something out. Then she nodded again.

"Why did he come back? And why didn't you tell the doctors you hadn't seen him for years? Why keep visiting him?"

"Why do we do anything?" Dr. Blunt shrugged. "Why did I marry him in the first place?" She laughed an unfunny laugh. "I can tell you that, actually. He got me pregnant. That's why I married him."

A day earlier if somebody had told me that Dr. Blunt was married to a man who'd got her pregnant outside wedlock, I would've laughed. Despite my own experience, I think I would've found the idea ridiculous. That day, it made sense.

"I got pregnant and so we had to marry." She glanced sideways at me. "You're from a different generation. You wouldn't understand."

"I do." I hadn't meant to say it that loudly, so my voice quivered around the high ceiling. "I do understand." And suddenly the story that I hadn't told – that I thought I'd never tell – gushed into the space between us. "I was engaged once – pretty much. He was a man I loved and I'm sure he loved me too, despite... Anyway, I said I'd marry him as soon as he liked, but I wasn't going to bed with him until that ring was on my finger. I thought that was for the best."

I made myself look at Dr. Blunt. Her eyes were locked on my face.

"Tom got drunk at a college party one night – completely unlike him, he hardly drank at all. I'd refused to go because I hated parties and he ended up sleeping with someone else who was as drunk as he was. It's funny – I never thought that could happen to us. Not just because I trusted him, but because I never thought anybody else would look twice at him. I mean, I thought he was handsome, but he was so un-cool. Like me. We were perfect together."

I didn't want to carry on with my betrayal of Tom, but it was as if the words were saying themselves. "She got pregnant and they got married a month later because even in 1991 there were still men – one man at least – who had some honour left.

"I watched them walk down this aisle." I looked past Dr. Blunt at the full stretch of the church. "And I knew that if I'd compromised what I believed in and had slept with Tom, it would've been me. And we would've been happy because we loved each other in a way she would never have loved him. It was ruined forever."

"I didn't know." Dr. Blunt's voice was soft for once. "Nobody ever said anything."

"Nobody except Dad knew."

"Tom wasn't a local man then?"

"He lived in the cottage on the beach. Maybe that's why I thought that Ben... that Ben..." I stopped. We both knew what I'd thought.

Dr. Blunt's eyes met mine and we studied each other. And I wondered what life would've been like if I'd been her – willing to have sex outside marriage for the sake of love. What if I'd gone to that party? Tom would have married me. Life would've been so different. For a minute – for the last time – I allowed myself to go back to those days and to wish I'd done things differently.

ROSEMARY

Behind Jenny's eyes something flared and died away again. A burst of pain, or maybe a memory of pain. When it was gone, her usual expression – the one I'd always thought of as rather silly – settled into place. But it didn't look so silly to me then. It didn't look sentimental and naive and weak. Not at all. And I wondered what my life would've been if I'd been like her – unwilling to have sex outside marriage even in the name of love. What if I hadn't gone to that party? What if I'd done things differently?

"Your baby," Jenny began, "did he..."

"She," I interrupted. "She died."

"I'm so sorry."

"You don't think it was God's judgment on me?"

Jenny laughed. It was the last sound I was expecting to hear in that dark church.

"Do I think God kills babies when people do things that he doesn't like? No, Dr. Blunt, I don't. Goodness me, the human race would've died out long ago."

"Then perhaps he made a special case for me," I said. "I've done some very stupid things in my life. If there is a god, I've let him down badly."

"If there is a god, he probably didn't ever need you to prop him up." Jenny shrugged. "I'm no expert. You'll have to ask him yourself."

"I will do. If I find him."

"Yes. When you find him."

There was a long silence after that. Not the quiet of a hospital room, with the tick of a clock and the squeak of a trolley. Complete silence.

It was Jenny who broke it. "Ben's not in love with me, is he?"

"No. I'm sorry."

"It's OK." She nodded. "I don't know if I was really in love with him either. And I'll try to make sure I never work it out." She paused before asking in a quieter voice. "Is Ben in love with you?"

"I don't think so."

"Are you in love with him?"

I thought of Ben: of flying a kite in a thunderstorm; of my red painting in his cottage; of the two envelopes in my bag. "I don't think so," I said again, and then added, more slowly, "But I think I might need him."

"Sounds as if you should find out."

We both stood, sensing that we'd said all that needed to be said.

"I won't tell Ben," she said. "I won't tell him about your husband."

"Thank-you."

At the end of the pew we turned in opposite directions – Jenny towards the altar, I towards the door. When I reached it, I looked back to see Jenny watching me. She raised her hand in farewell. "I like your hair by the way." Her voice echoed down the aisle. "It suits you."

I suddenly felt tiny. And for the first time since I was 17, it wasn't because somebody was trying to make me feel small. It was because I had met somebody bigger than I could ever be.

...

Letter from Julia to Rosemary.

Wednesday 15th August

Dear Rosemary,

What a rollercoaster you last letter was! As good as a Catherine Cookson. An artist acting as if he has something to hide, fraternising with a woman he can't possibly be in love with and then writing a cryptic note that explains nothing but excuses everything! I think the note was rather lovely. George never wrote anything like that to me. You have kissed and made-up, haven't you? I'm sure there's an innocent explanation to his behaviour. There's no way he's in love with Jenny – not if she's the woman you've made her out to be.

Anyway, despite the excitement of The Affair of the Brackton Artist, that's not the main point of my letter. I've been doing a little bit of sleuthing myself. I'm no Miss Marple, but a few calls and e-mails to the right people and even I can discover things. Do you remember that surprise I said I had for you? Well, I was going to hold out until I came to visit, but I received the e-mail this morning and I simply can't wait to tell you about it.

Promise me you won't be cross. I know you'll say I'm meddling, but it's for your own good, so you must forgive me. Say you will? I wrote to the authorities in Australia, you see. I thought if I could find out what happened to Michael, you'd be able to let go of all those terrible memories at last. I wanted to know once and for all, where he was. I can't stand to think of you never being able to move on, after all this time. Anyway, it took several e-mails and a lot of being passed from pillar to post, but I got there in the end. A lovely lady in Perth told me all I needed to know.

Michael's dead, Rosemary. He died in Queensland about 18 months ago. There's no doubt about it – I've checked it all out. The nice woman said she shouldn't do it, but she sent me a scan of Michael's immigration photo and it's definitely him. If you send them proof of your identity she'll even let you have a copy of his death certificate. She said they would've contacted the next of kin at the time and I suppose that would've been his brother – the one who was always having parties and the girls at school all had a crush on. Apparently Michael did quite well for himself in business, but never re-married. That's all the lady could tell me about him.

It's rather vulgar to say anybody's death is good news, but isn't it? You can forget him now, Rosemary. He's dead. He's been dead for well over a year. He's never coming back.

I hope this isn't too much of a shock for you. Please don't be cross with me. I thought it was for the best. Call me if you want to talk about it.

Lots of love, Julia

BEN

From the back of my studio, I watched Rosemary weaving her way up the sand in the last of the light. Even at that late stage, I hesitated, waiting until there was a real danger she would see me through the windows, before making up my mind. In the doorway, I took one last look at her, then went to the bathroom and shut myself in.

I waited for the knock. It didn't come. Instead, there was a clatter and soft shush as something was pushed through the bristle teeth of the letterbox. Then silence. I stayed in the bathroom another five minutes before letting myself out. Rosemary was nowhere to be seen.

The envelope on the mat contained five piles of paper, done up in elastic bands. Five bundles of cash. I didn't count them. Rosemary had said 5000 pounds, and it would be 5000 pounds. I was only thankful she hadn't insisted on handing it to me herself.

Ever since she'd left my cottage first thing that morning, I'd been unable to think of anything but her and my escape. They had become mutually exclusive in my mind, and that mind was still reeling from my change in fortune. Everything had happened so fast and so unexpectedly, I hadn't yet worked out whether everything had turned out for the best. On the face of it, I was sorted. I had the money, I had a few hours' head-start. But suddenly it didn't seem that simple.

I'd intended to tell Rosemary the truth that day. And, although I'd been reluctant at first, I felt as if fate had cheated me out of my confession. Rosemary had made it too easy not to finish what I'd started. I'd been planning to beg for advice, and before I'd got close to the truth, she'd given me a way out instead. No more swindling, cheating or lying. There was nothing to feel guilty about, was there? Rosemary had given me the money willingly. If she didn't know precisely why I needed it, that was her fault for interrupting. I hadn't stolen anything from her. God had shown up with his miracle in the nick of time. So why didn't it feel miraculous? And if it was God, why wasn't my painting finished?

I didn't turn the lights on, even as twilight faded into the night. I stood in my studio in the dark, on guard in front of my easel. I had the way out I was looking for, yet it didn't feel like the gift it should have been. If it'd come a week earlier I would've taken the money without a second thought. That night, I was torn. The money and escape? Or Rosemary and India? If I ran up to The Lookout straight away and finished my explanations, would Rosemary come with me or call the police? And did I dare risk finding out?

The dizzy, ecstatic rush of the previous night – when I'd promised India and not seen anything that could stop us – had trickled away in the long, lonely day. Now all I knew was that if I stayed, I'd have to face whatever came. I'd have to be in court the next morning and my fate would be out of my hands at last. I might not see India for a very long time. Yet, if I ran, Rosemary would never see India at all. How brave was I feeling?

My fingers felt the rough surface of the canvas, working their way inwards until they brushed the one point I'd failed to fill. In the dark, I felt for an answer. Should I stay and risk everything for this odd woman who'd caught my imagination – who'd made me the painter I'd thought I always had been? Should I trust her with the truth? Or should I run and leave her behind?

ROSEMARY

On Thursday 16th August – the Last Day – my alarm clock was redundant; the first pale glimmer of sunrise was only starting to seep into the horizon when I woke. I stood in my pyjamas in the garden, wrapped in dawn light and, for a moment, I wavered. I would miss the sea – the stretch of uncertainty beyond the safety of my back fence. Then I remembered the envelope I'd pushed through Ben's letterbox the previous evening, and the second envelope on the bed upstairs.

When I turned back towards the house, I caught sight of my reflection in the French windows. I ran a hand through unfamiliar hair. It'd been longer than I cared to remember since I'd done anything more than chop the bottom few inches off with the kitchen scissors and, from the look on the girl's face as she tried to decide what to do with it, that must've been obvious.

It was meant to be a symbol of my fresh start. I'd gone to Lockhaven to close the door that had stood ajar for too long, and to open a new window. I'd planned for a new wardrobe, new hair, new books to read. But while the girl fussed around me with clips and combs, I knew I didn't need all that. I didn't need symbols to show me who I was. Or what I'd done. For the first time since I'd set foot there over a year earlier, my visit to the hospital was clear in my mind. I knew why I'd done all those strange, mad things. I remembered how it felt to lose Michael for the second time in my life; to be determined not to let the third time catch me unawares. I remembered the night, a year earlier, where history had repeated itself in the kitchen of my house. I remembered it all, and yet somehow the knowledge didn't cripple me. My overriding feeling as I walked away was not remorse, it was the understanding that I'd never been myself. Not since the day Michael left for the first time. One Rosemary had taken over my life, but she wasn't the right one. She was a shadow.

I let the girl shape and feather and whatnot, and I'll admit I liked the end result, but that was all. The new dress I'd bought in the Debenhams sale on my way from hospital to salon wasn't needed. The shoes I'd planned to buy and the new necklace I'd seen in the jeweller's window could be forgotten. I wasn't going to show Ben that I could be somebody new. I was going to show him that I could be Rosemary. The right Rosemary.

My other errands, took much of the rest of the day, and I only just caught the last bus home. As we trundled out of Lockhaven, thoughts of the hospital and the papers I'd have to sign, the funeral I'd have to organise, tried to sneak into my conscience, but it all seemed far-off and unimportant. It was easy to replace the thoughts with more pleasant ones this time. At least, it was until the bus pulled into the last stop, and Jenny called me into the church.

That was my reality check. The easy simplicity of cutting loose from my madness – severing the strings – didn't seem so easy. Jenny had only guessed half the truth, but half was enough. An hour after leaving her in the church, as I made my way down to the beach with a jiffy bag stuffed with 50 pound notes, I still hadn't shaken the sense of unease. I was relieved to find Ben absent from Anchor Cottage. I needed the night to pull myself together.

By the next morning, when I stood in my garden, looking at my reflection in the windows, the unease had been replaced with a sense not of unreality, but hyper-reality. As if life had replaced whatever went before it. I padded through my silent house, leaving a trail of dew footprints. In the bedroom I sank down on to the bed, pulling the plane tickets from the envelope: India, First Class, One way. Those flimsy bits of cards would remove the last traces of my nightmare, would wake me from my sleepwalk. I glanced at them every few seconds as I dressed, unsure if they were real, or part of Michael's last, cruel illusion.

I'd left nothing to chance at the travel agency. I'd sorted out currency, compiled checklist of vaccinations and visas, discussed where to get anti-malarial tablets. I knew Ben would know it all already and I didn't want to give him the chance to be smug. The tickets were open, so we could book any available seats in the following month. We could plan it together. In a couple of weeks, maybe only a few days, we could be away. I wanted that more than I'd ever wanted anything.

All that morning and afternoon, I busied myself at home. After our escapades on the beach, Ben needed a good night's sleep, and I was rather hoping that a day to himself would allow him to finish the painting we were both waiting for. I wrote letters, settled bills, cancelled the small life I had no further use for, and I imagined Ben down in his cottage as I did so. I could picture him in his studio, smiling as he painted the last stroke, closing the gap on God. He would laugh and set his paintbrush to one side, and pull a Hobnob from the packet on the table. And when I arrived with my envelope he'd be waiting for me, eager to show me what he'd done. Irritating and infectious as ever.

At seven o'clock I couldn't wait any longer. For a moment I almost gave into temptation, and held my new dress against me in front of the mirror. It was deep purple with navy swirls, tiny flowers around hem and sleeves, with a hair comb to match. It was beautiful. It wasn't me. I laid it on the bed, pulled on my walking boots and headed for the beach.

I'd nearly reached the kissing gate, when I heard the shout.

"Dr. Blunt! Dr. Blunt!"

Jenny was tearing down the path from the village, glasses bouncing, hair pulling free from her bun as she struggled to pick up speed in a skirt that would've fitted two of her at once. I didn't want to see her. I didn't want to give myself time to doubt what I was doing. It seemed rude – especially after what had passed between us in the church – to pretend I hadn't heard her, but I thought I could deal with it later – go to see her the next day perhaps. Wasn't that what I'd been doing all year – all my life – anyway? Deciding what I wanted – needed – in the moment, and leaving the consequences until later? I could pretend Jenny didn't want to talk to me now, and I could confront her tomorrow instead. I could choose when to face her, just as I had convinced myself I could choose when Michael should die.

"Dr. Blunt! Wait a moment." She continued to call until I was far enough down the steps to be out of view from the top. "Dr. Blunt! Rosemary?"

Once on the sand I was too busy picking my way through the litter of towels and plastic buckets to look more than a few feet ahead of me. The storms had given way to sunshine, but the humidity was already building again, and during the day the beach had been packed with holidaymakers roasting themselves before the next band of rain swept in from the west. Even that late, the sand was covered with people encircling portable barbe-cues and crates of beer. I was nearly at the cottage before I'd worked my way free of the debris and could look up. I knew at once something was wrong.

The studio window, usually framing a collection of proud easels, was empty. In another couple of steps I could see through it all the way to the back of the room, to the bare trestle table. The door to the cottage was neither flung wide to the sun, nor shut to keep out the noise, but stood ajar. As I looked, a figure passed from the living area into the studio. It wasn't Ben.

I began to run. Sand poured into my shoes as I stumbled up the beach past the last few gawping children. I hurled the door open. A handful of boxes, filled with Ben's painting things, sat on the floor. A basket of crockery blocked the entrance. There were no clothes, no bags, no sheets on the bed. It was a blank canvas. He was gone.

I can still see that scene. If I close my eyes, I can picture the exact angle of every box, the position of every tube and brush within them. And on the periphery of it all, standing in the doorway to the studio, is the figure who wasn't Ben.

"Ms. Blunt." A nasty smile grew on Mrs. Baxter's face as she examined my new haircut. "I didn't expect to see you here. Haven't you heard the news?"

BEN

It's hard to explain how I ended up as I did, creeping away from Brackton in the dark of night. It might look as if it was a cowardly thing to do – walking all the way to Lockhaven, catching the first train to London, without so much as a goodbye. Maybe I was a coward. Art for me though was a need, not a desire. Nothing could come in between me and it. It consumed everything else – every*one* else. Art could never have been only a hobby to me. I had to paint. I couldn't not. Even if every teacher told me it was a waste of time. Even if my mother was disappointed and my father banned me from taking lessons. I had to do it. Even if it meant teaching myself.

I wasn't the first frustrated artist. I won't be the last. Take Hitler as an example. His dad wouldn't let him paint either. I'm not saying it's an excuse for what he did – of course not – but I wonder what the world would've been like if Adolf had spent his days painting watercolours of city squares and river banks. If he'd been happy.

Fast-forward half a century to another artist. One whose dad wouldn't let him work on his art either. One who had to take on the family architecture firm even though he had no head for business. Think of him in his office, staring at a print of *The Scream* on the wall opposite his desk, head reeling from trying to make the books balance, only wanting to be back in his flat with a paintbrush in hand. Think of the five architects he employs, and their families who depend on his ability to turn a profit to keep them in their nice houses with their nice neighbours and nice holidays twice a year.

How do you think he'd feel? With a dad who still owns the company – who hovers over every decision, only stepping in to criticise, never help. How do you think he'd feel to watch the business slipping from under him, losing everything his family fought to create? Wouldn't he do whatever it took to stop it? And would you blame him for that?

I *was* a painter you know. All those paintings I showed Rosemary, Jenny and Cheryl – they were all mine. Maybe life was six days a week at the office, but it was seven nights in front of an easel as well, and in a funny way I think Rosemary would've understood. Not wanting to be an artist – she'd never get that – but the idea that it's not what you do with your time that makes you who you are, but what you dream of when nobody's watching. When the cycle of euphoria and self-loathing finally ended, and I found myself in Brackton, that was who I really was. Not the pathetic man who could neither tell his dad to stick his job and go off to scrape a living selling pictures, nor the useless man who couldn't learn to run a business properly, but an artist.

When I buckled my seatbelt in preparation for take-off on the afternoon of 16th August, I was still telling myself that my crime was victimless. The stuff I did in Brackton might've hurt people – Jenny? Cheryl? – I don't know, but everything that came before was different. Tax fraud – who does that hurt? Nobody. I did it to save five jobs, to prevent an old man's heart from breaking as his business went under. That's not a crime. Even HMRC realise that. If I hadn't been so stupid about it all, I would've got away with a civil case, a hefty fine and a slapped wrist. But I didn't know when to stop. I kept doing it, and lying about it even when I was caught out. Like the suprematists, I didn't know when I'd reached zero-degree, and enough was enough.

When I started out in Brackton I only intended to make a few friends, paint a few pictures, tell a white lie or two to make myself into the artist I was deep down. I wasn't aiming for total abstraction. And it was the same with the business. The first time I fiddled the figures, it was meant to be the last time too. The rough patch we hit in 2002 was meant to end. All I did was forget to report a few contracts to avoid the VAT. Everything else was legitimate – all the loans and credit I pumped into the firm to keep it afloat. If it hadn't been for the recession we might've made it.

I still don't know whether I should've trusted Rosemary with the truth. Every step I took away from Brackton, made me more sure I should've tried. If she'd known I was nothing but a man who'd bankrupted himself through loans, who'd watched the family business collapse under his leadership, whose father had died a bitter, angry death, would she have thought any worse of me? Probably not. It probably wasn't possible. She might even have thought more of me if I'd seen it through. If I'd been brave enough to fiddle the VAT system on a scale that would've rescued the business once and for all, she might've respected that. But a little bit here, a little bit there, a decade of lies that only saw me squeaking through each month by the skin of my teeth – there was nothing noble in that.

The reason I hadn't confided in Rosemary wasn't fear she would call the police to tell them I'd breached my bail conditions and was planning to run. I hadn't told Rosemary because I couldn't bear to look at her face when she knew I'd been seduced into the madness of believing that one more loan, one more credit card, one more false report to the taxman could fix everything; that I was a fool who couldn't even cheat my way to success.

She wouldn't care that I had no job, or that my car and flat and everything else – other than my paintings, which nobody thought could be worth anything – had been sold to pay off my creditors. She wouldn't care the only cash I had was the pittance allowed to me by the bankruptcy order and the stash I'd hidden under the mattress. She wouldn't even have cared that I wasn't a professional artist. She would've cared the life I'd urged her to live, was one I hadn't had the guts to live myself. I couldn't tell her face-to-face for fear she would shrink before me – be sucked back into the small life she'd been ready to leave behind. But I also knew, I couldn't let her find out with the rest of them. And so, on my third and final train of the morning, I wrote her a letter explaining everything. I might not have tried to take over Europe, but I was as guilty of my crimes as anybody. And I still needed to confess.

Hours later, I was still thinking of that letter and all the things I should've said and didn't, when a man dropped into the seat next to me. After a few seconds of fiddling with his seatbelt he squinted past me, out of the window.

"Nice day for it." He leaned back again. "You on business or pleasure?"

"Business."

"Long trip?"

"I think so," I said. "I'm not sure."

"Sucks, doesn't it?" He rummaged in his bag and extracted a paperback thriller. "But there's no point going all that way for only a couple of days. My work always send me for at least a fortnight. How about you?"

"It's an open-ended visit," I said. "I'll be back when I'm back."

"God, I couldn't do that. I'd go crazy not knowing when I'd see the kids again." He smiled and tossed the bookmark on to the tray in front of him. "Still, absence makes the heart grow fonder, right?"

I looked away from him again, out at the sunlit tarmac of the runway. "I hope not. I really hope not."

JENNY

It was my fault the papers got hold of it. What started as a 30 second item on the local news, blew up into something impossibly big.

At first, it all seemed too ridiculous. Then things started falling into place. It took me a moment to recognise the photo on BBC South — the younger, more serious Ben, staring out of the screen. It took more than a moment to understand what the newsreader was saying. Police were appealing for anyone who knew where he was to get in touch. When he hadn't turned up at court they'd traced him to Brackton, but it was too late. He'd already gone.

I don't know where the reporter got my name from — somebody in the village presumably. I didn't tell him much, only that Ben was an artist as far as I was concerned. He'd never mentioned any business or anything about being prosecuted. Somehow my few words turned into a tale of deception and intrigue in the local paper, and when that was picked up by the nationals, the village was inundated. In three days Ben went from being the gentle, smiling man I knew, to a suppressed artist with a brilliant mind, or a charming con-man who had some dark power over people — depending on which paper you read. Every fact about him became news in a surreal tornado of headlines and misquotes. A simple case of tax evasion became something far more romantic. And I think that's what Ben would've wanted.

I should've been shocked. Dad was. But perhaps I'd known that something wasn't right about him. His odd mood swings from relaxed to intense, carefree to anxious, were easy to dismiss as artistic temperament. When he talked to me about art, everything fitted. The rest of the time it was hard to grab hold of him. And I suppose that's what we all fell for. Maybe we did know that a home-schooled bohemian shouldn't know Latin, and maybe we should've questioned how his mother had changed from sculptor to painter in a few short weeks, or any one of the other dozen inconsistencies in his stories. And maybe we chose to ignore it all because the abstract version of Ben he presented to us was the one we wanted to see. We didn't want a privately-educated only son of an architect. We wanted to be astonished.

It all seems simple in hindsight, yet I don't think I'd spot the signs if I lived that whole summer over again. Call me naive but it wouldn't occur to me that those hasty trips to London were to sign-in on bail, or his attempts to ingratiate himself were half genuine, half means of escape. When the journalists asked me if I'd known he was a businessman, the question was absurd. I hadn't known because he wasn't one. He might've lied about all sorts of things to me, but he wasn't hiding the fact he was a businessman. He was hiding the fact he had worked in his father's business. They're not the same thing at all.

Three days after the news broke, Vicar came to see me. He sat uncomfortably in Dad's armchair and asked how I was, without looking at my face.

"I'm fine thank-you. Very well."

"This business with the artist chap has been shocking." He shook his head, in the way he did in the pulpit over the stoning of Stephen. "A terrible thing to happen."

"It's caused quite a stir, hasn't it?" I poured the tea. "I'll be glad to get our village back again when the fuss has died down."

"Quite. I... ummm... I understand, you were friends with this man."

For once it wasn't me who blushed.

"I was, yes." I offered him the sugar tongs. "I like to think I still am."

In the awkward silence I had the urge to tell Vicar what I really thought. Even though what Ben did was illegal and wrong, even if he was a coward who wouldn't quit the job he hated, even if he cheated and then lied to the investigators, even if every word he spoke had been embellished, distorted, abstract – I couldn't hate him. I couldn't even disapprove of him.

"I hope you're not too upset by this whole thing," Vicar said at last. "If you want to talk about anything you.... ummm... you're very welcome."

"Thank-you, but I don't think that'll be necessary. I'm OK."

And I was. Because I'd known him, you see. The press didn't know Ben, however much they pretended to. I did. As a bohemian, Ben was two-dimensional; his life read like the blog of a teenage gap-year traveller, and I believed in it because I wanted it to be true. I was too smitten with the idea of the fraud – and the fraudster – to question it. But the fraud was only as a bohemian. As a person, he wasn't a fraud. He wasn't two-dimensional. I knew Ben, and I think he was possibly misunderstood. He was probably a good man. He was certainly an artist.

ROSEMARY

Letter from Julia to Rosemary.

Monday 20th August

Dearest Rosemary,

Please answer my calls. I've phoned three times a day at least since the news broke. I see all the pictures of Brackton on the television and I'm worried to death about you. If you need a refuge from it all, you're welcome here any time. You know that.

I feel awful. To think how much I encouraged you to be friends with him. It's Michael all over again. I'm so sorry. They keep making out on the news that he's a riddle wrapped in an enigma, shrouded in a mystery – the hype is quite absurd. How has a tax-evader become a figure of glamour? I suppose he's a man of mystery and everybody always likes that sort of thing. Every detail about him is being lapped up quite shamefully by the tabloids. I see some blonde thing has sold a kiss-and-tell story to the red tops today. Claims to have slept with the "fugitive" while he was staying in Brackton. I hope the lie was worth the disgusting amount of money she was paid to tell it.

As you haven't replied to either of my previous letters, I'm giving you until Wednesday. If I don't get a letter or call by then, I'm coming to Brackton, even if you're angry. I'd rather shouting than silence, Rosemary.

With lots of love always, Julia

. . .

Ben's letter was the truth. It makes me sound a fool to say it, but as I read it at my kitchen table the day after he left, I knew he was telling the truth. When you've been lied to enough, the truth is as stark and ugly as blood on snow.

All that stuff about wanting to be a painter, the angst-ridden melodrama of needing his father's acceptance and the financial security of a good job – it was all true, I suppose, and written in a way to tug at the heartstrings if you allowed it to. But it was the other things he said – and did – that mattered.

He could've run away at the start. He wasn't meant to have money. Bankrupts don't get to control their own finances. I suppose the police took that into account when they set his generous bail terms. They didn't know Ben had his secret store of cash. Even if they had known, they wouldn't have guessed that instead of using it to flee the country straight away, he'd use it to rent a cottage, buy paint and canvases, and to lead a big life for a few weeks. The life he'd wanted to lead all along. And if, sometime later, he'd got scared at the thought of this new freedom being taken away, and he'd done what he could to escape, I don't think I can blame him.

When I first met Ben, I thought we had nothing in common. I was wrong. We were both frauds. We were the two most suited people never to fall in love. Ben might not have been all he wanted us to believe he was, but the colour he brought to my life fought away the greyness that had enveloped it, and if it hadn't been for him, my madness might never have ended. I might have carried on pretending that the man in the bed was Michael until I was found out. I might've carried on believing it myself.

I'm not trying to tell you Ben wasn't an idiot. He was. I'd known that from the start. It came as no surprise to me that if he was the kind of man to commit fraud, he was also the kind of man who managed to get the civil investigation turned into a criminal one by continuing to lie and fiddle long after there was any point to it. Who am I to criticise him for that? One lie, one moment of madness that gets dragged out into something slow, creeping, grey; months passing and the hole getting deeper every day. Of course Ben should've stopped patching up his failures with more lies. Of course he should've had the courage to live the life he wanted from the start. And of course, I should've stopped trying to impress a man who'd abandoned me in my twenties. Of course I should've never told the paramedics that the man lying unconscious in my hallway was my husband.

I don't know exactly when I realised what I'd done. Sometime in those last few days before Ben disappeared. Perhaps not until my final visit to the hospital, when I looked down at a man who wasn't Michael – who had never been Michael, however much I needed him to be. Because I did need him to be, once. When the tramp had turned up at my door, begging for help, I'd needed him to be Michael, because I knew Michael was dead.

The letter had arrived two days before the tramp did – almost exactly a year to the day before Ben would appear in my life on the edge of an incoming storm. I was still Michael's next of kin – still his wife after all that time, and although it'd taken the Australian authorities several weeks to track me down, they'd managed it in the end. The letter they sent, telling me Michael would never be back to see what a success I'd made of my career, destroyed the neat order of my life – smashed open the doors to compartments that were meant to be locked for good. How dare he die? How dare he vanish without knowing how wrong he'd been about me? Everything had been about him – *everything*. Without him, who was I? Where were my edges and corners? I had no colour or form; I wasn't real. He'd got away with everything. And left me with nothing.

Losing Michael for the second time in my life was no less of a shock than the first. And this time, it was final. Except, it didn't have to be. If I didn't want Michael to have died, then I had to find a way of making him live again. When the tramp turned up on the doorstep, pleading for help, it felt like an answer to – yes – like an answer to prayer. Instead of the drooping, grimacing face of a stranger, I saw Michael. History repeated itself in front of me: the kitchen, the ranting man, the headache, the slurred words. It was my last night with Michael all over again. I didn't have to have lost him. I was being given a second-chance. This time, I could kill him before he died.

At the sight of the knife in my hands, the tramp tried to speak through twisted lips. He backed away into the hallway, staggered towards the door. Then he was on the floor and it took me a minute to realise I hadn't stabbed him after all. Michael had walked out and left me once; Michael had died and left me twice; and now, Michael was going to leave me for the third time. It was too easy. He couldn't be allowed to die again. So I called for an ambulance.

It was surprisingly easy for the man to become Michael. The panic the news of his death had stirred in me, was all gone. I could sit by Michael's bed and I could finally tell him about all the things I'd done since he'd walked out on me. And he had to lie there and listen. I knew the doctors were wrong when they said he was a vegetable. He had to be conscious or it wouldn't be fair. He wasn't dead; he wasn't unconscious; he was alive and listening, and this time *I* was in control. By the time Ben started questioning me about my trips to Lockhaven, there was nothing to tell as far as I was concerned. In Brackton, the man in the bed didn't exist; a blank space in my memory. In Lockhaven, he was Michael. To the doctors and to me.

If my Michael had died, I imagine I would've been caught out. Alarm bells would've rung somewhere when I tried to register his death. But he didn't die. That was the irony, the cruelty; what I wanted and what I feared. This time, I had to choose to kill him myself. The third time I lost Michael, it would have to be my own choice. And I couldn't choose it. I couldn't let him go. Until I met Ben.

I'm not sorry I gave Ben money. Not a bit. If he'd needed more, I would've given him more. If he'd asked, I would've gone with him. Probably. As I sat on the window-seat in my bedroom, his letter in my hand, looking down on a cottage at the edge of a sea the colour of madness, I was glad I'd helped him escape, even unwittingly. The press fracas hadn't yet taken hold and the beach was as deserted as it had been three nights earlier when God shook the world around us. It would take another few days for the details of Ben's movements to make the papers, but I didn't need the names of airlines or flight timetables to know where he was. Just as I didn't need the Sunday supplement art critics to tell me his paintings were rather good "for an amateur". I knew Ben was on the trail of an adventure; I knew his paintings were indescribable.

I re-read the last page of his letter, and wondered if he was thinking of me as he bought his ticket to Quito with my cash. Did he peer out as the south coast disappeared from view and picture me down there at my window watching vapour trails dissolve into the blue?

You should forget me, Rosie. Perhaps that won't be hard. But I won't forget you and, more importantly, you mustn't forget yourself. Don't forget to find that bigger life. I'm sorry I wasn't big enough to join you in it – that I couldn't bring myself to be honourable, return your money and head off to court to face the music. I'm sorry I didn't find God for you.

If we ever meet again I'll do whatever I can to make it up to you, I promise. Perhaps you'll let me take you to India and maybe you'll even tell me what you do on Mondays and Thursdays. Then I'll know I'm forgiven, though heaven knows I don't deserve it. Until then, I'll keep imagining you smuggling bootleg liquor or training to be an assassin. And I'll keep an eye out for God. You were right, Rosie, I have no idea what he looks like, but I still believe I'll find him one day.

I was going to sign off with the truth – a list of all the things I am, and all the things I'm not. I know I don't need to. You know it all already. So I'll only say that I am not the man I wanted to be. And I am sorry.

Di te incolumem custodiant, *Ben*

Di te incolumem custodiant; may the gods guard you safely. And in my head, I could hear Ben adding a postscript, laughing at me as he did so.

"Not too safely, Rosie. Don't let them keep you too safe."

BEN

It started with *The Scream*. I think so anyway. But it didn't stop there. I didn't stop at Munch's masterpiece and neither did art. We kept moving – impressionism, expressionism, cubism. Then, not long after the cubists got their thing going there came another movement like no other: futurism. Futurists embraced the violence of modern life: heat, noise, smells, speed, technology. They didn't care about representing the world, or even explaining it; they wanted to change it. They believed everything old should be destroyed to make way for the new. Nothing in the past mattered.

For a while, these Italian artists flourished, but they couldn't survive forever, because they were wrong. You can't destroy the past. You can't pretend it hasn't happened and keep pushing forward regardless, or you'll end up like they did – trying to embrace things that no sane person ever could. While the suprematists tried to escape the terrible reality of the Great War, futurists celebrated it as a driver for change. Many of them went further, linking themselves with fascism. Violence became worthy. They thought they could create a new world every day, one where the sins and blessings of the past had no place. They thought they could keep painting over the top of old pictures. And it didn't make sense. It was a fraud.

Futurism started off as something radical. Radical can't last forever. It became only another link in the chain of art history. It got left behind as art delved further and further into abstraction, until the truth was hidden from view, available only to those who knew the code, who realised that even when things don't look like what they're meant to be, they still contain reality. Art is a lie that makes us realise the truth.

I don't know why it was *The Scream* for me. Just as I don't know why Picasso started distorting his paintings, or why Mondrian couldn't hack diagonals. Psychologists would have a field day with the whole bloody lot of us. I've lost count of how many theories I've read on *The Scream* alone. Rosemary would laugh at all of them, of course, and say that Munch probably painted the sky red because he'd run out of blue. And maybe she'd be right. And maybe, just for once, she wouldn't.

Some people say *The Scream* is a symbol of Depersonalisation Disorder – a feeling of being an observer in your own life, watching it pass you by. It's a kind of madness. You feel as though you aren't yourself, as if the things you say and do are not by choice; it's not really you who is saying and doing them. Your world becomes a dream. And the danger of dreams is that one day, you might well wake up and find you no longer know where you are, or how you got there. Or where, indeed, you are heading.

ROSEMARY

Letter from Julia to Rosemary.

Wednesday 22nd August

Dear Rosemary,

I am writing this sitting at your kitchen table, and it feels very strange. I always imagined that when I saw your house for the first time, you would be in it. I certainly didn't imagine this.

I don't know whether to be flattered or annoyed that you were so certain I'd come here if I didn't hear from you. Am I that predictable? When I found your front door unlocked and a note addressed to me on the table, I was afraid – for one moment only – that you'd done something silly. Something that no man is worth. Even before I'd opened the envelope I knew I was wrong. You're not the suicide type. Although, I'm no longer sure I know what you're really like at all.

I read the copy of Ben's letter as you asked, and find it hard to hate him now. I suspect that was your intention. I can't say I find it as easy to forgive him as you do, but if he taught you what happiness looks like, then I'll try.

Your letter was a different matter, and I hardly know where to start with it. Why didn't you tell me? You could've told me that Michael had died. I might've been able to help – found you a counsellor or something. I can't believe you went through all that alone. I feel as if the person who did all those things is a different one from the person I've been writing to all these years. They can't both be you. Can they?

I've posted the letter you left for Dr. Richards, though I can't imagine what he'll think of it. Was what you did illegal? Can you be charged with impersonation on somebody else's behalf? I hope not. I wouldn't be at all surprised if they hushed the whole thing up, anyway. There must've been systems in place to stop cases of mistaken identity, surely? But perhaps that's unfair.

You were married to a Michael Blunt after all. And his lack of medical records really could be explained by his emigration to Australia decades ago. I suppose the doctors had no reason to check-up on you. And anyway, what sort of woman pretends to be the wife of a comatose man? I'm sure I don't know.

I found the present you left on your bed. It's beautiful. A size too small for me, but I think I can manage to do something about that by the wedding. I shall be the most glamorous Mother of the Groom you can imagine. The matching hair comb is very sweet – the flowers on it remind me of that hair clip I used to wear to all the parties as a teenager, do you remember? What a long time ago that was. Before Michael and Grace, George and grandchildren; before life became Life.

This afternoon I went down to Anchor Cottage. I wanted to see where Ben lived. The journalists have gone now, but Mrs. Baxter was busy clearing out the last traces of Ben. She's not a fan of yours, is she? When I introduced myself I could see how far I dropped in her estimation as soon as I said I was your friend. You know, she was going to burn Ben's paintings? I think I managed to persuade her that they were probably quite valuable now he's notorious. And anyway, they must belong to HMRC or something. Ten years of VAT fraud must add up – comfortably into six figures if the papers are to be believed. Mind you, with all the interest in Ben his pictures are probably worth enough money to discharge his debts after all. How ironic.

Mrs. Baxter (reluctantly) let me look through the canvases while she popped back to her house for more bin bags, and I thought they were quite good. One or two of the smaller ones were rather beautiful – though I couldn't tell which way up they were meant to go. There were some odd paintings in the stack too – different from the others: a dark mess of colour interrupted by red lines; a piece of scrappy paper filled with a swirl of green; an portrait of a young woman staring out of the canvas with a hungry expression.

Then there were the two canvases standing apart from the others. One of them was enormous, the other quite small. They seemed connected somehow, as if they were made to hang next to each other. They quite caught my imagination and I wondered if you knew what they were. I've enclosed a Polaroid of them for you (see – Polaroids have their uses!) Did Ben ever tell you what they were called?

It seems odd writing to you at a different address after the last six years. I hope this reaches you in time. I'll lock up when I leave and keep your keys safe until you need them again. Thank-you for the offer, but I'm not sure George would view Brackton as a viable holiday destination. Maybe we'll pop down for a weekend sometime though. If for no other reason than to look at this view while we eat our breakfast. I can see why you fell in love with it.

You will keep in touch, won't you? I miss you already. Whoever you are. With lots of love, Julia.

. . .

A photograph propped against the alarm clock. Muted colours of the Polaroid making it seem as if it was taken in another era. Perhaps it was. Two canvases stand side-by-side, propped against a whitewashed wall.

One of them is red. It has wild shapes and soft corners, spewed out on to the canvas in an explosion of different tones. It looks a little bit like Love, but it isn't romance. It's a funny kind of Love – full of spikes and tangles too.

The bigger painting is more complicated. It's a picture of God, and I know that not because God looks out at me, but because he doesn't. Strange patterns in orange and yellow crash up against blocks of blue and green; dark lines split the painting into squares and rectangles. And right in the centre, somewhere in the middle distance, there is a blank square. A nothingness.

Every time I look at the photograph I wonder what the paintings are trying to tell me about their artists. They are Love and they are God. They are 999 words and an absence. They don't quite look like what they are meant to be.

. . .

Letter from Rosemary to Julia.

From: Dr. R. Shelley
The Layla Lotus Hotel
Bangalore
India
Friday 12th October

Dear Julia,

After a bus journey best described as a bit hairy, I arrived three days ago and have put my shaken bones back together again. For the first time in my life, I wish I was better at describing things. It's incredible here. Even now, Bangalore is 30 degrees and, with the monsoons gone, the sunlight is intense. I'm writing this letter in the shade of a café, on the edge of a market so large I fear I'll never get out every time I go in. I do go in all the same.

Everything here is full. The heat, the noise, the colours – all of them hit you as soon as you step outside. Yesterday, I saw a stall covered in hundreds of dishes filled with brightly-coloured powder. I thought it was paint, but they turned out to be tikka powders: saffron, violet, shamrock green. There are spice sellers everywhere, with bowls of bark and seeds and pastes, and they shout for attention over the silk sellers and shoe makers. As I walk through the crowds, children swarm around me, hoping for coins. I give them sweets instead – garish squares of sugar and Kju Pista sausages of cashews and pistachios. They snatch them from the paper bag and squat under the tables to eat, constantly watching for anybody who might steal a bite.

There are so many things to tell you about, I couldn't possibly describe it all – not even if you gave me a million words to do it. So I won't try. Instead, I'll find somewhere that sells brushes and I'll paint you a picture.

I found God in the word-search this morning, Julia. It was odd because I wasn't looking for him there. To tell the truth, I haven't been looking for him anywhere. And yet, there he was on the back of the cereal packet, hanging down from the middle of igloo. Do you think that's where he's been all along? Hidden in plain sight? Maybe we can't lure him closer through meditation or donations to charity. Maybe he's not to be found in the marble eyes of statues or the corner of our bedroom ceiling where we direct our hasty prayers. While I was trying to remove him with physics and Ben was trying to pin him down to an infinitesimally small point in the centre of a canvas, was he here all along at the breakfast table, waiting to pass the milk? I don't know. I have a strange compulsion to find out.

I wonder if Ben has found him yet. Or did the police find Ben first? No, don't tell me. I haven't read a British newspaper for over a month and the last news I heard of him was that some gallery in London was planning an exhibition of paintings by 'the notorious fraudster, Ben Summers'. He'd like that.

I wonder if he knows. At any rate, I don't want to know if he's been caught. I prefer to think of him wandering the globe, meditating with monks and playing with Ouija boards in motels, and perhaps doing the word-search on the back of a cereal packet in a hotel restaurant somewhere.

I'm not coming back, Julia. Not for a long time – perhaps not ever. I'm going to stay in India until I need some personal space and then I'm going to Australia to track down where Michael's buried. I'm going to go to see him and I'm going to laugh, not because he's dead, but because I'm alive. Life, in all its smallness, is still worth having. It still belongs to me.

After that I'm not sure where I'll go. To buy a prayer wheel in Tibet, or to learn to scuba dive in Cuba. I'm going to hunt down every atom of life I can find and add it to my own until it expands beyond the box I put it in when I married Michael. I'm going to chase after a big life to see whether Ben was right after all – *crede quod habes et habes*; believe that you have it, and you do.

With love and all those other thousand-word things,

Rosemary

ENDS

Printed in Great Britain
by Amazon.co.uk, Ltd.,
Marston Gate.